M000203814

ECHOES IN TIME

ANDRE NORTON & SHERWOOD SMITH

Echoes in TIme

Copyright © 1999, 2021 Andre Norton and Sherwood Smith
All rights reserved.
This edition published 2021

Cover design by Augusta Scarlett, LLC (www.scarlettebooks.com)

ISBN: 978-1-68068-213-7

The characters and events portrayed in this book are fictitious. Any similarity to real persons, living or dead, is coincidental and not intended by the author.

No part of this book may be reproduced or stored in a retrieval system, or transmitted in any form or by any means, electronic, mechanical, photocopying, recording or otherwise, without express written permission of the publisher.

This book is published on behalf of the authors by the Ethan Ellenberg Literary Agency.

About the authors:
Andre Norton: http://www.andre-norton-books.com/
Sherwood Smith: https://www.sherwoodsmith.net/

ECHOES IN TIME

In this sixth entry in the Time Traders series, time agents Ross Murdock and Eveleen Riorden are recalled from their honeymoon to take part in a dangerous assignment: find a team of Russian scientists who vanished without a trace from a research mission in the past of a far-off planet. Along with a team of Russian time agents with their own mysterious agenda, and Saba, a new agent teamed with Gordon Ashe, they leap into the alien world's distant history.

There they encounter alien races whose appearance, language, and customs are incomprehensibly strange. Some mystery changed this world, and music seems the only tool that might prove a key to unlocking the planet's secrets. But as they try to decipher a digital alien Rosetta stone, time is running out. Ross must figure out how to save his team before they vanish forever.

This high-intensity race against time is filled with excitement and wonder in the grand, retro-scifi Time Traders tradition.

TABLE OF CONTENTS

PROLOGUE

The day's heat had diminished to only a residual shimmer from the cooling earth. The chitter and click of insects in the scrubby green brush formed a kind of musical accompaniment to the laughing and singing of the long, snaking line of children crouched together, one in front of the other, knees up near their chins.

"Here is our mother!
Our mother, our mother!
Here is our harvest,
Our fruit, our harvest!
Our mother, our fruit..."

The children laughed as they sang, their bare toes scrabbling forward in the dust as they waddled and hopped. Their dark brown skin was mottled and streaked with painted patterns, some chalk-white, others subtle earth tones. Sweat and dust marred the fine lines of the patterns, not that the children cared. They were only playing. They sang and laughed with the companionable abandon of children who know that the time for real skin painting, when they became adults with adult responsibilities for food and shelter, war and marriage, lay far in the sunny future, after many harvest games such as this.

Saba Mariam, watching from her post beside a jumble of rocks, felt as if she had been wafted back through time. So the children of the Surma had played and sang for count-less generations in this sere mountain region of southwest Ethiopia.

She looked down at her hands, the skin dark against the plain khaki of her trousers. She and her recorder were the only jarring notes in this scene out of history, the only intru-sion of modernity—though at any time an airplane might roar overhead, causing children and adults alike to pause, like startled deer, before they scampered off to hide.

Saba glanced at her tape recorder, working silently behind a warm gray boulder. The Surma tolerated her strange ways because she did not interfere with them, and she had proved that she was not in fact sent by their age-old enemies, the Bumi. She looked strange to men and women alike, with her ears and lips unpierced. She was, to the Surma, a child walking around in a grown body, for she did not display the ritual markings of a responsible adult, but they dismissed her strangeness with a kind of humorous tolerance.

Saba had learned to sit quietly, patiently, drawing no attention to herself. After her long stretches of neutral observance, she knew that the people would forget her pres-ence. She would become no more interesting than another boulder, or a patch of scrubby grass, and it was then that she turned on the recorder, making a record of music that had been handed down through families over centuries and centuries of time.

It was good work. Important work. Saba was proud to be one of many who quietly went about recording the songs and myths that had sustained human beings since the cra-dle of civilization. Progress had brought to the Earth untold advantages, but its pervasive growth was choking off in ever-increasing numbers the very old languages, customs, and cultures of peoples who had lived in harmony with the land since humans first crossed the great continents.

It was indeed important work, Saba thought as one very small three-year-old tripped and went rolling in the dust. The song broke up into laughter. The children re-formed into their line; one girl at the front began singing again, soon joined by the others, as in the distance a group of mothers and young unmarried women chattered and prepared food.

Important work—and involving work. It kept one busy, which in its turn prevented one from worrying about those things that could not be solved—

As she thought this, she became aware of a sound that perhaps had warned her subliminally of approaching intrusions.

The faint hum, reminiscent of bees bumbling around flowers, resolved into a battered old motorcycle drawing a three-wheeled side car. The rusty machine was probably older than Saba herself.

The children heard it as well. For a moment they all went still, and then their leader dashed through the dust to her mother. The other children followed, some still laughing, others singing bits of song. The mothers gathered their young and vanished into the sun-dried brush.

Saba climbed up on a boulder and shaded her eyes against the great, bloodred late October sun. The driver of the motorcycle revved the engine and zoomed around brush and scraggly trees, halting two meters from Saba's rocks.

Saba held her breath as the wafting odors of petrol and exhaust blew past, so unfamiliar after her month here in the wild mountainous region. The driver, meanwhile, pulled off sunglasses and a tight baseball cap, shaking free a cloud of curling brown hair. The clothing—tough, anonymous bush garb—had made gender difficult to guess at; a gloved hand pulled out a kerchief and mopped some of the dust and grit from a middle-aged female face as Saba approached.

The driver looked up, shoving the kerchief into a pocket.

"*La Professeur Mariam? Vous êtes Saba Mariam?*" she asked.

Saba nodded, adding in French, "Is there an emergency?"

"*Oui.*" French was obviously no more the driver's native tongue than it was Saba's, but Saba had gotten used to polyglot conversations—often in tongues chosen because possible surrounding listeners would not understand the conversation. Not that any listeners were around now.

The woman said, "*Je m'appelle Taski Aleyescoglu. Je suis avec L'Étoile Projet.*"

Project Star.

For a moment Saba stood staring at the unfamiliar woman, angry at this breach of promise.

L'Étoile Projet—Project Star—was the bland name for one of the most secret organizations in the world, one for which Saba had given her strength, her spirit, and nearly her life.

Saba turned her gaze on the Time Agent courier. "I was promised a year," she said in French. "A year to recover."

"It is an emergency," Agent Aleyescoglu replied.

"Answer me this first: has Lisette Al-Aseer reported in?"

The Time Agent did not pretend to not know the name. Her lips pressed into a line, and she shook her head. "I am sorry, Professor Mariam."

Saba drew a deep breath. "And they expect me to cut short my recovery time? And return?"

The agent said, "Whatever is going on is classified over my head—as is whatever your former partner is still working on. All I was told was to find you and bring you back.

Whatever it is that has them scrambling now, apparently only you can solve it."

Saba turned her gaze to the last limb of the sun, sinking beyond the western peaks. Shadows blended softly now, making it difficult to see the woman's face. If she was to leave, she'd have to go now; they were miles from any road, and driving about at night in Ethiopia in the dark was no simple matter.

She looked back. "Me as a musicologist?"

"You as you. That's all I was told: it must be you, it can be no other person."

Strange. But time travel was strange, that Saba knew. Strange, alien, and even more remorseless than the natural passage of time.

She looked over the distant clumps of trees, knowing that the Surma crouched there, and she smiled sadly to herself. All very well to fancy that she had stepped back in time while recording these people celebrating the year's harvest. Apparently she was to be drawn back into real time travel, in a machine designed and built by beings never born on Earth. How many agents had been lost in the quest to understand this technology from beyond the stars?

She shook her head.

"Can you tell me at least where this emergency is taking place?"

"I wasn't told. Of course," Taski said, settling onto the motorcycle and pulling on her goggles. "But when I was on my way out, I overheard an order for someone to contact the American Embassy for your visa."

"New York! So this new emergency involves the Americans?" Saba shook her head. She knew that Project Star had originated with the United States, but so far her connection with the Americans had been peripheral at best.

Taski grinned as she yanked the baseball cap over her forehead. "Big boss will probably be out here next, and you can ply him with all the questions you like."

Saba sat back on her rock. "If there is so urgent a need," she said, "why did he not come here instead of you?"

Taski revved the engine, which roared, sending some distant birds flapping skyward from the shrubs. Their cries echoed back, faint as the laughter of children, as the motor died down to an uneven growl.

"Might have," Taski called. "But he's still in Mother Russia."

Russia?

Saba mouthed the word, but did not speak. In amazement—and apprehension—she gazed at the courier, who gave her a careless salute, revved the engine once more, then drove off into the twilight, leaving a cloud of light brown dust hanging in the still air.

Russia? And the Americans? Could there be a connection?

She might not have been able to conquer her bitterness, but one thing she had learned was patience.

Saba bent over the recorder, pressed the ON button, then settled back to wait for the Surma to emerge, like shy ghosts, from the shelter of the brush.

"*Vikhodite! Ruki v' verkh!*"

"Like hell I'll come out with my hands up." Mikhail Petrovich Nikulin smashed the butt of his pistol into a corner of window, and stuck the muzzle through the hole. Bitter Siberian air smote his sweaty face.

Two things happened almost at once.

From behind came a shout: "Nikulin! You know the orders!"

From outside the rickety old building came the *klatch!* and *click!*s as two of the half-hidden gangsters dropped bullets into the chambers of their rifles.

Phwup. A large-callibre bullet burrowed into the half-frozen slush just below Misha's window, kicking up splatters of mud.

Footsteps from behind. A moment later a short, dark-haired figure crouched below the level of the windowsill. "Nikulin!"

Misha did not have to look down; he knew that voice, and he knew the expression on the older man's face.

"You *know* the orders. No violence. If we have to, we activate the destruction device on the ship," Gaspardin said.

White hot anger flared through Misha Nikulin. "We are not going to lose that ship," he stated, his gaze staying on the figures in the bulky coats creeping foward from the cars to the old stone fence.

He fired once, and heard a shouted curse. Outside, one of the gangsters flung up his weapon and dropped, rolling in the muddy slush, hand clasped around his wounded knee.

"Misha—"

On the periphery of his vision Nikulin saw Gaspardin reach up for his pistol. "Don't touch me."

The hand vanished. "You will answer to the Colonel for contravening orders."

"If that ship is blown up, she will answer to me," Misha said, and again he fired, winging a second figure in the arm.

The trefoil flicker of automatic weapons fire glowed outside, and all around Misha wood splintered. Glass shattered and rained down in a musical tinkle. He dropped to the dusty wooden floor and belly-crawled, not back to the inner room, as Gaspardin did, but to the kitchen annex, where he'd stashed an old wartime teargas pistol.

As the furious automatic fire stitched across the weatherworn, dilapidated building, Misha loaded the pistol with a teargas cannister, used the butt to knock out a corner of the brittle glass, and then took aim.

He fired into the midst of the attackers. Heard choked, angry cries. A whiff of teargas drifted on the cold air, making him sneeze, just as raking bullets smashed into the antique ceramic oven, sending out a lethal spray of shards.

Warmth creased Misha's ribs. He ignored it. Steadied his grip. Shot a second time, then flung aside the tear gas weapon and picked up his pistol. Dropped the magazine. Checked to see if it still had ammunition. Slid the magazine home and jacked a round into the chamber.

He kept crawling from place to place, forcing himself to make each shot count, until the roaring outside grew louder than the roar in his ears.

The shooting had ceased. He leaned against a window, glanced outside, and realized the gangsters had retreated to their vehicles and roared away.

Misha stared through the window, trying to make sense of the endless gray Siberian sky meeting the distant horizon. But it didn't make sense. Nothing made sense except the fact that the mission was safe. The alien ship was safe.

"...realize it, don't you?"

Misha looked over his shoulder, made out in the swiftly gathering darkness Gaspardin's anger-narrowed eyes, his mouth white in his grizzled jowls.

"You defied orders," Gaspardin repeated. Then his expression changed as his gaze worked down Misha's shirt.

Misha glanced down, but all he saw were billowing clouds of darkness. He lifted his free hand to his side, and felt the wet warmth there.

"Damn," he said, and slid into the darkness.

He woke staring up at a low sod ceiling. He smelled generations of cabbage and potato meals and unwashed wool. Heard the creak of a chair.

"So you are awake, young man." That voice belonged to Colonel Vasilyeva. Misha turned his head, saw her sitting by a narrow window set into the thick stone wall. Through the window he glimpsed hayricks, and the long white Russian sky. He knew this place; it was the fallback position for their team, in case of disaster. His hand lifted to his ribs, encountered a taped bandage there.

He said, finding his throat dry, "The mission is safe."

"No thanks to you."

The Colonel's face was calm, her gaze unwavering. Like others who had spent childhood under the shadow of Stalin, she seemed to have no emotions whatsoever.

Misha knew that was wrong.

He said, "The ship?"

"It is safe enough. Now." Her voice was as immovable as granite. When she was angry, her demeanor carried all the force of a rockslide. "But that will not be the case if any of your victims die, and the government turns its attention back on us."

Misha fought against blinding anger, and winced as he moved restlessly on the bed.

"If," she stated in a low, soft voice, "I give orders for that alien ship to be destroyed, it will be done."

Misha gritted his teeth and forced himself to sit up against the wall.

The Colonel went on, "They were just a bunch of opportunists, there to take over the energy plant, and use it for some easy piracy by price gouging. They had no idea that we are time agents, and that we have an alien ship. And of course they are going to come back, in bigger numbers. We have to make certain that what they find will be a hydroelectric plant. Nothing more. Nothing less. Nothing," she said in a slow, cold voice, "to raise questions."

"I'm sorry," Misha said at last, though it cost him more effort than sitting up had.

The Colonel sat back, one blunt hand working at her temples as if she had a headache. If one were to interpret that gesture as weakness, that would be equally wrong.

"The Americans have a ship," she said. "We are now allied with them. The Germans have a ship. The French have a ship, as do the Norwegians, and Africans. May I remind you, Mikhail Petrovich, that these are all our allies now? The Time Agency is worldwide. This mission will be carried through, even if one of us loses a ship."

Misha shook his head, then winced as corresponding pain racketed through his skull. "I'm sorry. I just don't believe the Americans are going to help. Or if they do, what their price is going to be."

"None of us know," the Colonel said. "My entire life I have not trusted them, but necessity forces change. You forced it sooner than I would have wished."

Misha winced.

The Colonel said, "Our people should be finishing up at the energy plant right now. Then on their way to St. Petersburg to get ready for the journey." She dropped her hands to her knees. "None of us trust the Americans. But balanced against that is the reality of our government struggling to survive, and the unrest so very close. No one must find out about these alien artifacts—either the ships or the time-travel mechanisms. You know that as well as I. Rather than let anyone find out, anyone at all, we blow up the ship—we blow ourselves up. These secrets cannot fall into the wrong hands. Every single government who knows the secrets agrees. And so necessity forces us all to compromise. To work together. To solve the mysteries we've been presented, before we find ourselves with bigger problems from outside our gravity well than we're causing for one another within it."

She sat back.

Misha sighed, presing his hand against his side. It hurt. "The mission?"

"The flight to New York leaves tomorrow. We begin the training there."

Lightning flared behind Misha's eyes. He strugged up, made it to his feet. "I'm going," he said, not caring that his voice broke. "Get me on that flight."

"But the doctor—"

"I don't care. I *will* be on that mission, if I have to blast my way across eight time zones to do it. And you know I never make empty threats."

They stared at one another.

"Zina." He relented at last. "Please."

The Colonel's lips creased. Just faintly.

Misha sank down onto the hay-stuffed bed. The effort of standing had made him dizzy. But that no longer mattered. He knew he'd won.

"We will leave tomorrow," she said, "but without you. As soon as your fever is down, you will follow us." She pointed at the bed. "Now get some sleep." The door shut behind her.

CHAPTER ONE

The phone rang. Ross Murdock looked up, startled. For a moment his eyes met his wife's across the room. Eveleen paused in the act of patting down the folded tablecloth on the basket they'd both just finished packing.

Strange, to hear a phone ring. It'd been days since they'd been so rudely interrupted—long, glorious autumn days there at Safeharbor, on the coast of Maine. No phone, no TV, no newspapers—nothing but seabirds, and the sound of the breakers crashing on the rocks down the hill from the house, and each other. Heaven.

"Let's ignore it," Ross said.

Eveleen shook her head. "This isn't our house, it's Gordon's, and it might be someone who needs to get in touch with him."

"Who?" Ross asked as the phone rang a second time.

Eveleen's expressive brown eyes glanced at him, rounded with amused patience. "Friends? Family?"

"Outside of the Project, he doesn't have any friends," Ross said, half joking. "And I don't think there's any family either. The Project is his friends and family."

Eveleen said, "I really think we should answer it."

"Then I'll get it," Ross said. "I'm closer."

On the fourth ring he picked it up. "Ashe residence."

1

"Ross." The voice was immediately familiar—Major Kelgarries. "I've been trying to reach you. We've got an emergency—"

Ross slammed down the receiver. "Phone sales," he said, forcing a smile. "Let's get going on that picnic before the weather drives us back inside again."

Eveleen smiled back, hefted the basket, and opened the door.

Ross closed the door on the sound of the phone ringing again. "Looks like we might luck out weather-wise after all," he said in a voice of loud, hearty cheer.

Eveleen looked at him with her brows quirked, but she said nothing as he slid his hand next to hers on the basket, and with their picnic lunch swinging between them, the two started up the trail behind the house.

An hour later Ross lay stretched out on the cool grass, staring up at the cloud formations.

Emergency, he thought. Yeah, sure. There *always* was some damned emergency on Project Star, and it seemed to Ross that he'd been stuck in the middle of most of them.

Well, he'd done his time. They'd promised Eveleen and him a honeymoon, and he meant to have it. A honeymoon meant just the two of them, no interruptions, nothing more dangerous than the occasional bumblebee.

He glanced at Eveleen, who had been watching the wheeling seabirds swooping and circling above the Maine breakers. She had turned her attention to him. Their eyes met, and hers narrowed.

"Phone sales?" she repeated.

Surprised, Ross said, "What?"

Eveleen's mouth deepened at the corners. "I might be dense, but it seems odd to me that you'd still be angry an hour after hanging up on a junk sales call."

Ross snorted. "Angry?"

Eveleen reached over and traced her finger over his jawline. "Clenched. Just like some movie hero about to be blasted by twenty machine-gun-totin' bad guys." She tapped his hand, which—he belatedly noticed—had been drumming on the grass. "Not quite white knuckles, but the next thing to it."

Ross gave her a reluctant grin. "It was Kelgarries."

Eveleen whistled. Beyond her, a gull cawed, and far below, as if picking up the sound, came the mews and cries of myriad seabirds.

"This is our time," Ross stated. "I resent like hell their breaking their promise."

"But you know it has to be an emergency, or they wouldn't," Eveleen said. "Did he have a chance to say anything?"

Ross, remembering that same word *emergency,* gave a shrug.

"Darling." Eveleen looked sardonic. "Don't even waste the breath claiming you don't care. Or that they don't care. The fact is, Kelgarries's ghost is sitting right here between us, or you wouldn't be so tense. We might as well go back and find out what the problem is."

"Dammit." Ross got up, and began repacking the basket.

"Does 'dammit' mean that I'm right?" Eveleen asked, grinning. "A spouse likes to be able to decode these little clues."

"Dammit means dammit," Ross said, slinging the basket over his shoulder.

"I'll remember that," Eveleen said, chuckling, as they started back down the trail.

Within half an hour of their reaching Gordon Ashe's house, the phone rang again. Eveleen gave Ross that sardonic look again. "I'll get it this time," she said, and picked up the phone. "Gordon Ashe's residence," she said in a polite voice. "Eveleen Riordan speaking. May I take a message?"

Ross wished—absurdly, he knew—that she would follow that with "Sorry, wrong number," or maybe "No, we don't need any aluminum siding."

But ten seconds passed. Thirty. She still hadn't spoken. Ross crossed the room to her side and waited in silence.

She finally said, "I understand, Major. And we appreciate the extra time you've allowed us. See you tomorrow."

She gently laid the receiver back into the cradle, and turned her face up to Ross. "Emergency indeed."

"Project Star." Ross swore, then added, "We should have used the damn transfer machine to blast us forward, or back, or somewhere in time when they couldn't find us." He sighed. "What kind of emergency? He say? No, he wouldn't—not over the phone."

"Correct. All he said was that they need us to report to the Center."

"What about Gordon?"

"He's already there."

Ross let out a long sigh. "It was too good to last, I guess," he muttered, biting down what he really wanted to say. But cursing fate, the world, and his bosses wouldn't change anything. So he added only, "Tomorrow?"

"They're sending a copter to pick us up. At least we don't have to drive all million and a half of those windy roads back down the coast again."

"If it meant we could be alone a little longer..." Ross started.

Eveleen grinned, and wiggled her brows suggestively. "We have the rest of tonight. Let's make the most of it."

He had no objections to that.

Gordon Ashe poured a cup of fresh coffee and sat down at the briefing table. He looked up at Major Kelgarries, who gave him a somewhat lopsided smile before saying, "They'll be here tomorrow."

"Was Ross pretty fluent?" Gordon asked, trying for lightness.

Kelgarries—a tall, hatchet-faced man—said, "Ross hung up on me. Ten tries later I spoke with Eveleen. When I mentioned an emergency, she seemed to appreciate our having given them as much time as we have. I suspect Ross might have had a more, ah, characteristic and colorful reaction, but she was the one to hear it—not me."

Gordon Ashe nodded, smiling. Truth was, he was impatient to get Ross and Eveleen back, to plunge directly into what promised to be a tough assignment. He'd never permitted himself to indulge in what he considered to be a dangerous luxury, romance. It was too much like weakness. Yet he had to admit that Eveleen Riordan and Ross Murdock made an excellent partnership.

The catch was that Ross and Gordon were no longer partners.

So would he go solo this time? Or would he, Ross, and Eveleen make a threesome?

Wait. Hadn't Nelson Milliard, the top boss, said something about a later discussion concerning personnel for the mission?

Gordon sipped at his coffee, resigning himself to a day's wait. His years of archaeological study had forced him to learn patience.

5

❧ ❧ ❧

At midday the next day, Ross and Eveleen's second copter ride ended outside a nondescript building located on the outskirts of a small town in upstate New York.

They stepped out of the copter, bending low against the powerful blasts of air generated by the slowing blades—and by a cold rain-laden wind.

As if nature had agreed that their honeymoon was over, a powerful storm had swept down from the north during the night, and it had chased them steadily as they transferred from copter to small plane to copter again.

Ross was peripherally aware of his scarred hand flexing and then tightening into a fist as he and Eveleen crossed the tarmac to the front of the building blandly labeled NORTHSIDE RESEARCH INSTITUTE. His danger sense—whether sparked by the storm or by anticipation of whatever news awaited them inside—made him edgy.

He glanced at Eveleen as a security guard opened the thick glass doors for them. She looked neat and competent as always, her brown hair swept up into a chignon, her slacks and shirt attractive but easy to move in. Only someone who had been trained in martial arts recognized in her controlled grace the mark of the expert who was poised for action; though her face was pleasant, even smiling, Ross realized that she, too, was tense.

Just then she glanced across at him, a quick, assessing gaze. He grinned, she grinned.

So they were beginning to read each other's moods.

The elevator opened then, and they passed inside. Instead of going up one floor to what Ross figured were ordinary offices, they went down the equivalent of five or six floors, deep underground.

6

They did not speak during the short ride down. When the doors slid open again, they looked out on a familiar scene: the main offices of what had been known merely as Project Star, the work of a government agency so secret that there wasn't even any acronym to spark the interest of the curious.

Full-spectrum lighting and lots of potted indoor plants made the best of an underground facility sealed fifty feet below light and air. Ross and Eveleen strode past cubicles and desks, glancing at the busy support staff who researched projects for the Time Agents—and then sorted the data that resulted from the agents' excursions into the past.

How many of these people, most of whom he did not know, had had to read Ross's reports, and write up reports of their own?

He supposed he could find out if he wanted to, he thought as they passed through the double doors at the other end of the big room. But did he really want to know how much work he was making for someone else?

The thought caused him to repress a grin as they reached the outer office belonging to Nelson Milliard, the head boss of the Project.

At their entrance, three men and a woman glanced up. Milliard looked like a typical CEO—big, gray-haired, abrupt in movement, a man to whom time was precious. Major Kelgarries, Ross's very first contact in the Project, could never be mistaken for anything but a military man. But the third man, Gordon Ashe, looked to the uninitiated like an outdoorsman: brown-skinned, blue eyes, brown hair with blond sunstreaks, and very fit. It was not obvious to the casual observer that Ashe was also a doctor of archaeology, and a leader with a very subtle mind.

The fourth person, a woman, was unknown to Ross. Short, middle-aged, and gray-haired, dressed in a plain suit of blue linen, she displayed the same characteristics as Milliard; whoever she was, Ross decided after a second's evaluation, she was important.

"Ross. Eveleen," Milliard said in greeting. "Permit me to introduce you to Colonel Zinaida Vasilyeva."

A Russian?

Milliard turned to the woman. "Colonel Vasilyeva, these are Eveleen Riordan and Ross Murdock, two of our best troubleshooters."

The woman gave a short nod and a brief smile. "I have read much about you." Her English was excellent, if heavily accented.

I'll bet you have, Ross thought grimly. Question is, our reports—or those written by your spies?

"Please, sit down," Milliard said, indicating two waiting chairs. "Coffee? Something to eat?"

Just then the smell of fresh coffee registered on Ross, and he rose to help himself. As he poured out two mugs, he looked over his shoulder at Ashe, who watched, smiling faintly. "Russian?" he mouthed the word—knowing the others couldn't see.

Ashe's only response was a slight crinkling of the skin around his eyes.

Milliard went on. "We're still expecting Colonel Vasilyeva's colleagues, and one of our own people, all of whom were delayed by the weather in Washington, D.C. The Colonel came on ahead so that we could begin the preliminary briefings. The Major will give you the general outline of what we're up against." He nodded at Kelgarries, and sat down.

Kelgarries turned to Vasilyeva. "Would you care to begin, Colonel?"

The Russian Colonel gave a short nod, and folded her hands. "We have come to request your aid," she said slowly,

8

in accented but excellent English. "In the past the politics of our governments have made us rivals, and perhaps we Time Agents fostered that rivalry in an intellectual sense even after the political issues were resolved."

Kelgarries grinned, and the. Colonel's eyes narrowed in unexpected humor.

Ross found himself grinning as well. Early on during Project Star, the diminishing Cold War had kept the two Terran nations apart, even when they seemed to be fighting the same enemy. Later, after the Cold War was officially considered at an end, the race for knowledge had seemed less political and more of a game to see who learned the most the quickest. Except it had been a game full of danger.

"But you had reason to be wary about approaching us before this."

Milliard's diplomatic statement brought a sour smile to Ross's lips. He hid it by sipping coffee.

"That is so." The Colonel gave an abrupt nod. "In the very beginning, when we encountered the entities you Americans nicknamed the Baldies, we assumed incorrectly that they might be allies of yours. Their actions—destroying our bases without provocation—made investigation into your possible motives seem dangerous. It was deemed better to trust only ourselves."

Remembering those days, Ross felt a twinge in his hands. He nodded grimly.

"I see you agree, Agent Murdock," the Colonel said, comprehension clear in her dark eyes. "These Baldies are dangerous, and even after we discovered that you, too, worked against them, we did not know how far they had penetrated your own establishments."

Ross spoke for the first time. "So what's the score here? Baldies pulling a fast one on you?"

9

"Fast...one?" The Colonel repeated, frowning slightly.

"Baseball slang." Kelgarries turned to Ross. "No—at least not directly. Our target is a world, not a people, though the Baldies might very well be involved."

"But—" Ross looked from the Major to Ashe. "Dominion—"

"Is still safe," Gordon Ashe said quietly. "What this concerns is the world we first visited aboard that derelict, with Travis and Renfry. Remember?"

Ross grimaced, recalling the terrifying journey aboard a ship whose controls were totally alien, the worlds they'd nearly lost their lives on not once but several times. "How can I forget?"

The Colonel said, "When you returned, as you will probably remember, the tapes you brought back were shared among those governments who wished to exploit the knowledge on them. The random draw awarded to us the tapes that focused on that particular world."

"I remember that," Ross said. "And I was just as glad we were officially rid of that planet!"

The Colonel smiled, then continued. "We surmised, as apparently you did, that the ruined city you had visited was once a major starport, a center for many different starfaring species. Our immediate goal was to learn what we could about the Baldies to protect ourselves against another attack like the one that was so devastating to us. Our decoding of the tapes was frustratingly slow, and funding in our country is always an issue. Since we—I speak now of the Time Project—must remain a secret from the general public, and thus we win the government little advantage in the eyes of the citizens, the government wants maximum results for minimum funding."

Kelgarries and Milliard nodded, exchanging glances. Ross felt an unexpected spurt of sympathy for the Russians.

"It is much the same here, then?"

"Much the same," Kelgarries said.

The Colonel smiled again, this time her mouth curving in irony. "Well, you will understand, then, when I tell you that it was decided at high levels in our government to speed our research along by sending a party of scientists back to when the starport was flourishing in order to gather more data."

Ross whistled on a low, soft note.

Colonel Vasilyeva's brows quirked. "Yes, it seemed ... premature to us as well. We planned what we believed to be a more cautious approach. Our time-travel team jumped back to when the tower you identified as a library was still functional, or at least intact, but after a time when we had adjudged the starport was no longer in use. After all, for all we knew, the starport might be peopled entirely by the Baldies, and we had no faith in their welcoming human beings into their midst."

"We'd probably plan an approach similar to yours," Ashe said. "I take it something went wrong?"

"That's what we need to find out." The Colonel turned to face him, her hands now tightly clasped. "Except for an abandoned Time Capsule, our scientists sent back to the past have vanished utterly, leaving no trace."

11

CHAPTER TWO

"No trace," Ross repeated. "But wouldn't that give a hint?"

"The Time Capsule's log was ended abruptly, so abruptly that we do not believe that Katarina, the team archivist, had time to add a warning or even a summation," the Colonel said.

"Can you describe your general plan of approach?" Gordon asked, leaning forward, his fingertips together.

"We send our exploratory teams out in doubles, the time-travel team, and the base team. While the travel team of scientists go back in time, the others stay and guard the ship and the transfer apparatus, and gather scientific data while waiting. Our travel teams can't reset the time from the far end—our technology was severely set back by the destruction the Baldies caused us—so time in the past marches parallel to time in the present. Our teams cannot appear moments after they left; that would require resetting the apparatus from the far end, which is impossible, since the far-end equipment is merely a projection, or image, of the present-end apparatus."

Kelgarries said, "Our own practices have brought us to much the same rule, if possible. There are ways to force micro-jumps within a given time: they are incredibly energy-costly, but even more risky, we've found after some disasters,

12

is that they somehow stretch the fabric of time dangerously. We try to keep missions running parallel to current time."

The Colonel nodded in agreement. "We still do not really understand this alien technology—either how it works, or why."

Ross spoke up. "But the Time Capsule?"

"We have a standard schedule," the Colonel said. "Forgive me for what must seem circumlocution, but I believe it is necessary to describe all this in detail."

"We understand," Ashe said. "Please. Continue."

The Colonel paused to sip at her coffee, and then she sat back tiredly in her chair. "We never know if the travel team will execute their orders in hours, or weeks, so we arrange scientific gathering in a priority order. The guard team takes samples of the immediate surroundings, and analyzes them. They set up posts for observing local denizens. In this instance, the orders included finding the tower that you once found, Dr. Ashe, and exploring it, if the indigenous flying peoples permitted. We had included in our equipment items we thought to trade for the ancient spools—if there were any left for us to collect."

"And were there?" Gordon asked.

She gave her head a quick shake. "You and your colleagues had gotten the prime specimens," she said with a nod of approval. "But we wanted to double-check. We expected our travel team to be able to get far better materials from the functioning library—which would correlate with the present. Anything we gathered would, of course, be missing in our portion of the timeline."

Everyone nodded.

"After that, they were to start exploring farther out, excluding only the hostile weasel folk and their territory. Some of our people were to examine the buildings, and others to work in widening circles through the jungle area, taking samples and analyzing them." She frowned down into her coffee cup, her gaze going distant. "We found the remains of one of our travel team on the third sweep."

The room was completely silent.

"On the sixth, we picked up a signal," she continued. "It meant that the travel team had buried a Time Capsule, for whatever reason."

Ross made an impatient movement, caught Eveleen's eye, and controlled it. Major Kelgarries looked over at him, his upper lip lengthened as if he repressed the urge to smile, but he said nothing.

The Colonel, however, noticed the movement, and gave Ross a courteous nod. "You have a question, Mr. Murdock?"

"I just wonder why your team didn't detect their Time Capsule on arrival?"

"If they had, they wouldn't have jumped," Ashe said, grinning.

Eveleen grimaced. "Sometimes this time stuff makes my brain ache."

"Mine as well," Milliard admitted.

"Is same thing as quantum mechanics, Schrödinger's Cat, you know?" the Colonel said, leaning forward. In her intensity to convey her thoughts, her Russian accent was very strong. "The Time Capsule both was and was not detectable until the first team jumped. Then the superposition collapsed. After that the Time Capsule *was*." She shook her head. "Nah! Is easier to say this in Russian."

"Comparable to the Baldies' interference with our station up north, several years ago," Kelgarries said. "We didn't see the evidence of their tampering when we arrived and set up base, until after the events—and we knew what to look for."

Ross realized his surprise must have shown, because Kelgarries went on. "Yes, we've already exchanged detailed briefings on all missions, on both sides. We each need to know everything if there's to be any hope of rescuing that survey team."

How detailed? Ross wanted to ask. He hid his reaction as the Colonel said, "We can explain the specifics this way: where would our team have searched? Should they spend countless weeks searching the entire planet for a possible Time Capsule, which could be anywhere? There was no signal at the transfer site, remember, so our base team had no clue that a search ought to be made. The sixth circle was quite far out."

"Got it," Ross said, still trying to assimilate Kelgarries's matter-of-fact statement about exchanging info. "Sorry about the interruption."

Colonel Vasilyeva gave her head a quick shake. "All questions are important when we deal with the past and present, and how they are interlocked. And I have little more to tell you. The Time Capsule was an almost daily report, ending abruptly after Day Sixty-two—correlating with the present—about three weeks before the Capsule was found. The only common item among them all was a feeling of malaise—an allergic reaction, we judged—but this was also felt by our scientists in the present time, only not as severe. And once they returned to the globe ship, their symptoms disappeared."

"A broad-spectrum course of anti-allergens will take care of that," Kelgarries said.

The Colonel nodded. "We had not taken this precaution as the report made by your team," she nodded at Gordon, "had not indicated illnesses."

"Nothing serious," Gordon said. "Could be a seasonal thing?"

"This is what we assume," the Colonel said.

Eveleen said quietly, "Any evidence of the vanished team turn up?"

The Colonel shook her head. "At that point, of course, new orders superseded the old priority, and our team searched. Except for the remains of the biologist, there was no forensic evidence whatsoever, not for many miles. Either they were buried on one of the other islands, or they just vanished. Our search team widened their circles of exploration until time and supplies ran out, and they were forced to return home."

"Grim," Ross admitted. "So where do we come in?"

Kelgarries said, "As the Colonel mentioned, the Baldies did severe damage to their bases and equipment a while back. They are still recovering."

"Slowly—too slowly," the Colonel said, her frustration evident in her voice. "Our government does not want to give us funds without results, and we cannot produce results if we do not have the funds to continue our work. So much of our energy has been forced into reconstruction!" She spread her hands, then shrugged. "And so, when the Major contacted us with the proposal to share information, we came instead to ask for help."

"Which we plan to give," Milliard said. "This planet is obviously important—only the treaty, which gave the data to you, according to the division of the spools, has kept us from exploring it further. We, too, would like to learn more about that spaceport, and maybe the Baldies. If we can solve some of the mysteries about them, we might be able to defend ourselves better against them, should their attention come this way again. And we have to assume that it will."

Ashe tapped his fingers on the arm of his chair. "I agree. The only protection we have, and it's mighty slim, is our second-guessing their assumption that in destroying the

Russians' bases they dissolved any Terran threat. But they might find evidence of us elsewhere—"

"Or they might just decide to come back here and mess around again with the primitive natives," Ross finished sourly. "I'm with you. So, what's the plan?"

"That my best agents go back with a Russian team to the starport planet, and find the missing Russians—and whatever information you can," Kelgarries said, grinning.

"Three of us?" Ross asked, indicating himself, Eveleen, and Gordon.

"No," the Major said. "Four agents from our agency will join four Russian Time Agents. Our fourth will not be American, however. I've other excellent operatives, from projects you three know little about. One of them seems fated to be assigned to this project."

"Fated?" Ross and Eveleen spoke together, looked at each other, and laughed.

"Fated," the Major said.

He reached behind the desk and carefully pulled out an archaeologist's specimen box. Ross could see Cyrillic lettering on the side.

Kelgarries looked over at the Colonel, as if for permission, and when the Russian nodded, he opened the box. With reverent care he removed a small piece of what looked like dark wood.

"The Russian science team found this in the rubble at the library building. It was buried deeply—they found it after a week of careful sifting for artifacts."

He held it up, and Ross saw that it was indeed wood, carved—ancient-looking. A closer examination showed a woman's face. Human, singularly beautiful, and incredibly detailed. Ross, glancing at it, felt that he'd know the model on sight, were he ever to see her.

Just then a quiet beep sounded in the room. The Major moved to the desk computer and looked down at the message pad at the corner of the terminal. "Ah," he said, "just in time." He looked up. "Ross, you and Eveleen will go back as partners. Gordon, meet your new partner."

At that moment, the door opened, and a tall, well-built woman walked through the door. Dressed in an expensive business suit, the woman moved with grace and assurance.

Ross looked up into her night-dark face, her black eyes, and he swallowed against sudden shock.

"Professor Saba Mariam," the Major went on. "These are Colonel Vasilyeva..." He went on with the introductions, which Ross barely heard.

Instead, he tried to process the fact that this woman and the carving had exactly the same face.

Chapter Three

Gordon Ashe sighed as he sank back into an upholstered chair.

He and Ross were alone, finally.

Eveleen had volunteered to show Saba around the facility; Ross flopped down and idly flicked on a video.

Ashe just sat. The eternal full-spectrum lighting in the den of the suite they'd been assigned gave no hint at the time. Gordon did not need to turn his aching neck to glance at the clock in order to know that it was late. His body knew it, his mind knew it.

The rest of the Russians—all except one—had arrived shortly after Saba, and Milliard had called a break for dinner, saying that they could all get acquainted over a meal.

Gordon hated that kind of gathering, banal chatter between people who did not trust one another, but who were forced by circumstance into the pretense that they did.

He'd managed to exchange half a dozen painfully polite comments with his new partner, and fewer with the new Russians. A poor reward for what had seemed an interminable meal. Boredom and stress combined to give him a headache.

"Okay," Ross said, killing the video with a careless swipe of his scarred hand. "I can feel your mood from here. Spit it out."

19

"I'm just tired," Gordon said.

"And?" Ross prompted.

"And so what part of 'I'm just tired' is unclear?". Gordon said, knowing that when he resorted to sarcasm, he belonged in bed, asleep.

Ross just laughed at him. "You don't want a woman as a partner. Go on, admit it."

Gordon shut his eyes and leaned his head against the back of his chair.

"You were so polite to Saba at dinner," Ross went on inexorably. "You sure as hell weren't to me when we first met. You only fall back on that lady-and-gentleman routine when you're peeved. Dead giveaway, Dr. Ashe."

Gordon sighed. "Not peeved. Not that. Too strong a word."

"So what's wrong with Saba? She's got intellectual qualifications enough to spare for three scholars—Professor of Musicology in Addis Ababa, plays a dozen musical intruments at concert level, knows Western classical music as well as Ethiopian, which, I'm told, is ancient and fascinating both. And she's made a couple jumps on super-secret African missions, one of which involved Baldy interference at about the time we tangled with them, so it's not like she's ignorant of that aspect of our job."

"It's not Saba," Gordon said. "Her credentials are better than mine, and she's probably everything Kelgarries claims, and more. But..."

"She's female?" Ross prompted.

Gordon sighed again. "I'm not against women in the Project—despite the way I was raised. The last of my old prejudices was knocked out of me when I first met Eveleen's former boss and thought I'd better go easy on this tiny, gray-haired lady martial-arts instructor, and she proceeded to dry-mop the practice mats with me. I know that our female agents are every bit as bright, as courageous, as capable as we are. But a partner...living in such close proximity with one. Especially a highly cultured, refined one."

Gordon remembered the appraisal in those beautiful dark eyes. She'd looked at him with the same intellectual curiosity one might give a fossil, and a not very interesting one at that.

He knew such a judgment might be unfair. It could very well be that she was as reserved as he was; he had no idea what kind of impression his own expression had conveyed. Probably lousy, he decided, grimacing.

Meanwhile, Ross chuckled. "Don't tell me. You think Saba won't be inspired by the vision of you in the morning with a night's stubble on your face and your clothes rumpled and mussed? And then there are the niceties of who gets the bathroom—or what passes for a bathroom on these luxury jaunts to the past—first?"

"All right, all right." Gordon grimaced. "Enough needling."

Ross was still grinning. "It's just that you're being absurd. Believe me, I had all that to contend with on Hawaika and Dominion, and the women managed pretty much like the men do."

"But I'm not used to it," Gordon said. "My experience, even my studies, all pertained to prehistory, when women's movements were largely curtailed, and thus few female agents made the jaunts. It's what I'm used to, good or bad."

"Then it's high time you *got* used to something new," Ross retorted heartlessly. "You won't find any sympathy here, boss. You're the one who told me—on my first mission— that we learn or we petrify. And you know we're going to need Saba's skills too much, from what few hints the Russkis dropped about our mission. She's perfect for this jaunt, and we've got lives to save."

"All right," Gordon said. "I concede."

"And if our positions were reversed, you would have just fed me the very same line," Ross went on. "Okay. I'm done lecturing."

"Then I'll get some sleep," Gordon said, rising from his chair. "What seems impossible at night is often merely improbable by morning."

Ross laughed and flicked the video back on. "Night, Gordon."

Ross watched Gordon Ashe close the door to his room. He shook his head, then sank back on the couch. There was an action video on, one of the latest releases thoughtfully provided by the Project, but Ross found his mind wandering.

Too much had happened that day. Russians as allies— the prospect of visiting a planet that he'd profoundly hoped he'd never see again—Gordon's dilemma.

Going on a mission, which could be dangerous, with his wife.

He winced. He could talk over with Eveleen all three of the first set of problems, and he'd welcome her fair-mindedness and acute observations. If he brought up his last worry, it would only annoy her. She'd see it as a mistrust of her abilities, but he didn't feel any mistrust on that score. He'd seen her competence proved too many times; in hand-to-hand combat, in fact, she was better than he.

No, having women along as partners didn't bother him.

What bothered him was something he'd never thought to feel—the protective instinct fostered by love. He'd been a loner his entire life, and he'd only had himself to worry about. Now everything had changed, his entire worldview had changed. He still had nightmares about that terrible day on Dominion when Eveleen's mount had fallen on her, nearly killing her. Until he knew she would pull through he'd thought his own life would end.

This, he felt, he couldn't discuss with Eveleen. It was too hard to articulate—too easy to misstate himself, and create a misunderstanding. He didn't really trust words, when it came right down to it. He trusted action.

At the same time he knew if anything happened to her, he wouldn't survive it. He'd rather disaster strike him first. It would be easier to take.

He wouldn't discuss it with Kelgarries or Milliard either; he wouldn't refuse the mission, not when they needed him, and to bring up what seemed like complaints went against his own code of honor. So why bring it up at all?

Instead, just after dinner—when everyone was still standing around outside of Milliard's office, waiting for coffee, and chattering about nothing—he'd checked the computer records that he had access to. He'd found two other married agent teams on the roster. With an idea of talking to them he'd checked on their status, to find out that one team was in Iceland, doing a run that was heavily classified, and the other team was in South America, training for yet another classified project. He hadn't had a chance to send then an Email inquiry—thinking out the wording for *that* would take time—but he sure was tempted.

The door slid open, and Eveleen came in, her stride still full of bounce, her eyes clear and sparkling.

"Have a good time?" Ross asked.

She bent to kiss him. "Great!" she said. "Saba's one smart lady. She's going to be a tremendous asset for this mission. She's got a wicked sense of humor, too. Jokes in that soft voice, with that cultured accent, and a totally straight face—she was quite funny about how we have ads everywhere, literally everywhere, in America. And I nearly split my sides laughing at her assessment of the general-issue 'artwork' on the walls in the big data-processing room."

"The people down there are supposed to be working, not living in a museum," Ross protested.

"Work progresses better in congenial surroundings. You know that, I know that," Eveleen corrected.

"It's not exactly a Beaker-trader cave down there," Ross said, secretly enjoying setting her off.

Eveleen's eyes narrowed. "No, but you can just imagine who did the decor. Some government functionary who wanted to save a few pennies on the budget and bought those awful prints at a bargain sell-off from some super-cheap department store. 'Order me artwork in earth tones to match the chairs and cubicle dividers.' And then those pictures are nailed to the walls, as if anyone would even think of walking off with one!"

Ross finally gave vent to his laughter. "All right, all right. So we Americans are cultural no-tastes and upstarts. Come on, let's hit the sack. If we don't get some shut-eye, we'll be sorry tomorrow."

"She's not a snob, Ross," Eveleen said quickly, twining her fingers in his as they walked to their room. "It's just that Ethiopia is such an *old* culture. She can't help seeing us from a vastly different worldview."

"All I know is, we've got a vastly different worldview to start cramming into our brains tomorrow," he said. "Or should I call that universe-view?"

Eveleen laughed.

Ross was still thinking about that conversation the next morning.

He rose early, while Eveleen still slumbered, and went straight to the gym. His years of experience with Project Star's routines made the next day's schedule predictable: he and the others would spend hours sitting around and listening to field tapes.

Ross did a lot better riding desks for long stretches after a session with the machines and on the practice mats.

As he worked he wondered about the success of this assignment they'd been forced into. Impatience gnawed at him, the more maddening because there was no single person to blame. Milliard and Kelgarries both had been sincere in their regrets for the curtailed honeymoon. They were both plainspoken men, honest, and hardworking. They did not demand more of the agents than they demanded of themselves.

Yet the truth was, Ross did not want to go blasting across the galaxy in a ship designed and made for unknown beings, to a planet as weird as it was dangerous. He wouldn't want to go again with other Americans he knew; double that a bunch of Russians; and triple that for going with his wife.

"Dammit," he snarled, and sent a punishing roundhouse kick to the padded target. The sound he made was a satisfying *whump!* but the top of his foot stung.

Wincing, he glanced at the clock—and realized how late it had gotten. He was still in a frosty mood when he dashed out of the gym, his wet hair cold.

Down the hall to the main corridor—and at the sight of two people he stopped short.

One, a tall man with long blond hair, had his arms around the other.

And the other was Eveleen.

CHAPTER FOUR

Lightening flashed through Ross's brain.

He wasn't aware of crossing the hall. Suddenly he was next to them, drawing in his breath preparatory to choking the life out of that yellow-haired sleazebag, but then Eveleen stepped back, her arms moving with calm deliberation.

Somehow she was outside the guy's grip—and somehow she was also between Ross and his target.

"Ross," Eveleen said with determined cordiality. "Allow me to introduce you to Mikhail Nikulin. The last of the Russian team," she added, with just enough emphasis to keep Ross from moving, or speaking. Her head turned, and in the same voice she said to the newcomer, "My husband. Ross Murdock."

Nikulin raised his hands and stepped back, miming surprise. "Now, why is it that the most beautiful ones are always taken first? And I thought it so promising a beginning." His accent was strong, but his English was quite good.

Ross realized his jaw was clenched so hard his teeth hurt. He forced himself to relax. The desire to punch that challenging grin was almost overwhelming, but he had to control it. Nothing had happened.

Nothing had happened.

27

"I had hoped to meet you eventually, Ross Murdock," the fellow went on. He talked in a lazy drawl that did not fool Ross for a second; the guy's stance, the assessment in his gaze, made it clear he was quite ready for any sort of action Ross might offer.

He knew who she was, Ross realized. And he did that on purpose.

It made him angry all over again, but at the same time he had to admit it was a fast way of testing the territory.

"We have heard much about your experiences," Nikulin went on, still with the smile and the appraising gaze. "There are questions I have. We shall share a drink and talk, you and I."

Ross forced himself to shrug, and to speak. He was glad his voice came out sounding natural. "We shall sit and listen to a lot of tapes—and sooner than later."

"It's true, we are a bit late," Eveleen said. Ross did not mistake the relief in her eyes. "If you will follow this way, Mr. Nikulin."

"Misha Petrovich," the man corrected. "You must call me Misha."

Eveleen slid her arm into Ross's and led the way. Misha fell in on her other side, his long stride easy. Ross glanced over, still saw that readiness, caught sight' of callused palms. This Misha had obviously seen plenty of action. Ross then comprehended what he'd said, and realized that *he* was not unknown to the Russians.

So was Misha Petrovich Nikulin, Ross's Russian counterpart?

The thought did not give Ross any added pleasure in the prospect of this mission.

They reached one of the all-purpose rooms where they found Kelgarries and the rest of the team—Russian,

Ethiopian, and American—waiting. Ross saw the short Russian woman he'd met at the dinner the night before (what was her name? Irina something?) smile for the very first time. She greeted Misha in fast Russian. As the tall blond guy sauntered over to talk to his group, Eveleen squeezed Ross's arm.

He turned his attention to her.

She whispered, "You let me handle him."

"He knew who you were," Ross said, angry all over again.

"Of course he did," she whispered back. "It's a verbal martial-arts trick—he wants you off-balance. And as long as you come snorting around like a bull before a red cape, he's going to keep pestering me." She grinned. "Think of it as a compliment to your reputation. It is, after all, in a kind of backhanded way."

"If he wanted to compliment me, he could have said, 'Nice work! Glad to have you on the mission.' Or is that unknown in Russia?"

Eveleen gave a soft laugh, but then she whispered more firmly, "I repeat: you let me handle him."

"Please," Kelgarries said. "We need to get started. Everyone, please find a desk."

Ross gritted his teeth again. This mission was already a disaster as far as he was concerned. But he spotted his own laptop waiting, and dropped down behind the desk where it lay. Sitting next to it was a pair of earphones.

Gordon Ashe had the desk next to his. Eveleen had gone over to sit near Saba Mariam.

"All right. We will begin with the tapes found in the Time Capsule. On your terminal, you'll see choices for your language preference. My people, you know the drill," Kelgarries said. "For the benefit of our visitors, let me explain

29

how we usually proceed. We'll listen all the way through just once. Feel free to make notes. When we're done, we'll begin again, this time stopping for questions and explication. But we all need a basis from which to start, so without any further talk, let's proceed."

Ross settled into his chair, yanked his laptop over, and plugged it into the database terminal. As he pulled the headphones on, he stole a look at his wife; she had her head supported in her hands, her favorite listening position. To all appearances she had forgotten the existence of the blond Russian.

Ashe was already making notes, as was Saba. Interesting. The Russians all sat, polite and impassive. They'd heard this before, of course.

The tape began. The translator's voice was a bland, professional actor's voice. "This begins the Record of Exploration Team A, recorded by Katarina Semyonova, team archivist. Day One. We have just arrived..."

Ross looked down, saw his hand tapping on his laptop case. He stopped it, and sat up straight. He was restless, but didn't want to show it.

He wasn't just annoyed with that blasted Russian version of Don Juan. He also hated the beginnings of these Project tapes. It was always the same, the recordings went on in great detail about every single thing, most of which usually turned out to be insignificant later, when the team had gathered more data.

"...what seem to be feathered cats."

Ross grinned to himself. Feathered cats! He remembered those. Now, that was one weird thing. What kind of biological niche would feathered cats possibly fit into?

Ross looked down at his laptop and typed out a quick note. You never know, he thought, what details turn out *not* to be insignificant later.

When he was done typing, he turned his attention to his earphones—and discovered that the Russians had already made their jump into the past. He listened closely—and sure enough, the voice reported that their biologist had gone missing.

The Russians, because of time pressure and a lack of clues so far, had regrouped into doubles and proceeded more cautiously, their priorities being to search for their missing member and to stay hidden.

About a week into their stay in the past, Ross felt his mind wandering again—returning to the feathered cats. Feathered cats—what purpose could they serve? How would they evolve?

The voice changed suddenly, and Ross caught the end of a real surprise.

"...no evidence of the winged folk, contrary to what we had been led to believe from the tapes of the American Expedition. But this is our third sighting of the beings we call, for lack of data, the weasel folk—as the Americans did. Only at night, and within the great city, have we seen them. During the day, we have seen other beings, but no weasel folk. We have not made ourselves known as yet, though again, unlike what the Americans reported on their tapes, these beings exhibit no signs of aggressive behavior..."

Weaslies? No winged beings?

Had someone else gone back in time and caused a major rupture in the timeline? But everything else had checked out—

Ross shook his head, as if to chase away his thoughts. That was the problem with time travel, all the blasted ramifications. It was enough to give any super-scientist a brain sprain, much less an everyday guy.

So Ross decided not to think. He turned his attention back to the tape, and this time he kept his attention on the bland voice detailing a daily load of new surprises.

Chapter Five

When the tape was done, the first question was from Ross, which did not surprise Eveleen. "The *Weaslies* are the dominant culture?"

Eveleen bent her head, hiding a smile. Her husband was an acknowledged top agent, brave, intelligent, and altogether wonderful—but he was also impetuous, impatient of rules, and a maverick.

And she adored him for it.

Kelgarries's hatchet face didn't change in expression, but Eveleen sensed very strongly that he was trying to hide a smile. Some of the Russians looked a little startled at the outburst. Only Ashe remained, at least outwardly, unmoved—he and Saba both, she noted belatedly.

"Yes," Kelgarries said. "You are correct."

"But the winged people in the ruined tower were still there in the present," Ross stated. "*Are* still there."

"Yes, they are," the Colonel affirmed.

"And the Weaslies are still feral."

"Again, you are correct."

Kelgarries went on, when the Colonel sat back, "So we can assume that the timeline has not been tampered with—though I guess we'll never really know. But for our purposes, we can assume not."

33

Ross sighed, clapping down the lid on his laptop. "Weaslies. When I think of that fight we had—well, this is beginning to look like a puzzle where half the pieces are missing. These Weaslies in the past sound like some kind of ancient Chinese culture, only even older and more stratified—so what happened? There was sure no sign of any culture at all when we met 'em."

"The violence is there," Eveleen spoke. "Remember the biologist, whose only crime seems to have been to enter an enclave without identity or place. How did all that change so drastically?"

"That's one of the mysteries we are going to have to solve," Ashe spoke up.

Ross groaned theatrically, clutching his head. "I don't think we're the ones to send. This is sounding more and more like a case for a regiment of brainiacs. Not a handful of agents."

Kelgarries shook his head—echoed by the Colonel.

"No. These people—we may as well get used to their term, Yilayil—would, to all appearances, not tolerate being studied. We need skilled agents—yourselves—to adapt to their culture in the ways outlined by the missing team, and work from within."

"But it sounds like we're going to be a cross between servants, and ... and house pets!" Ross protested.

A soft laugh and a swift exchange of Russian reminded Eveleen of the presence of Misha Nikulin. She did not turn her head. Her long years of martial-arts training had already inured her to certain types of men—of which Project Star inevitably had its fair share. One sure way to provoke Mr. Nikulin would be to look at him—a glare just as much as a smile would be equally challenging.

"Being house pets is an easier assignment than running after mastodons in winter, wearing nothing but a wolfskin mini skirt and a coat of grease," Ashe said, laughing.

Saba smiled slightly. Eveleen caught her glance, and Saba's smile increased.

The Russians were now deep in conversation, the Colonel illustrating something. Ashe leaned over to speak with Kelgarries and Ross.

Under cover of the other conversations, Saba murmured softly, "Your husband. Very like my first partner, Lisette Al-Aseer." Saba's dark eyes were difficult to read. Humor? Sadness? Eveleen sensed a little of both.

"Tell me about her," Eveleen whispered back.

Saba gave a little shrug. "She was just as impetuous. Always in trouble with the authorities—while pulling off brilliant coups. I learned a great deal from her."

"Where is she now?" Eveleen asked.

"One of the first ones sent off-world," Saba answered, her expression now sober. "I have had no word for over two years. In the data banks she's listed as 'On Assignment' and whatever that assignment is has been classified beyond my level."

Eveleen nodded. If anything had happened to Saba's friend, the other agents might never find out. There was too deep a need for secrecy; though the world knew about space exploration, the governments had made a concerted effort to keep all hints of news about time travel from ever reaching the media. The chance of unscrupulous individuals getting hold of a time machine for their own uses was too great a danger.

So the Project was veiled in secrecy, and that meant strict data control even among agents, always judged on a need-to-know basis.

Unfortunately.

As Kelgarries paused to answer a question from one of the Russians, Eveleen thought back over the night before. While Ross had been watching his video, she'd been in the library using the E-mail to query the three teams of married agents that she had found after a quick scan through the data banks.

I'm so used to taking care of myself, she thought as Kelgarries, the Russian with the query, and the Colonel now talked in quiet voices.

Eveleen felt a little sad to have even one secret so early in a marriage, but she hesitated to discuss this with Ross—especially after seeing his reaction at Misha's absurdity.

What good would telling him do, except make him worry? Men had been blithely launching into action for millennia. Women had been equal partners with men relatively recently—but they had been champion worriers since the dawn of time. Better to ask some married couples with more experience in partnerships under dangerous conditions how they coped with the fear of loss of a partner.

She watched Ross typing notes into his laptop, a little frown between his brows.

I'd rather get lost than lose him, she thought bleakly, and then scolded herself for defeatist thinking. The idea was to keep them both safe.

Kelgarries looked up then. "The Colonel suggests that we might actually speed the training along if we split for the language-assimilation portion. We'll get together again when we start training for specific positions on the world. Gordon? Summation?"

Gordon Ashe looked up. "I'll give us all a quick synopsis of what kind of civilization we're looking at, so we can keep the worldview in mind as we crash-learn it in pieces."

He cleared his throat.

"One. The Yilayil people are the dominant culture, a hyper-complex civilization trying to maintain the diversity of an interstellar culture that—for some reason—has no new entries showing up. But the process for assimilation has already begun, through a complex of behaviors that are both cultural and ritualistic, called ti[*trill*]kee—" He whistled the middle part with difficulty. "It seems to mean deportment, but it's more than just that; it's a way of life accepted by all, and deviation, once one has been accepted by the Yilayil, is not tolerated. Since there is no mention in the Time Capsule of the winged people, we must assume they arrived later—"

"From a crashed spaceship, perhaps?" one of the Russians asked, enunciating carefully in English. "Or from one of the islands on the far side of the planet from the spaceport?"

"It is a possibility, though unlikely—not if they have any kind of culture with technical capabilities," the Colonel said. "When our globe ship skirted the planet, we did energy readings. Energy use is uniformly low, except on the island containing the spaceport. There it is exceptionally high."

Kelgarries said, "We assume from the observable drive to conformity that any other race with technical capabilities is eventually drawn to the capital island and conformity in order to have access to data and technology."

"The flyers are not tech-capable in the present time-line," Ross spoke up. "Of course, none of the three races we encountered were. They were a lot more civilized than those feral humanoids or the Weaslies."

"The flyers might be indigenous and hidden, and might be latecomers. We will be looking for clues, of course," Ashe said, nodding. "Second: the Yilayil are the only nocturnal land-living intelligence on the planet, and all the diurnal creatures exist lower in the cultural hierarchy, locked into rigid castes that determine their status and duties. Divergence means ostracism; obedience is rewarded with privileges which translate to various forms of wealth, leisure, etc."

Ashe stopped, looking around for questions. No one spoke, but Ross frowned, flexing his scarred hand. Eveleen bit her lip.

Ashe said, "Ross?"

The scarred hand balled into a fist, and then opened. Eveleen watched her husband force his feelings behind a polite mask as he said, "It sounds a little like we're expected to fit into a society of robots."

"Not robots," Ashe said, smiling. "If they were, there would not be a question of conformity, would there?"

"Conformity," Ross repeated, grimacing. "I have to admit that's what sticks in my craw. Conformity seems another word for—" He looked over at the Russians, and Eveleen saw Misha nod and give Ross a thumbs-up.

It was an unexpected gesture. Eveleen was relieved to see Ross flick a hand up in salute. Then he went on, "I don't know what. Main thing is, I didn't catch who decides if any given race has 'conformed' properly."

"That's because the First Team didn't say." Ashe sat back, scanning his notes. "Until we find out, we can assume that the Yilayil decide. Anything more to add?"

Ross shook his head.

"Then I'll continue with the Yilayil," Gordon said. "They dwell in tunnels and caves, vast spaces underground. At first they had seemed unable to deal with the sudden appearance of the First Team whose place of origin they—obviously—couldn't figure out. This is important to remember:

they are, of course, aware of other races—we will apparently meet several—and their way of dealing with them has been to assimilate them into the hierarchy through ti[*trill*]kee. Every race has its enclave somewhere on the world—yet the spaceport on the main island is closed, so no new ones are coming in. We don't know if this is by accident or design. We will have to find out."

He paused. Again, no questions.

"As for interaction, the races are segregated, save for a single exception: the mysterious House of Knowledge— which, apparently, is what Ross and I called the library— where the Russians found that carving."

Eveleen cast another quick glance at Saba. It was clear what her job would be: she'd have to penetrate the House of Knowledge, to learn what she could about the missing Russians. The evidence was already there, if the carving could be believed, that Saba had *been* there. Her visit had already happened—hopefully safely.

What is my job to be? Eveleen thought.

She looked down to hide a grim smile.

She'd find out soon enough.

Saba excused herself from dinner as early as was polite, and left the common room. Much as she enjoyed watching the impetuous Americans strive to find congenial topics to discuss with the reserved, rather dour Russians—and the way the two male agents, Misha and Ross, watched each other speculatively when the other was not aware—she felt the pressure of time tightening the muscles on the back of her neck.

She'd seen the looks on all their faces when a sample from the language tapes was played. If the stakes had not been so high, she would have laughed at the restrained disgust of the Russians (who had apparently just begun struggling with the Russian version of the tapes) to Eveleen's shock and Ross Murdock's blank despair. Only Gordon Ashe had displayed little reaction, a slight frown between his brows, his head bowed as he concentrated.

She crossed the short hallway to her room, turning on the light and her computer at the same time. Calling up the tapes, she tabbed the sound to the speakers, and paced back and forth in the tiny space as she listened.

Saba was grateful to Katarina, the unknown but gifted Russian linguist/archivist on the missing team, for having done a superlative job on the preliminaries. As it was, learning this language was going to be a terrific challenge.

The translator's voice began.

"The Yilayil language has one component in common with English: it seems to be a tremendously flexible language, adopting words from all the others, altering them and making them its own.

"That is *all* the Yilayil tongue has in common with English."

And next was an example. The sound was strange, midway between a whistle and a drone, with ululations and note alterations rather like a chant, or music, modifying it.

The Yilayil people, with their muzzles that resembled those of earth weasels, were not likely to make the labial sounds of human languages. The. humans who were to approximate the Yilayil language would first of all have to know how to whistle—and then would have to learn to hum while doing it.

But harder, much harder, was the prospect of hearing the language and then speaking it. Chinese, often regarded as the toughest language to learn, used to take at least a couple of years for a linguistically gifted individual; now, with the hypno-tape method used by government agencies, it took several months. Chinese seemed easy compared to this utterly alien, bizarrely weird tongue.

Especially since the hypno-tapes she had used until now were complete and these weren't. These tapes left whole levels of expression fragmentary and confusing.

And they had a limited time in which to learn it—the duration of their flight to the planet.

Saba had seen the unspoken reaction in all the others' faces. She knew it matched her own: dread. Everyone was very aware that the First Team's lack of knowledge might have been related to why they disappeared.

Luckily Katarina had taped a great deal of indigenous talk—which her team had been in the midst of studying when they disappeared. Saba, on hearing her tapes, vowed she was going to master it before planetfall. This meant that she had to find the key to the language, its music, even though its speakers had utterly nothing in common with human beings, whose various language-musics carried subtle but definite similarities.

So she'd better get started right away.

Gordon Ashe looked at Saba's closed door. From beyond it came faint sounds: he recognized the weird noises of the Yilayil language. Annoyance and admiration twisted at his guts.

The admiration was easy to acknowledge. He had a lot of respect for any agent who got right to business when a mission was at hand, especially one that carried this much

41

firepower. The annoyance...why the hell couldn't she call them all in and share her expertise? Did she have to get ahead, just to show off?

He shook his head, hard. No. Stop attributing competitive American motivations to someone from a totally different culture.

He raised his hand to knock, then sighed. What would he say? Would he just be interrupting her for little purpose?

Better to get busy with his own tapes, he decided. So he retreated to his room and fired up his computer.

He paused the tape after that first Yilayil example, then replayed it.

"Weird, isn't it?" Ross spoke from the open doorway.

Ashe turned around, saw Ross and Eveleen standing there.

"Come in," he said. "I take it you had the same idea?"

"I saw Saba leave," Eveleen said, smiling. "Ross and I made a bet she was itching to get cracking on her tapes."

"Where are the Russians?" Ashe asked.

Ross jerked a thumb over his shoulder. "Finished dinner, Colonel gave them the high-sign, and they vamoosed in a group. My guess is, they're hunkered down right now with their versions of Katarina's tape. Learn fast, make the decadent Americans look bad."

"Be fair," Eveleen retorted, elbowing Ross in the side. "That missing team was their friends. If our friends went missing, we'd do the same."

"I don't want to be fair," Ross said. "I want to be first."

"So much for scheduled recreational time," Eveleen added with a grin.

"We can do recreation on shipboard," Ashe said, and he hit the replay again.

At the end, Eveleen had a faint crease between her brows. "It's like chanting, more than speech," she said. "Speech sounds monotone after it," Ross added, his eyes closed.

"Mellifluous," Eveleen put in. "That's the word I was looking for."

"Mellifluous—or demented?" Ashe said, and activated the tape again.

The translator's voice filled the room: "The normal word order is: Speaker identity, status, location, time, verb, subject, indirect object, direct object."

She followed with a trill/drone in Yilayil, then said, in English, "This is, roughly translated: 'I, Yeeyee Sight-of-stars, at pathway-meets-water at dawn offer trade of scent-bearers-from-beyond-sun their gili-blossom mat."

Ashe paused the tape.

"That takes forever," Ross complained.

"The Yilayil statement took half the time the English translation did," Eveleen said. "Are all those flowery things names or noun-identifiers that you have to invent every time you speak?"

Ashe shook his head. "Too little information yet. Let's listen further."

"This is the word order of neutral statements. There are other word orders for different challenges and deferences, for commands, for questions. We will address the matter of questions later, for these constitute another form entirely: briefly, we have questions of challenge, questions of debate, questions of personal consequence—"

"Huh," Ross interrupted, rubbing his chin. "What about 'Are my shoes untied'?"

"That, I imagine, would be a question of personal consequence," Ashe said, smiling.

. "If they wear shoes," Eveleen put in. "Now hush, and let's hear this thing through, or we'll never get any sleep tonight!"

Ross subsided with a willingness that he had never exhibited to any of his male partners in the past, and they proceeded through the tape in silence.

At the end, Ashe shut off his computer, and sat back in his chair. "Well?"

. Ross pursed his lips, and let out a long liquid trill. "Guess we better practice wetting our whistlers. Think they have beer?"

Eveleen snorted a laugh. "*Will* you be serious?"

Ross sighed. "I think we're going to go nuts trying to learn that mess. I can't hear anything but bird-tweeting. Some cabbie I'll be."

"We'll be," Eveleen said. "Just as well we both are assigned to transportation. One of us is going to have to learn this stuff."

"You learn it. I'll drive." Ross grinned.

Ashe shook his head. "Oh, go to sleep."

CHAPTER SIX

"What happened with this new Russian, Misha Petrovich Nikulin?" Saba asked the next day as Eveleen and she worked out side by side on the stationary bikes. "Something. There was too much tension yesterday that I cannot otherwise explain."

"Oh-h-h-h-h yes," Eveleen said, rolling her eyes. "I was just going down to the training room when I looked up and there was this handsome blond guy strolling along looking at the door numbers. Before I could open my mouth to ask him if he needed directions he walked up, introduced himself, threw his arms around me, and tried to kiss me."

"No warning?"

"Nothing. Because coming along right behind was Ross."

Saba took her lower lip between her teeth. "Did you know this man?"

"Misha? Never saw him before in my life. But I will wager any amount of money he knew who we were, though he pretended not to. And furthermore it was not my devastating beauty that brought on that excess of affection—it was some kind of crazy challenge because he wasn't the least surprised to see Ross there."

Saba, to Eveleen's surprise, nodded in agreement. "I know that type. In truth, I think this agency the world over

45

selects for just that sort—both male and female. My former partner was like that. I could see her doing this to your spouse, just to see what would happen."

"And I would probably have decked her," Eveleen admitted. "Yes." She winced. "You know, I *would* have. It's all very well to tell Ross that I can take care of myself, thank you, but instinct is faster than thought, and it does go both ways."

Saba smiled, her dark eyes steady.

"Huh," Eveleen said. "I hadn't thought of *that*. Well. One of those unpleasant little insights that one needs now and again to keep one humble. I'll remember that, in case Misha starts it up again and Ross breathes fire."

Saba put her head to one side, but said nothing.

Eveleen gave a sigh, short and sharp, and forced her mind back onto the job. "Speaking of Russians—and Yilayil challenges. It makes a kind of sense, if what the Russian linguist surmised is correct, in challenge mode one gets very flowery—the more challenging, the more oblique. This would give the other person time to frame a response, and decide who gets preference, who defers. This must mean that everyday activities require relatively simple language—not just with outsiders, but among themselves. Otherwise it just doesn't seem reasonable."

Saba's eyes narrowed as she considered. "I would take care," she said slowly, "in assuming what might seem reasonable to Yilayil culture. Especially given the hints of multiple layers to the language, the odd tenses and sensory aspects."

"I just assumed those were artifacts of a limited data set," said Eveleen. "Just misunderstood."

"I am not so sure," said Saba carefully. "But, yes, otherwise I do agree that far: quick modes of speech for the minutiae of everyday business makes good sense. It does seem, though, that almost every aspect of life involves a challenge of some kind or other—at least when encountering beings outside one's own group."

"If a few months' studies can be trusted," Eveleen said. "I keep thinking of that poor biologist." She winced as she recalled the grief and shock expressed by Katarina when her team discovered the remains of their fellow agent, just after they had made their first encounter.

Saba also reacted, her face tightening, her gaze lowered. Eveleen felt the lance of remorse, and wished she hadn't spoken. She had momentarily forgotten about Saba's first partner. Did the woman lie in some unknown grave worlds and centuries away? Or had something wrenched time out of alignment so that she was forever lost—as had apparently happened to one of Gordon Ashe's former agents?

Eveleen bit her lip, wondering if Gordon or Saba would talk about that. They both had this experience in common, but they were both so very reserved.

Saba looked up, and said in her calm voice, "This has occurred to me as well. Often. The challenge aspect might be emphasized only with newly arrived outsiders."

"We'll be getting that treatment," Eveleen said, relieved that the moment seemed to have passed.

"Perhaps. As for the specifics, most of them sound like they are ritual challenges, and both sides know the question and answer before it's even spoken," Saba said. "It's a kind of right-of-way etiquette."

Eveleen nodded, glad that, so far, her instincts were corresponding with the better-trained Saba's. "And the Russians were still in the early stages of establishing themselves within the hierarchy, so they were exposed to the more formal challenge-speech..."

Eveleen thought she heard doubt in the Ethiopian's soft, musical tones. "Except?" she prompted.

Saba shook her head slightly. "It means little to query at this early point."

"I know," Eveleen said. "Just for the sake of discussion— and because, hard as we are working, we're not exactly going anywhere ..." She pointed at their bicycles.

Saba smiled. "All right, then. It does seem to me that the Yilayils do little that is sudden or impulsive, if what we are learning conveys a true sense of their culture. And yet we come back to the fact that the First Team disappeared— abruptly—without any sign or signal."

"That we've yet discovered," Eveleen amended. "When we get back, we might still find something."

"And, barring that?"

Eveleen bit her lip. "I have to admit it's been bothering me too. I suppose the problem, if problem there was, might not originate from the Yilayils at all—but from one of the other races living on the planet. We don't know anything about these as yet, except for some names and some superficial characteristics. Our Russians didn't have enough time, apparently, to learn much of them between the time they made themselves known and when they disappeared. They spent so much time living in the jungle outside the city, just watching!"

"And?" Saba prompted. .

Eveleen sighed. "Well, I know it's not fair to judge, but I can't help thinking about what the Yilayils became down at our end of the timeline—those Weaslies. There certainly was no sign of hierarchy, or structure, or music, when Ross and Ashe encountered them! Just bloodshed!"

"I, too, have pondered this," Saba admitted.

Encouraged, Eveleen warmed to her theme. "So far, in every culture I've studied or encountered, there is at least some trace of the former. But here—we are presented with the Yilayils, whose culture is intricate in the extreme. It reminds me of medieval guilds, only much more complex. Each individual seems to be born into a specific guild, to which they appear to belong for a lifetime. Their name and location indicates their guild, family status, and field of mastery—and everyone has a place. Strangers are not tolerated; they have to be integrated slowly, but integrated they are. No evidence of war, the Russians said. And yet—we always come back to this disappearance."

Saba nodded again. "Since it is my lot to go to this House of Knowledge, I have to hope to find some clues there."

"Except that's another mystery," Eveleen said.

Saba smiled grimly. "When was I there for that statue to be carved? Or am I going to arrive to find a group of women, from some other planet, who look just like me—and if so, where might *they* have come from—and why?"

Eveleen shuddered. "I know it's cowardly to say so, but I'm glad that my 'skill' is just going to be a cabbie. That is, assuming we get *that* far."

The timer went off then, indicating the end of the workout. Saba went off to the showers, but Eveleen lingered. Since this was not officially rec time, she was hoping to find someone for a good workout on the practice mats. There was no better stress reliever, she firmly believed, than sparring and grappling with some feisty martial-arts expert whose skills were as good as her own.

She moved to the gym—but just as she was opening the door, her pager buzzed quietly against her wrist. She peeled back her leotard sleeve and glanced down, then sighed.

Milliard! There was no putting *him* off.

She showered and changed in record time, then raced to an elevator to go to the top brass levels.

When she emerged, she found another surprise—Ross was just getting out of the second elevator.

"Hey," he said, grabbing her hand.

"What's the problem—do you know? Is this meeting an 'uh oh,' or an 'oh yeah'?" she asked, sneaking a peek around the corridor.

"I don't know anything beyond the fact that it's just thou and I, O wife," Ross said, grinning.

"So you haven't pounded Misha Nikulin into paste."

Ross laughed. "I haven't even seen him. Besides, you're the paste-pounder in the family. You could dispose of him faster than I could."

Eveleen nodded, not showing her relief. Especially after her discussion with Saba, she was doubly glad that she hadn't further hassled Ross about that disastrous first meeting with Misha, after they'd retired for the night. Apparently Ross had thought it through on his own. "And don't you forget it," she said, mock commanding.

No one was in sight. She leaned up for a kiss, then Ross knocked at Milliard's door.

"Come in."

The big boss was seated behind his desk, his gray hair disheveled as if he'd just been running his hands through it.

"Something's wrong?" Ross said as he and Eveleen entered and sat down in the overpadded chairs before the desk.

"Many somethings," Milliard said with a twisted smile. "But that's my headache. I called you two in for a last-minute talk. I know it's late in the game, and I'm not sure what to do if there's a problem, but I have to talk to you if only to ease my own mind."

"We're here," Eveleen said, feeling apprehension.

"If its these Russians," Ross began.

"No." Milliard sighed, shuffling a couple of papers on his desk without really looking at them. Then he sat back. "I know we railroaded you two into this project. That's because I desperately want you both there. You're both in tiptop physical shape—the medicos gave you green lights after your evaluations following your return from Dominium. But it's been pointed out to me by several people whose job it is to keep track of these things that we usually keep married pairs at home flying desk jobs for at least a year, until they feel their relationship is stable enough for the intense stress of fieldwork. You two have barely had a honeymoon. How do you feel about rushing off right away?"

Eveleen was so surprised she couldn't think. "Is this," she asked with care, "in reference to specific team members?"

Milliard gave her a quizzical glance. "Not specifically. Has there been a problem?"

"No," Ross said at the same time as Eveleen said, "No."

They looked at each other and smiled.

Eveleen realized that the incident with Misha had in fact stayed between the three of them. Four, counting Saba, but Eveleen did not believe that the Ethiopian woman would have talked about it. So she considered the question in general.

During her single years the emphasis on the Project had always been the work at hand. Of course people did socialize—and match up. She'd dated briefly among the men at HQ during her days as a martial-arts instructor. She'd even briefly dated outside the Project, knowing that she could deflect superficial questions about what she did by just claiming to teach martial arts. Except how could you really get serious with someone you had to lie to if he asked lots of detailed questions about your career?

Nothing—until Ross—had been serious. And her relationship with him had begun off-world, away from therapists, psychologists, and other Project personnel. She'd made her own way, and on her return, had expected to continue making her own way. It hadn't occurred to her that there existed an official policy for such contingencies as marriage among agents.

She looked over at Ross, to find him watching her, and a pang smote her heart. Was he just now beginning to think along the same tracks that had worried her?

She wanted to spare him that. "Oh, I don't see a problem," she said, smiling, infusing her voice with as much confidence as she could. "Remember, we did have a lot of time together on Dominium, so we know we can handle fieldwork together."

Ross sat back, drumming one hand idly on his chair arm. "She's right." He grinned. "And if something happens, I know she can protect me!"

He laughed, Milliard laughed, and Eveleen snorted a laugh as well.

"Are you sure? Any doubts? Because I'd rather pull you off the Project now, and find some other agents, than put you at further risk—"

"No," Ross said firmly, and—

"No!" Eveleen exclaimed at the very same moment.

Their eyes met and again they laughed.

Ross isn't worried, she thought. That's what I want. I *will* protect him, but not in the ways he was joking about.

The door to Milliard's office opened, and Gordon Ashe almost ran into Ross and Eveleen, who were just coming out. Both of the pair were grinning.

"You too?" he asked.

Ross raised his hands. "We're not in trouble. I promise!"

Eveleen laughed. "Twit," she said, not at all angrily, and the two of them headed for the elevators.

Ashe walked in, to find the big boss looking tired.

"Case Renfry and Mikhail Nikulin took off for Russia last night with the load of scientific equipment," Milliard said without preamble. "You haven't seen Case for a time, but he's been taking intensive training in Russian. With his background—having gone with you on that first run to the Yilayil planet—he's been welcomed by the Russian science team to join their number."

"Good," Gordon said.

"Now. This is the last chance for us to do anything to help you before you take off." Milliard rubbed his jaw. "Anything you foresee as a problem?"

"No," Ashe said. "Beyond the usual range of unforeseen disasters that comes with fieldwork."

"I mean with the personnel," Milliard asked. "Too many untried aspects to this setup. Could spell success—or a major headache."

Ashe nodded. Pairing Russians and Americans was new, and one didn't need to be psychic to see that mutual trust was going to take time. Sending two agents just married was against policy. So was pairing partners of both opposite genders and different cultures. But, at least so far, driving necessity fostered the needed mental readjustments. Except— "Ross and Nikulin might be a problem."

"I suspect that the Colonel was not completely happy with Nikulin either," Milliard went on. "Which may or may not be why he was only here one day."

Ashe waited for an explanation, but Milliard just shrugged. "No, nothing has been said to me. Internal problems, maybe. He's volatile, I've learned that much. There is also the fact that their agent-base is so small that they are perforce thrown together for extended years."

Ashe nodded. "Small because of those successful Baldy attacks. That's got to warp their psyches a little."

"The Colonel says that some of them exhibit what could be called combat fatigue—but what can they do? They can't hire more agents, not until they can show their government positive results. So they cope with the sorts of problems we are able to prevent by reassignment and protracted leaves, when necessary. To get from general comments to specifics, the Colonel thinks Nikulin had some kind of relationship with one of the missing team—and with at least one of the Russians assigned to your team, as well. He's a loose cannon, Nikulin is. Here's his file. You'll have to watch out for him—"

Ashe nodded, picking up the folder. He read rapidly through it, then glanced up. "Right. Or Ross will resolve things his own way. I understand."

"Which brings us to us," Milliard said. "How are you getting along with Saba?" His eyes narrowed shrewdly.

Ashe thought briefly of the tall, handsome woman. "She's like me," he said slowly. "All business."

"Good. I don't require you two to become best friends, but I do need you to work together well. Your lives may be at stake, and you have to be able to depend on each other."

"I believe I can depend on her," Ashe said, with conviction. "And I try to be dependable."

"That's all I can ask," Milliard said. "Anything else?"

Ashe shook his head slowly. Anything else would stay within his skull and not be spoken. It was up to him to solve any problems that arose.

"The Colonel is coming in next; when we've had our interview, if there are no insurmountable problems, we'll start the clock on takeoff."

"Right." Ashe handed back Nikulin's file and rose from his seat. "Then I'll get back to work."

He went out, encountering the gray-haired Russian commander as she emerged from the elevator. She greeted him courteously, then continued to Milliard's office.

Ashe heard the door close behind her. The elevator door stood open, but he paused, his hand on the wall, and looked around.

Silence.

Soon he'd be aboard a ship accompanied by Russians—one of whom, Mikhail Petrovich Nikulin, used to be a major headache to American time agents back in the bad old days—a pair of newlyweds, and a partner who seemed as wary of him as he was of her. And he'd be in command of this jaunt into the past of a planet that was no part of human history.

He'd told Milliard that there were no problems, which wasn't true, but he promised himself that he'd solve them, which was true. The many problems of time, logistics, language barriers, and the rest could indeed be solved. Emotional reactions simply didn't count, not when there were lives at stake.

But the real truth was, with his best friend now married, he'd never felt more isolated in his life.

CHAPTER SEVEN

Ross Murdock peered out the window of the airliner. Russia!

He had to shake his head as he looked over the last of the Gulf of Finland gleaming with gray-green highlights in the weak sun. At home in the northeastern states, autumn meant chilly, rainy days interspersed with mellow warm ones, and driving around to view the glorious changing of the leaves. Here it was already winter—and so it would remain, he was told, until May.

Who would have thought he would ever set foot in Russia?

He looked around the plane. It was full of tourists, and Russian citizens going home. He detected a mixture of languages in the chatter.

The rest of his team was scattered throughout the plane. Next to him Eveleen dozed lightly, a mystery novel in her lap. Two seats behind, Ashe's sunbleached brown hair was visible. By craning his neck, Ross could see that the archaeologist was reading a history of St. Petersburg. Ross had done a little excavation on his own, just before departure. What he'd read was fascinating, and grim in places. He hadn't realized what an ancient land Russia was. But then, Ethiopia was even older, he thought, catching sight of Saba in the next row. She was calmly working away at her laptop computer, headphones on. Occasionally she glanced out the window. At the very end of his row he could make out Renfry's thinning hair. The technical expert was looking down as well, probably busy on his own laptop.

Ross turned the other way, and looked at Ashe again. Why hadn't he sat with Saba? He shook his head silently. Not his place to interfere—anyway, if he did, he'd probably make things worse. But Gordon and Saba didn't seem to mesh as a team. Ross just hoped this wasn't going to make things tough when the real action started happening.

The engine noise changed; the plane tipped downward, starting to lose altitude.

The seat-belt light flashed on, and people murmured as the plane decelerated, bumping occasionally in the turbulent air currents. Ross thought about launching from the planet again—not in a U.S. spacecraft, but in one of those weird alien globe ships. Somehow a little turbulence didn't seem very scary.

Eveleen woke up, alert within seconds. She clicked her seat belt on, and yawned.

"Great book, eh?" Ross cracked.

Eveleen grinned. "Actually, it's pretty good. But even the most brilliant book is not going to keep me awake after only two hours of shut-eye."

Ross shook his head. "Told you that crazy stunt would be a mistake."

"Wrong," Eveleen said. "Not a mistake. Being tired and headachy is worth it—I really think we started to get to know each other." She nodded toward some of the Russians, three or four rows back.

Ross grimaced. "We'll be doing that, and plenty, when we're all stuck together on that blasted fishbowl."

Eveleen grinned unrepentantly. Ross had been against her going out on their last evening in Washington, D.C., with Saba and some of the Russians to see some folk dance performance. The weather had been wild, and as the hours crawled by, he'd prowled restlessly around HQ, sure they'd met with some accident.

Turned out that they'd gone after the performance to an old dive frequented by Eastern Europeans, and there they'd drunk vodka, and slivovitz, and roared folk songs for half the night. When they returned, they'd all been tired, tipsy, but the atmosphere of tension had somehow lessened markedly.

The engines cut in, loud and vibrating, and the plane heeled.

Ross looked down at St. Petersburg, sprawled over the delta of the Neva River. From the air the old section looked almost like a fairy-tale city, and as he stared at those onion domes-gleaming in the low northern sun, once again he was struck by a sense of strangeness.

Then the plane touched down, and taxied slowly to the terminal. At once the cabin was full of chatter as people gathered their belongings and prepared to disembark.

Their passports stated that they were tourists, but once they reached the front of the long line, Ross was not surprised to see the official squint at his passport, look at a computer printout, and wave him out of line. He waited; Eveleen joined him a moment later, pulling her suitcase on its wheels.

They were taken to a special room for customs, which was a mere formality. Ashe and Sabe both joined them, both of them looking noncommittal as always. Eveleen looked about with undisguised interest as they were led down corridors and hallways, then out into the wintry sun and bitterly cold air. Snow drifted lazily as they were waved to an official-looking car.

The driver loaded their luggage into the trunk, then took his seat without speaking. Pretty soon they were zooming along the handsome boulevards of the Admiralty district. Bridges and canals were everywhere in evidence, amid spectacularly beautiful baroque edifices. To Ross the buildings looked heavy and solid—the kind of buildings that would withstand long winters.

"Oh! That's got to be the Hermitage," Eveleen breathed.

"I think so," Gordon said. "The Winter Palace—"

"That is correct," the driver said in heavily accented English. "I give you little tour before destination."

In silence Ross watched the city slide by. The cars all looked strange, and despite the cold weather, there was quite a bit of pedestrian and bicycle traffic about. The buildings really were handsome—most of them—and he found it quite interesting, very different from any American city he'd ever seen.

Before long they stopped outside an older stone building with a plain facade. Ross was just opening his mouth to ask where the rest of their team might be when he saw another car pull up behind theirs, and the Russians climbed out, all chattering with a freedom he had never seen them use back in the States.

Before long they found themselves in a big, warm room with high ceilings and ancient plaster, drinking sweet, strong coffee out of little glass cups encased in holders.

Colonel Vasilyeva sat down, smiling broadly. "Welcome to the Russian Federation," she said. "I apologize for the lack of time for a proper tour. When we return successfully from our mission, you can be sure we shall show you everything our city has to offer. Tomorrow morning, early, we will call for you, and a special train will take us to our destination. Tonight, we will relax..."

Interesting, Ross thought. She doesn't say anything of the mission that could be overheard. A habit of caution or necessity?

Then he thought about how he'd act if they were located in a hotel somewhere in the States. He wouldn't be blabbing either.

"...supper, and afterward you have free time," she was saying.

Gordon Ashe said, "We'll use that time to work on our studies, if that is possible."

The Colonel nodded soberly. "We will provide equipment with headphones."

"Thank you," Gordon said, sliding a glance from under his brows at Saba, who nodded, her demeanor calm as always.

"Then if there are no further questions, you may establish yourselves in your rooms, and meet back here for supper," the Colonel said, rising.

Five minutes later, Ross and Eveleen stood in their room, which was another with very high ceilings. Ross stared round at the remainders of some unknown Russian's aristocratic past in the moldings at the edges of the walls and around windows. The plaster was old, and the furnishings sparse, plain, but comfortable. A radiator hissed quietly in a corner.

Eveleen went to the window and gazed out over the Russian rooftops. She rocked back and forth on the balls of her feet, silent, looking pensive.

"Problem?" Ross asked, watching her.

She smiled back over her shoulder. "Nothing more serious than trying to decide if I want a workout to stretch the kinks from my muscles after that long plane flight, or if I would rather get a shower."

Ross prowled the perimeter of the room, inspecting the doors. One revealed a small closet, almost a little room; he flicked a low-voltage light on to illuminate a bathroom, complete with tub on feet. "I don't think a shower is an option," he said.

Eveleen appeared at his shoulder, and grinned. "If the water pressure is anything like Vera warned me, I guess my dilemma is solved." So saying she turned on the faucet full blast, and they both watched the thin stream of gently steaming water.

"It's going to take a while for that tub to fill," Ross said.

Eveleen snapped her fingers. "Workout first."

Ross sighed. "I'll turn on the Yilayil tape. We can whistle as we work."

Eveleen groaned and threw a pillow at him.

Dinner was noticeably different from meals in America.

The food was spicy and interesting, but that wasn't what caught at Ross's attention. They'd been joined by more Russians—but somehow Ross began to see them in a different light, and it wasn't just Renfry's ability to speak with them that made the difference.

Back in America, Colonel Vasilyeva and these four of her agents had been quiet, polite, and had moved as a group. Except for that damned Nikulin, Ross hadn't really considered the Russians as individuals; he'd looked on them as a kind of unit, and their tight silence had underscored his own lack of trust.

All he'd known about these people was that three of them were the Russian time agents. One, the lanky, bespectacled Valentin Svetlanin, was a scientist.

Back on their home territory, the Russians seemed changed people. Or maybe it was that night out; Ross couldn't imagine Valentin, for example, roaring folk songs—or any other kind of song—but Eveleen insisted he'd in fact been the most lively. He not only knew every single song, but variations on most of those!

Ross wondered if Mikhail Nikulin on his home turf was going to become even more obnoxious—like challenging someone to a duel with pistols at dawn?

Better not borrow trouble, Ross thought, and tried to force Nikulin out of his thoughts.

Instead, he tried to match names with faces.

Vera Pavlova was the redhead who laughed a lot.

Irina Bazarov was short, thin, dark-haired, and subtle-featured. In America she'd moved with a kind of compact neatness that here—on her home ground—Ross recognized as grace.

As the conversation got lively, Ross leaned over and whispered to Eveleen, "That Irina. She into some kind of dance?"

Eveleen's brows arched. "Ballet." She grinned. "About as many years as I studied martial arts. If not more."

Ross awkwardly whistled the Yilayil equivalent of praise.

And from the doorway came another whistle—liquid and pure, and correct in intonation.

"Misha!" the cry went up from the Russians.

Misha lounged against the doorjamb, his coat slung over his shoulder, his shirt open at the neck. Ross eyed the familiar waving blond hair and rakish, smile, trying to hide his instant reaction of dislike and distrust.

Misha laughed, said something in Russian, then immediately turned to Saba and Eveleen, bowing debonairly. Ross forced himself to just sit, but inwardly he thought, *If that jerk tries to smooch either of them, Eveleen had better paste him one, or else I will.*

"So much beauty in my beautiful country! It is poetry for the senses." He kissed Saba's hands, and then, sending a laughing glance Ross's way, bent and kissed Eveleen's as well.

Eveleen snorted a soft laugh, and then took her hands back.

Misha turned to the group and said, "I was sent along, obedient dog that I am, to guard the equipment the Americans contributed. But I assure you I was most diligent with my tapes. So, how far are the rest of you in this accursed tongue?" And he added a fast phrase in Yilayil, whistling and droning expertly.

Ross saw Eveleen whispering a translation to herself; he didn't even try. On the other side of the room the Colonel nodded once in silent approval, and then Saba leaned forward and responded, her intonations correct, as far as Ross could hear. Ashe added a short phrase.

"Chalk one up for us," Ross muttered under his breath.

Eveleen smothered a grin behind her hand. "I wonder if we'll find out if he was sent because he was in trouble or because he's the expert?" she whispered back.

"Somehow I doubt the second choice—despite the grandstanding." Ross leaned forward to sip more of the strong Russian coffee.

"Are we ready?" Misha asked, looking around.

"We leave tomorrow," Vera, the redhead, said. "You timed your arrival close, Misha."

"Ah, Zina said she'd have my ears for breakfast if I was late." Misha dropped into a waiting chair.

Ross glanced over at Colonel Vasilyeva; though she had, at the very first dinner, invited everyone to call her "Zina" he'd found her too formidable for that. But she smiled now, the kind of smile a fond parent would bestow on a favorite child.

Irina leaned over to touch Misha's arm, and she addressed him in rapid Russian.

"English," Vera said quickly, giving Irina a look of challenge.

Misha sat back, smiling. "Not a way to show our gratitude for the technical gifts, yes?"

Viktor Ushanov, one of the other time agents, said something quietly in Russian, and Misha sent an appraising glance at Ashe and Ross, all the irony gone from his face.

"English, English," the Colonel said. "Tomorrow we all begin speaking Yilayil, but tonight, we relax, and we practice the tongue of our guests."

The rest of the dinner conversation was innocuous; after dinner was over, while everyone was milling around the coffee service, Ross made his way to Ashe. "Did you get what was going on when our new boy came in?"

"Nothing bad," Gordon said. "My Russian is pretty rusty, but it was pretty clear that Valentin is coming down hard on our side. He's the young hotshot tech, and I guess Milliard gave the Russians everything they asked for, equipment-wise."

Ross nodded trying for fairness. "No small item, if they're still recovering from what the Baldies did to 'em."

Gordon nodded, his manner approving, then turned away.

The rest of the evening, Ross circulated, trying to get a feel for these new team members. The mission was beginning to take on a sense of reality at last.

The two oldest agents, one man and one woman, spoke very poor English. They were also the quietest and most dour—like Russian agents of old stories, almost, though both were in fact scientists, and would be staying at the base camp in the present, monitoring the time-transfer equipment and making tests. Still, Ross learned their names: Gregori Sidorov and Elizaveta Kaliginova.

The rest spoke English with varying abilities, as they all chatted about scientific developments and some of the problems endemic to secret governmental projects. Nothing classified or politically touchy—just the sometimes funny logistical glitches and exasperating hassles inevitable when dealing with bureaucrats. Those were apparently universal. Renfry became quite loquacious—willingly trading stories with his Russian tech counterparts. From there they moved on to subjects of general interest: movies, television, music, sports.

When the evening ended, Ross was in a good mood.

As he and Eveleen settled into their room, he asked, "So what did you think?"

Eveleen went to the window again, looking out. Then she turned around. "A whole evening of just chatter, but I don't think the time was wasted."

Ross grinned. "That Colonel—Zina. I've got to get used to that. She's no fool."

Eveleen. nodded. "The other night, at the folk festival. Tonight. Somehow these Russians seem less and less like ali ens, and more like, well, like us."

"Human," Ross said.

"Considering where we're going," Eveleen added, "that's a distinction that might just preserve our lives."

Chapter Eight

When the bleak sun rimmed the eastern horizon the next day, Gordon Ashe and his Eastern and Western agency colleagues were squeezed onto worn bench seats aboard a rattletrap of a cargo plane that might have seen service during the Second World War.

He looked down through a window at St. Petersburg dwindling rapidly away between two huge bodies of water, then the plane banked and headed north.

Conversation was minimal; the plane was not heated, and everyone seemed to prefer huddling into their coats, sipping at warm drinks. Just as well. Gordon sat back, watching his breath cloud, as he considered the twist their fortunes had taken.

Were there going to be problems with Misha and Ross? Young as he was, Misha had quite a reputation on both sides of what used to be the Iron Curtain. Of course, Gordon knew that Ross had a reputation as well. Gordon knew a little Russian, and he'd overheard some of them talking about Ross the other night. They all knew the story about Ross's burned hand—how he got it, and why.

There were not many who had survived direct encounters with Baldies. Ross was one—and Misha was another. In fact, if reports were accurate, Misha had apparently delighted in acting as a decoy in order to draw the Baldies off. What had happened to the Baldies he'd fooled wasn't clear, but Kelgarries, in a private conversation just before the team's departure, had wondered if the violence of the Baldies' attacks on the Russians had something to do with the kinds of games the humans might have been playing with the inimical XTees.

Apparently Misha had insisted on being included on this mission. It argued not just a dedication to tough causes. Agents on both sides, supposedly, only found out about missions for which they were being considered. Misha's knowing about this one meant either a high status, despite his young age, or an uncanny ability to winnow out secret information.

Was his reckless courage going to be an asset—or a liability? What were his real motivations for wanting to be sent on this mission?

And what caused the almost palpable tension between Misha and Ross?

Misha's sudden laugh punctuated the silence. Gordon lifted his head, listening.

"...not since I was small. One fall through the ice was enough," Viktor was saying in Russian.

Misha retorted, "Floe hopping was the biggest spring sport in my village."

"It was the only spring sport in your village," Irina said, deadpan.

Misha laughed again. "True!"

Gordon listened to Misha's melodious tenor voice, wavering about what he ought to do. He wanted the team to be safe. Of course. But they also had to work together, and trust one another.

He grimaced, wishing that he knew why the Russian agent had insisted on being included in the mission. Zina

Vasilyeva had been noncommittal; it was Milliard who had said something about some sort of relationship with one of the missing scientists. After watching Misha's flirting for an evening, Gordon was convinced Misha had a relationship of some sort with every single female in the Russian agency. Yet whenever Misha had gotten too outrageous, Zina had spoken a soft word, and the blond agent had raised his hands in truce, and subsided.

Gordon glanced over at the gray-haired woman, who was busy with a laptop computer. What kind of internal politics had the Russians been working through?

The engine sputtered suddenly as a buffet of wind hit them hard. The juddering vibration increased suddenly, causing Saba to glance up and Eveleen to look worried. Only the Russians seemed unconcerned.

Gordon sat back, letting out his breath slowly. He was glad when the plane banked again, and started dropping down. Through the window they could see the White Sea, just barely, a ghost outline through thick white clouds. The world this far north was shades of gray and silver and white—definitely the land of winter.

The plane landed without a problem, and silent Russian workers appeared from a rickety shed and began unloading baggage into trucks. Apparently the scientific equipment had been sent on ahead by train, a precaution against being bumped and banged around in the air.

Someone handed around thermoses of hot, sweet coffee and spicy soup as they piled out of the plane and into the waiting trucks.

Soon they were zooming down a freshly plowed road into what seemed the middle of nowhere. Again, no one spoke much; the truck was unheated. Gordon hunkered in his corner, listening to the growl of the engine and the clash of gears, wondering when he would see the States again. If.

Not if, he thought, angry with himself for permitting even one defeatist thought. And since his own thoughts were lousy company, he turned his attention to the others.

A couple of the Russians murmured softly, their breath clouding in the frigid air. Gordon glanced over—and saw that they were playing cards on a upturned gasoline drum.

He watched idly, listening to the chatter. The Russians were talking about family members, it seemed; after a while he realized they were indulging in the same kind of "what if" he wouldn't permit himself.

He turned his shoulder and glanced at Ross, whose face was grim and stony, his unwavering gaze on his wife. Eveleen had headphones on, running to a portable CD player in her coat pocket. Gordon wondered if it was Yilayil language practice—or something altogether different.

Saba, as well, was listening to earphones. Gordon had no question about what Saba might be doing. Of course she was working ahead on Yilayil nuances. But that was part of her job.

Across from her, Case Renry sat with a laptop on his skinny knees, equally absorbed in his work.

Gordon's attention came back when the truck gave a roar and slowed.

Soon they piled out—to see, sitting out on a barren tarmac launch pad, a globe ship exactly like the one that had inadvertently taken him, Ross, Renfry, and Travis Fox to the other world.

Travis. There was another subject to brood about. Gordon hated to think about Travis lost forever—and he regarded it as his fault, no matter what his superiors said to the contrary. How many would go missing this time—under his command?

As he thought it, he realized that that was his real fear. Not what would happen to him. But the fear that once again he'd lose an agent.

He shook his head; no use brooding. What he had to do was make damn sure that this time, everyone came back. Or he wouldn't.

Making this internal vow, he clambered out after the others.

"Whew," Ross was saying as he tipped his head back and grimaced at the globe ship. "Never thought I'd see one of these things again. Which was all right with me!"

Eveleen walked right up to the ship, and squinted at the dull, pearlescent hull. "Some kind of alloy?"

"Looks like a type of ceramic," Saba said, coming up on the other side.

"You'll have plenty of time to discuss this with Renfry and the other big brains during the trip," Gordon said, forcing an attempt at a light tone. "We'd better lend a hand in getting the gear stowed."

They all joined the line of Russians who were helping the truck driver to load equipment into the ship. Gordon saw Renfry and one of the Russians following a couple of crates with anxious looks—obviously delicate machinery of some type or other.

"At least the Russians seem to have made the inside a little more like home," Ross commented, peering up at the round opening as he muscled his load up the ramp.

"Could hardly be less," Gordon cracked, doing his best to lighten his own mood as he followed Ross inside.

Eveleen snorted a laugh.

"We bunk up here," Zina called down from the level above. "Choose where you wish to sleep. We did not assign."

This globe ship was slightly larger than the one he'd made the trip in before, Gordon noted. The Russians had fitted the big, circular space with movable panels, creating little double cabins that afforded a semblance of privacy.

Gordon hesitated, watching Ross and Eveleen go into one of the small cabins. Out of the corner of his eye he saw Saba hesitate, then she walked with dignity into the next cabin over. Gordon was free to join her—or not.

He looked around, saw that the other cabins were all claimed, and winced. A moment later Ross appeared as if propelled, followed by Eveleen, who whispered, "... make it any more difficult than it already is."

Out loud she said in a cheery voice, "How about if we females bunk together, and you fellows do the same? I know you and Gordon are used to each other's habits from old missions."

Ross rather sheepishly beckoned to Gordon, and Eveleen swung her bags into the cabin Saba had chosen.

Gordon did not hear the conversation between the two women, though he could hear the murmur of their voices.

Ross didn't say anything. He just stowed his stuff in a locker beneath the bunk he'd chosen, leaving the other one to Gordon.

Gordon got his stuff stashed neatly inside of a minute, and went out to see where he could lend a hand. He was not surprised to see that Renfry and the weedy Russian tech-whiz, Valentin, had chosen to bunk together. The Russian women had also paired off, the older two together, and the younger, and Misha and the dark-eyed silent Viktor had also chosen a cabin together, leaving the dour Gregori to bunk with the pilot, a quiet man in his forties who was introduced as Boris Snegiryov.

"We do not wait," Boris said almost immediately. "We lift soon. Get into your bunks. Strap in."

Gordon remembered that last trip. "I take it you haven't modified that plus-gees acceleration?"

"Two point sixty-seven gees," Boris corrected. "It is the same. We cannot interfere with the engines—we still do not completely understand them. We can only work around their given function."

"I don't need a second warning," Ross commented, waving a careless hand. "I'm for my bunk."

As soon as the equipment was stored to the techs' satisfaction, everyone retreated to their bunks, strapping themselves securely in.

Gordon listened to the sudden quiet. Neither he nor Ross spoke.

"We are lifting off," Boris reported over the intercom.

The first warning was the vibration. Gordon remembered that; his heartbeat accelerated.

The vibration increased steadily, until it became a low, subsonic moan that resonated through bones and teeth. Gordon shut his eyes—there was nothing to look at anyway—and waited.

The sound changed abruptly, and the cosmic hand swatted them, pressing him into his bunk.

His consciousness receded to a dim awareness of a virulently glowing red eye; suddenly it was the pit of a volcano he was falling into. He struggled against the nightmare, his body spasmed, and the pit dwindled and resolved into the red-lit numerals on a clock mounted near the door of the cabin.

But his inner ear thought he was still falling, so insistently that he barely noticed the aching of his body in every joint and socket. But he forced himself to unstrap and sit up—and immediately he floated free.

Grabbing the webbing of his bunk, he propelled himself toward the door. His stomach fought, but he recognized the zero gravity-induced nausea for what it was, and looked around, forcing his eyes to impose up and down on his surroundings.

It worked. After a few white-knuckled moments his innards settled, and he hit the door tab. "Ross?" He turned his head.

"Give me a minute." The agent gripped his bunk, his scarred hand showing white.

Gordon turned away and watched the door slide silently into the wall.

Somewhere he heard someone being sick, another person moaned, the baffling of the portable walls only muffling the sound.

A Russian voice called out, "Take your anti-nausea meds!"

A deep voice responded unhappily, "I cannot open my eyes."

Misha's laughter rang out. It sounded heartless. But then came his voice: "Here, Valentin. I'll find it for you—get on your bunk."

There was no sound from any of the women's cabins. Gordon hesitated, then tapped lightly at Saba and Eveleen's—grabbing hastily at a handhold to prevent himself from ricocheting back.

"Yes?" that was Eveleen.

"Gordon here. You all right?"

"We're fine."

Gordon handed himself up the ladder into the circular command center, where one of those cardboard-thin view-screens they'd nicknamed plates on their last journey now showed the blackness of space.

Boris was busy at a console that had been wired to the mysterious guidance console installed by the unknown makers of the ship.

A moment later Gordon was aware of a flicker at his side. He looked up into Zina Vasilyeva's face. Her chin jutted slightly, but otherwise she seemed composed and calm.

"We are safely launched," she said. "Are your people all right?"

"Adjusting to free fall," Gordon said.

"Shall we turn our attention to making a schedule for our people?"

"Let's," Gordon said.

The mission had begun.

CHAPTER NINE

Eveleen launched herself onto the next level, then looked around in delight.

Vera smiled, looking like a kind of cheery cherub with her red curls floating around her face. The other women who had longer hair had braided it and wore it pinned up to keep it from floating in their faces.

"You like?" Vera asked.

"It's great," Eveleen exclaimed. "When we were on the ground, all this space seemed wasted—I forgot about nullgrav."

Saba said, "Whoever made these ships must have spent a lot of time in space."

Irina, from behind, said soberly, "That is why we called them scoutcraft. We think they were sent out to investigate other worlds. They might have gone long times between actual landings."

Irina, Eveleen knew, was by profession a data analyst— apparently formidably good. Her finely chiseled face was also impossible to read, Eveleen had decided after covertly watching them all. Not so Vera, whose every mood was clear in her expression. Vera was gifted at communication; her missions had involved, apparently, getting people to talk. Eveleen hoped her talents would extend to alien races.

Eveleen turned her attention from the Russian women to the rest of the globe ship. The inner skin of the globe's

75

rec room was lined with recording instruments for the journey, as there was no real cargo space, but it also boasted entertainment—including a pair of VCRs (with a stash of tapes in in English and Russian) and a stereo system with half a dozen headsets so several people could listen to music at once.

In their cabins they also had headsets, but those were wired to the master computer on which the Yilayil language, and other pertinent data, were stored.

Near the Terran entertainment mods were the strange compartments and storage racks of the aliens who had built the ship. Among them were the rectangular boxes that were activated on being handled—and showed pictures of whatever the user wished to see.

Eveleen ran her hands over it, wondering what the hands of the original users had been like. Were they brown, or blue, or rainbow—were they five-fingered, or nine-fingered? What kind of places had been depicted, and what kinds of emotions had been inspired?

She thought about the sonic shower that Vera had nicknamed the Bubble Room. They only had one, but it was enough; she'd stepped out feeling not just clean, but with a sense of well-being that indicated the unknown owners of the globe ship were not so very alien from humans.

"There are two mysteries we have to solve," she said out loud, without thinking.

Saba nodded. "The Russian team—and these people." She nodded at the storage compartments.

They already knew the story of this particular globe ship; like the one Ross and Gordon had found fifteen thousand years ago, the Russians had also found theirs back in the past, the crew dead. Only unlike the American ship, whose owners had been newly killed, the Russian ship's crew had died some time before, of mysterious causes. Had another ship attacked them? Their skeletons had been intact, which argued against local predators. Was disease to blame?

That was still being investigated by teams of XT forensic specialists at home, working under as much secrecy as the time agents.

Meanwhile, the new team had to live together on this ship, and then they had to make it successfully back again after living in the midst of a third alien race.

Eveleen gently put the rectangle back in its place and turned away. Irina was gone; the other two were examining things.

Glancing at one of the clocks the Russians had wired in each cabin, she said, "Our rec time is about over. Shall we get busy?"

Saba nodded soberly, and Vera gave her a quick salute.

They found Irina in the small cabin that had been designated the study area. Zina and Gordon had declared that once people walked into the study cabin, no more English or Russian could be spoken—only Yilayil.

"Here in place of knowledge I—conveyance-motivator—work," Eveleen trilled.

Strange. She was actually getting comfortable with the word order when she used Yilayil—but if she tried thinking in English and translating it over, she got mentally tangled.

Saba added something about repetition, to which the others agreed, then they sat down to the tapes.

A week of ship's days later found her again in the study cabin, working with the other women. Each had found a favorite place to rest, and a mutually agreed-on method of study: they listened to a segment of tape, then went round in the circle repeating the new phrases. Then they asked one another questions that required answers based on the new material. At the end of the practice session, Saba would explain what they'd be hearing next, so they could either listen in their cabins, or review the old, however they learned best. As they advanced, Eveleen had begun to struggle with the odd tenses and sensory contradictions layered into the more formal challenge language.

"What is a green taste?" Vera asked suddenly. "Are we understanding this correctly?"

"It is correct," Irina said, checking her laptop. "But I do not comprehend it."

They all turned to Saba, who said slowly, "It is possible it means some kind of complicated insult, but that's only a guess. Let's proceed; maybe these contradictions will begin to make more sense."

Eveleen nodded, and reached to flick the tape back on.

Now, as Eveleen worked, her eyes observed the others, and her mind considered her own life. It was the human way, she had decided, to make crazy circumstances into a seemingly normal pattern. One created habits, and habits became customs, if enough people practiced them. When there was a semblance of order, one could function. In a totally chaotic or alien environment, the effect on one's mental health was profound enough to affect the physical self.

During the long days of space travel, the time-travel and scientific teams had all worked assiduously at their language studies, so much so that now and then even during rec time, whistle drones would punctuate chatter, particularly between those whose Russian or English was especially spotty.

The scientific team was also learning it—as Eveleen discovered on a rec shift when Valentin moved too quickly and inadvertently squeezed his bulb of coffee. Eveleen had watched in horrified fascination as the liquid spread into a cloud of droplets.

It was Vera who thought fast, grabbing the weird little device that they'd nicknamed the handvac, and chased after the droplets sucking them up.

As she worked, Renfry trilled, "Make it didn't happen!"

Everyone laughed—or almost everyone. Eveleen saw Saba frown slightly, then purse her lips and repeat the trill to herself.

What was she noticing? Eveleen mentally reviewed the trill. It was deceptively simple. In English it made no sense, but in Yilayil it sounded natural. Could it, she suddenly wondered, perhaps have some religious significance?

She brought it up with the study group later—and as usual, no one was certain. Irina said warningly, "Perhaps this House of Knowledge is a religious cult."

"You think this a bad thing?" Eveleen asked.

Irina's dark eyes flicked to her face for a moment, then down to the laptop that Irina never seemed to be without. "Perhaps," she said. "It depends on what they might worship—and why."

Eveleen thought about this for a time, then decided not to add to her worries—they'd find out when they found out. Meanwhile, there was plenty that she *could* learn.

The ship "day" had been divided into two watches of twelve hours each. The science team had taken the "night" watch, and the time-travel team the "day"—enabling everyone to have a full stint of time at the tapes and people with whom to practice.

Eveleen and Irina had concocted a set of exercises to keep everyone physically fit despite their weightlessness, most of them on a peculiar Russian universal exerciser.

79

The best time, though, was the overlap when the "night" team and the "day" team shared awake time. They watched movies together, or played cards together (the older Russians in particular seemed especially fond of complicated card games), or—Eveleen's favorite—made music. Not just listened, but made. Viktor played the violin, and Elizaveta could perform on a flute, clarinet, and recorder. Misha played a guitar, and he had a mellow singing voice. Just watching him leaning against a wall, singing ancient folk songs in shivery minor keys, was a distinct pleasure. He looked like something out of one of the romantic Russian films.

Misha. Eveleen grinned privately to herself. The guy seemed constitutionally unable to resist flirting—and not just with Vera and Irina, but with all the women. Saba held him at arm's distance. Nothing provoked her out of her calm dignity. Eveleen herself pretended not to understand some of his ambiguous remarks. So far, Ross hadn't seen any of it—which was just as well. Despite their agreement of before, Eveleen knew that Ross was not one for hiding his emotions, and the ship was simply too small for feuds.

And it had to be admitted he flirted with her rarely. Most of his attention was equally divided between Vera and Irina, the former of whom showed a very strong interest right back, and the latter of whom responded with a kind of intense coldness that Eveleen could not quite fathom. Misha, of course, seemed to pester Irina the most, to Vera's unhidden (but unexpressed) annoyance. Eveleen felt uneasy about this triangle—and hoped the rivalry wasn't going to translate into trouble later.

Zina turned to her, whistling something—and Eveleen realized she had let her attention wander too long. She dismissed her speculations and turned her mind to the work at hand.

From the circular accessway, Ross watched the women in the study cabin. They rested on several surfaces, but all their heads pointed in one direction, indicating a mutually agreed-on "up" and "down." What was funny was, the men's customary "up" and "down" was totally different.

How strange it was that the women seemed to have gravitated into one group, and the men into another. No one had set a rule about this—it just happened.

He glanced back at the cabin he shared with Gordon, and sighed. And he had been worried about married life on a mission! Except for that piece of legalese called a marriage license back home, he didn't feel married, not anymore. Most of his time was spent with the men, except for those rec periods at the end of the shift, when everyone got together to watch a movie or listen to music. He could sit next to Eveleen and steal a few minutes for talk, but that was about it for Quality Time.

"Countdown for the first landing just began." Gordon appeared, handing himself down the corridor. "Want to grab some grub now?"

"Sure thing." Ross followed him to the galley. Remembering the weird food he and his three fellow adventurers had been forced to eat on their inadvertent jouney last time, Ross grimaced.

Those areas of the galley were closed and sealed off. The Russians had installed a freezer and microwave unit, with a refrigerator housing drink bulbs.

His hand hovered over the panel of choices. Back in the States, he and the others had filled out a form for the Russians, indicating food preferences and aversions. The result was a selection of choices that took into consideration the highest number of "I like this" marks and the least "Won't eat it on a bet" indicators.

He liked the food—but eating in zero gravity was a hassle. He had realized, while laboring through his first meal, that the aliens had been smart, with their solids and pastes. Rice, mashed potatoes, sauces, were a messy chore. Chunky soup was a dream—and Ross wasn't sure he could swallow it even if they'd put it in bulbs. Food *felt* different going down, when it had mass but no weight. His first meal or two had made him gag, and he'd noted a similar reaction in some of the others.

He'd stuck to the pureed vegetables in juice form, and other liquids, until he trusted his stomach. Now he was used to it, and chose a pita-bread sandwich as well as his usual coffee and vegetable juice. Gordon had the same.

Ross slid his choice into the microwave, then broke the seal on his drink bulb. He took a long sip. The coffee, which was contained in a special unit, was fresh and scalding hot.

"Did I understand Boris right?" he asked. "I know we're going to hit the refueling planet pretty soon."

Gordon nodded.

"But what about that other world in Yilayil's system, the one with the furred critters. Did he say we're going to bypass them?"

"He did indeed. The Russians were able to program that particular landing out of the tape, which incidentally saves on fuel."

"Good."

"Our experiences there were apparently enough to convince them against any investigation of that planet. That will lie on some future team's plate—luckily our mission is definitely on the Yilayil planet."

The microwave light went off, and Ross reached in to get his meal. He shoved himself over to one of the rests, and hooked a leg around a curved handhold in order to anchor himself. He breathed deeply of the ship air—faintly metallic still, reminding him of the taste of the alien water from his previous journey—and then bit into his sandwich. He liked the spices the Russians favored.

"Good cooks."

Gordon grunted, swallowed, then whistle/droned a comment about food. While Ross was cudgeling his brain to make an answer, a perfectly pitched response came from behind them, and both Ross and Gordon turned to see Misha lounging in the hatchway, his blond hair drifting.

With a lazy smile, the Russian time agent moved with expert grace to the food dispenser, chose a meal with a light stab of his finger, and then chucked it into the microwave—all without causing his body to recoil. Ross kept his face impassive, wondering how many had witnessed his own first day or so, when he'd forgotten that any use of force will have an equal reaction, which meant he was left windmilling in the middle of a room until he drifted near enough to a wall to reorient himself. Had Misha seen? Probably.

His food was heated. Misha snagged it, grabbed a bulb of coffee, then pushed himself over to join the two Americans. Gordon made space for him.

Misha waved his bulb at Ross. "Your wife. She is very beautiful."

Ross nodded, instantly wary.

"But so prudish." Misha's brows quirked, and his mouth smiled, but his intelligent gray eyes were direct in their assessment.

Like the first time he'd seen Misha, Ross's instant reaction was a lightning stab of anger. He hid it, though, guessing immediately that he was being goaded. This guy couldn't possibly have the hots for Eveleen—not when he had an equally attractive woman like Vera sitting up and smiling every time he entered a cabin. And he hadn't exactly been ignoring Irina, Ross had noticed.

He's still testing me, Ross thought. And if I take a swing at him, he's just going to see it as weakness, and make a game of needling me.

So he forced himself to shrug, and grin. "I can only speak for myself. And no, I don't think I'm a prude, but I don't find you the least bit attractive."

Misha's laughter rang out—he was clearly surprised, and delighted, at the crack.

Gordon's lips twitched; Ross feigned unconcern, and took a bite from his sandwich.

"She likes to fight, your wife?" Misha continued.

"She's good at it," Ross said. Ordinarily he'd say *Ask her* but he wasn't going to offer this guy what might be interpreted as tacit permission to harass Eveleen.

"Ah, I like to fight. I shall offer her a fall, when we have gravity again."

Ross shrugged. "Be my guest." He knew Eveleen's practice mat persona—all professional. If this clown was looking for a chance to flirt, he'd find a robot more responsive if he planned to try it during martial-arts practice.

The thought made him grin. Misha gave him a speculative look, then turned his attention to Gordon, and he fired several rapid, acute questions about the library they'd found on their last journey, and whether or not the Weaslies had exhibited any signs of even rudimentary language.

84

By the time Gordon was done talking, Misha had finished his food, and he launched himself out again; they heard his voice floating back from the command cabin.

"Testing you." Gordon pointed with his chin in Misha's direction.

"I'm not an idiot."

"No, but you're the same kind—adrenaline seeker," Gordon retorted.

"Me?" Ross frowned, thinking back. Slowly, almost unconsciously, he flexed his burned hand, then he said, "Maybe. Once. But no more."

"No?" Gordon grinned. "No one, from Milliard on down, would have faulted you for not taking this assignment. Hell, the rules forbid newly married agents from being sent into the field."

Ross snorted a laugh. "Well, maybe a little. Eveleen as well. But not like that guy. What's pushing him?"

"I don't know," Gordon said slowly. "All I know is, he pulled every string to get assigned to this mission. Even to the extent of causing a shootout with gangsters in order to save this ship from discovery."

"You think it's just adrenaline, then? Or there's some other motivator?" Ross asked.

Gordon shook his head. "As yet, I have no clue. The guy willingly talks to everyone, and will even talk about himself, but only what he's done, never what he thinks. And we have to remember what all of them have lived through, finding out about comrades being killed in those Baldy attacks."

"I just hope he's not going to make trouble just to get things stirred up," Ross muttered.

"Zina thinks he's too smart for that. Nevertheless, I'm glad he'll be mostly away from us on his search job."

"Yeah." Ross crushed his empty bulb in his hand.

CHAPTER TEN

Gordon Ashe obediently swallowed his anti-nausea meds, and settled gratefully into the webbing of one of the extra seats in the command cabin. Next to him, Zina Vasilyeva waited silently, her gaze on the viewscreen. They'd just endured the hideous wrenching of the transfer from other-dimensional space; centered on the viewscreen was a small, blue-green crescent. A larger black disk with a corona flaring around it marked the planet's primary. The crescent swelled rapidly as the ship followed its programmed course toward the huge, ancient spaceport at which the globe ships refueled.

Gordon's unvoiced worry was that some other ship would show up, and they'd have to deal with the beings—somehow—though the Terrans knew little about how to control the communications of the globe ship.

He did voice one worry—that the reprogramming might somehow interfere with the communications. "When so much of the ship function is automatic," he said. "I wonder if tampering with it might cause some kind of signal to go out?"

"We debated this," Zina replied without taking her gaze from the screen. "There is no way to know if we have sent a signal. We decided to take the chance. The question of fuel, and of defense against the inimical beings on that one planet, made us feel the benefits outweighed the risk."

Gordon glanced at the communication board—still a total mystery. Was a signal going out—or not? There was no clue in the complicated series of lights and buttons.

At least no other ships were in sight, he noted, as the globe sped toward the mysterious refuel planet. Now gees pulled at them, and the ship reacted to floating trash: even after the lapse of millennia, the nameless planet was surrounded by a haze of detritus left behind by visiting star-ships.

The blue-green crescent resolved into a lush planet swirled with cloud systems. Gordon felt his body pressing into his webbing with more authority. Suddenly his viewpoint changed, though the position of the ship vis-à-vis the planet didn't: his inner ear registered *down*, and vertigo seized him.

At the controls Boris now held his hands ready above his console, watching lights flickering and measurements of various types streaming across his computer terminal as the autopilot brought the ship down toward the apparently endless stretch of white cement that marked the ancient starport.

Gordon swallowed fast, closed his eyes, and tried breathing slowly. They were in flight now, subject to the planet's 0.92 standard gee, which settled his stomach rapidly. The transition from orbit was not as bad as the emergence from the weird hyper-dimensional travel that none of the Terran techs—either Western or Eastern—could duplicate.

Silence gripped the ship, except for the creaks and subsonic groans of entry into a gravity well. All the crew members were in their bunks, on Zina's orders—all except Boris, the pilot, and Zina and Gordon as senior officers.

Gordon and Zina stayed with Boris as a kind of insurance—what kind, Gordon didn't know. He certainly couldn't operate the ship if something went wrong. It would have made more sense to have Renfry on hand—of course, Renfry and Valentin probably had wired up a viewscreen to their terminals, and were following the action from their cabin.

It's probably a political gesture, Gordon thought. *Showing us that everything's on the up-and-up, without having to say it. Establishing trust, which we've got to have if this mission is to succeed.*

Gordon opened his eyes again.

They were almost down. There was the peculiar blue-green sky again; memory smote him with unexpected force. No moisture was evident in that sky. If the planet had weather, it was all elsewhere. Of course, that would make sense—to locate a spaceport in a desert.

With a gentle bump, the ship settled onto the wide sweep of white cement. There was the rusty red ruin. There were the ghost ships, untouched since their last visit.

The globe ship's position with respect to the nearest ghost ship even looked the same—Gordon wondered if the globes were programmed to set down on the very same landing pad.

They'd have to, he realized belatedly. Or would the refueling bots come out no matter what kind of ship set down—and would they know what kind of fuel to administer?

Fueling bots!

He turned his head; his neck cricked at the unexpected weight. "When we were here, the fuel bot was broken—"

"We saw that, on your mission tape," Zina replied. Her voice was hoarse. "Our first mission was prepared for this problem, and were able to effect repairs on the robot."

Of course. He'd forgotten that first Russian mission—the reason they were here!

Gordon was embarrassed at his own stupidity, but only for a moment. From the way Zina rubbed at her temples, she was having difficulty adjusting to gravity again as well. Thinking was at least as difficult as moving.

"Here he comes," Boris said, for the first time during the entire journey showing some emotion. "Good work, Vasili!"

Gordon watched the viewscreen. The snakelike fuel robot slithered out to the ship and disappeared from view. But a moment later Boris gave a grunt of satisfaction, and indicated one of his measures. "Fuel."

"What type of fuel does this ship run on? Your people figure that out?" Gordon asked.

Boris shook his head. "Our analysis is much the same as yours—a type of slurry encapsulating some of the super-heavy elements, triggered by a catalytic environment that we do not yet have the technology to fully understand."

Gordon nodded. All the more reason to take extreme care when using the globe ships. The autopilot tapes might be safe enough—but the only fuel, as yet, was from this ancient star-port, and who knew when it would run out?

Boris gave another grunt, and touched a pair of controls. On the viewscreen, the robot hose began its steady retreat.

The globe lifted again, accelerating rapidly. The journey out was far faster, and Gordon realized that some of the inbound maneuvering might be programmed in accordance with planetary defense strictures. Speculation about the gauntlet of ancient weapons they might have faced occupied him until he felt his weight disappear. Soon after came the wrenching transition to hyperspace.

When that was over, he lay in his webbing until he felt recovered. According to that first journey, they now had exactly a week of travel before they planeted on the Yilayil world.

Everyone was progressing well with the language, thanks to assiduous use of the hypno-tapes and keeping to the rules about only using the language in work sessions. They were about as well prepared as they could be, given the incomplete and somewhat bizarre data in the language tapes, and their scanty knowledge of a very complicated culture.

What remained was the Terrans themselves.

Gordon had made a point of trying to get to know each of the crew. Easiest were the younger Russians; at least, easy to talk to, he amended, thinking them over. Misha talked at least as much as Vera, but not about anything personal. He kept his inner self well hidden behind an impervious shield of friendly, joking insouciance.

Hardest were the older Russians. Gordon's instincts told him not to press. He didn't think that Gregori or Elizaveta necessarily hated the Americans and didn't want to work with them, but their younger years had been spent in a rough political climate, wherein one did not reveal oneself easily. That they did talk to him—on such bland, unexceptionable topics as linguistic studies, science, and so forth— meant to him that they were trying their best.

The last, one was the toughest—Saba.

Thinking of those intelligent dark eyes, and the smooth, softly accented voice, Gordon decided he'd lain inactive long enough.

Time to get started.

He unfastened his webbing, nodded to Boris, and pushed himself out. Glancing at the time as he sailed through the rounded corridor, he gave the schedule a quick mental review, and headed for the rec room.

The noise of a video made him stop and peek in. Three of the Russians and Renfry were watching some documentary in Russian. He knew that several of the others were in the study right then, which meant that Saba was probably in her cabin.

He stopped himself outside her door, grabbed a handhold, and tapped.

The door slid open. Eveleen was gone; Saba was alone. Gordon saw her laptop terminal lit, the machine anchored down to the little desk. Earphones floated in the air next to the terminal.

"Gordon?" she said politely.

"May I talk to you?" he asked.

She nodded once. "Of course."

"Sorry to interrupt," he said, entering the cabin, which was small and very tidy.

"It is all right," Saba said with a graceful gesture. She swiftly saved her work, then closed the laptop and laid her folded hands on it. "Now. What did you wish to discuss?"

The cabins were too small for visitor space. Gordon had hitched himself over Eveleen's bunk.

"I've been thinking ahead," Gordon began. "We have no idea why that statue of you exists, but we can assume that our mission has something to do with it. It was probably carved as a result of our visit."

Saba nodded; they all knew that.

"Your assignment is to enter the House of Knowledge, about which we only know one thing: that only selected beings are permitted entry, and everyone else stays out."

Again, common knowledge. Yet she exhibited no impatience—she knew, then, that he was establishing the background to his thoughts.

"I might not be able to get in, even as your ******." He whistle/droned the word for *runner/caregiver.*

"I have thought of that," she admitted. "But we do not have any evidence that the inhabitants of the House of Knowledge are prisoners, or how could the First Team have learned even what they did? I must assume that I can come out to visit you if need be."

"No evidence except those anomalies in the language," he insisted. "You yourself noted that the odd tenses seem to deny free will at times, that they might indicate a cultural means of coercion. So I don't think we can count on that. What I'd like to do is establish a code, in both languages— English and Yilayil—that ideally we can use on our radio connection. One code for pulses—for emergencies—and another for spoken communication."

"So you are assuming that we are going to be in a hostile environment, then," she said.

He shook his head. "Given how many pieces are missing from the puzzle, I think it's best. I talked it over with Zina before we strapped down for the refuel, and she says she's had thoughts along the same line."

Saba sighed a little, flexing her hands. Gordon realized she was tense, though she gave no overt signs.

"Look," he said, "I hate to pile on the pressure."

She shook her head, smiling a little. "It is already there."

Gordon smiled back. This was her first admission of real human emotion. And he knew that the same thing could be said of him—that he hid his real reactions. But it would be a mistake to assume that he didn't have any, just as he couldn't assume that she did not feel normal human emotion.

"Well, we can't get around the fact that you are going to be important in some way—if not for us, for them. Let's just hope that this means they think you're great, and give you a cushy position somewhere, doing something poetic in one of their rituals. Meantime ..."

Saba nodded again. "Your code is an excellent idea. Have you designed something?"

"I thought that we could do that together," he suggested. "We got a little time before our shift turns in for sleep—how about getting a start on it now?"

Her smile widened, just a bit. "I think that's a very good plan," she said.

The hour after Gordon came into her cabin to speak passed quickly for Saba. Once they'd begun to work, the man's remote countenance relaxed; his slow, careful speech—as if he were reluctant to speak at all—became normal. He was still too controlled for Saba to hear his natural rhythm. Controlled, cautious, but not inflexible. She could be patient.

All people made music of some kind, Saba had discovered when she was a girl beginning her studies in English and French. In Ethiopia, music was very much a part of life for the peoples she had known, traveling about with her father, who was a doctor—the Dorze, her mother's people, and all the other peoples of Ethiopia, from Eritrea to the elusive Danakil, made music all the time, in every aspect of life.

But in listening to the language instructors at her school, she had discovered that there was music in speech. Each language had a different music, and each individual interpreted that music differently.

She'd lost that conviction for a time, when she moved to Addis Ababa to attend university. But after a time life in the large, sophisticated city had brought her old convictions back, once she'd gotten used to the noise of technology. There was a kind of music even in modern life. Some people made very little music, but what they had was dark, angry, ugly—jangling with disharmony. Some made the muscle-tightening music of fear. Others made quiet music, repeating patterns they had learned from generations of equally quiet people.

Some—very complex persons—kept their music to themselves until they trusted. At first she'd wondered if Gordon Ashe had any music, but she'd come to realize he was one of these latter. He had a fast mind, and an attention to detail that she appreciated.

In that hour of study that he had come so suddenly to request, they laid the groundwork for a series of signals, ranked according to need, that they could build on.

When the bell toned for the shift change, Gordon seemed as surprised as she was how quickly the time had vanished. He said a polite good night—once again careful and remote—and left.

Saba stayed in the open door, her mind ranging over the past hour. As yet Eveleen had not shown up. Saba wondered if she and Ross had managed to find a little time alone, and hoped it was so. Eveleen never complained, but there was a wistful expression in her eyes when she referred to her husband, so newly wed. Her voice, so pleasant, with sunny music very close to the surface, would convey shades of longing.

A flash of long yellow hair caught Saba by surprise, and she looked up to see Mikhail Petrovich Nikulin hanging upside down, just a meter from her face.

With a quick gesture, he oriented himself so that they were aligned in the same direction, then he gave her one of his grins.

"Nice night for pairs," he said, pointing back over his shoulder in the direction Gordon had gone. His own music was exotic, quick with control and unexpected percussive accents. This Mikhail—called Misha by his Russian colleagues—was another complex person.

"Perhaps," she said, feeling a spurt of amusement at his assumption that she and Gordon were romantically involved.

"So do you like old men only, or have you a smile for me?"

"Old? Men?" Saba asked.

"Gordon Ashe might be tough as nails, but I'm younger and much more handsome," came the immediate retort.

"Thank you for the information, Mikhail," Saba murmured.

"Misha! I want two things, and I shall have them: you will call me Misha, and you will smile at me."

"I will give you both, willingly, if I can then retire for rest," she said. "Good night, Misha." And she gave him a very polite smile.

"A challenge!" He laughed. "That's a challenge, Saba."

She closed the cabin door, and heard his laughter echo as he moved away.

Eveleen appeared a moment later. "That guy!" she exclaimed. "Does he ever give up?"

"You too?" Saba asked.

"Ohhh, yes. I noticed him talking to you during rec time, what was it, day before yesterday? It's so easy to lose track—one day so much like another." Eveleen grinned as she wrestled out of her clothes and into her sleepwear. "You know," she added, her head muffled in her top, "I could get used to this nullgrav—all except getting dressed. I feel like an octopus, writhing around in midair!"

Saba chuckled. "You are right. It is difficult."

"So, back to Misha." Eveleen's head popped out, and she fixed her floating hair into its night braid. "He's, what, pressuring you for a date? Or does he just want you to admire his oh-so-fascinating handsome blond self."

"He wants to make me smile," Saba said.

"Well, that sounds harmless enough."

"I have said it wrong," Saba corrected, and she lowered her voice, trying for his characteristic tone of voice—partly humor, partly challenge. "He wants to *make* me smile." She gave the verb a slight emphasis.

Eveleen's brows winged up, and she whistled one of the Yilayil challenge responses. "So. What do you do?"

"Continue to ignore him, and hope that Vera or perhaps even Irina will eventually occupy his attention."

Eveleen hooked herself into her webbing, and fastened it over herself. "Never a dull moment, that's the name for this mission, right?"

"Right," Saba said, giving in to laughter at last. Then she too composed herself for sleep, and doused the light.

And so the last days of zero grav passed. Saba felt the pressure of the imminent landing—they all did. No need to check the schedule anymore. Everyone was putting in as much preparation time as they could, the science team readying their equipment.

Saba continued to meet with Gordon each day, and they rapidly set up a communication code that both could remember with very little prompting. They'd covered as many contingencies as they could invent, leaving room for possible combinations as the mission progressed.

Misha, of course, continued his campaign, but even he seemed rather absentminded—as if he continued out of habit, or to hide how he, too, had emotions about what was soon to take place. She found those emotions difficult to interpret—but she was certain that they were there.

Finally Boris sent the signal for the emergence from the transdimension, and they all retreated to strap into their bunks.

Saba knew that landing on the Yilayil planet was now a short time away. She took her anti-nausea medication. Very shortly thereafter the wrenching weirdness seized her in its grip, making her body feel as if it had been turned inside out and then right again.

When at last it was over, and she had recovered, she opened her eyes to see Eveleen groggily sitting up from her webbing, which was swaying gently from her movements.

She unstrapped and hooked a foot around a hold, working through a series of movements that Saba had learned were very good for restoring circulation and muscle tone.

In silence Saba joined her.

When the two women were done, they left the cabin, and found the others gathered round the command center.

There, on the viewscreen, was the system they were headed toward. A blue-white crescent loomed on one side, slipped away.

"Passing second planet now," Boris reported.

"Good riddance," Ross Murdock cracked.

"Amen to that," Case Renfry said softly.

Not long after, they saw Yilayil—a big blue-green crescent, not unlike Earth at this distance—rapidly growing dead center on the screen.

It swelled, until they could make out the islands thickly straddling the equator, and the white, sere land masses at the poles, all hazed by the atmosphere and obscure under swirling weather systems.

"Back to the bunks," Zina commanded. "We are shortly to planet—our work is to begin."

No one had anything to say to that—even Misha seemed subdued.

In silence the two women retreated to their cabin, and prepared for landing.

CHAPTER ELEVEN

Ross felt gravity close its fist on his vitals, and he concentrated on his breathing. The ship was now under flight; the globe creaked and vibrated as it arrowed down toward Yilayil.

Ross tried to picture the planet, a series of island clusters belting the brilliant blue ocean that girdled the entire world. The spaceport was not located on the largest island—just the flattest. Most of the rest had active volcanoes on them: not good choices for any kind of city. Ross wondered if they'd be there long enough for the science team to actually explore some of those islands; there had to be tens of thousands of them, if not more.

He hoped not.

It seemed the landing was faster this time than the last, but maybe that was because he knew what to expect. At any rate, they finally set down with a gentle bump, and Ross bounced and swayed in his bunk webbing, stretching his limbs experimentally.

Sounds came from the other cabins. The others emerged, one by one. Some of them had wasted no time in getting their equipment ready for deployment. Gordon was already out of his bunk, overseeing things; Ross listened to the quick American voices as he and Renfry spoke.

"Damn," Renfry was saying. "This stuff is heavy. I sure wish we knew we could safely run power off the ship."

Ross thought about the mysterious fuel, and wondered how they'd power the globe if they suddenly ran empty. They couldn't do it—of course. The idea of floating through space forever, maybe caught in the weird transdimensional plane, gave him the willies.

It was enough to get him to unstrap and swing out of the bunk. He slipped his shoes on and left the cabin.

"Ah. Ross." Renfry hailed him with obvious relief. "Gotta get this generator stuff out first thing, and get us a power supply set up."

Ross nodded, feeling his muscles protest as he lifted a heavy box. After the weeks of weightlessness—despite the workouts—everything seemed to weigh about a ton.

"Misha and Viktor gone out scouting?" Ross asked.

"Soon's Boris lowered the ramp," Renfry said. "That guy Misha acts like he's been in two gees for a month. He was out there with enough bounce to make a Marine drill sergeant happy."

Ross snorted—and then grunted with effort as he started down the ladder after Renfry. He was just as happy not to see Misha lounging around and grinning at his laboring movements under all that weight.

They made it to the outer port, and Ross glanced out. Like before, the rich; scent-laden air hit him at once, and he' nearly dropped his burden as a violent sneeze took him.

Renfry sneezed right after, and then sneezed again. He rather hastily set his own box down and sneezed a third time, then sheepishly wiped his nose.

Ross sniffed, trying to get his sinuses acclimated; he looked around as he waited. They'd landed at dawn. Gaudy pink and orange and yellow light filtered through the lush growth at the cracks in the old spaceport paving.

"Phew!" Eveleen appeared next to him, her arms piled with several flat boxes. "Smells like an explosion in a perfume factory!"

"It is just as well we brought a large supply of anti-allergens," Valentin said soberly, appearing behind Eveleen.

"We didn't get sick on our run," Renfry said, "but maybe that was luck. I'm just glad we're immune—at least we can hope we're immune," he amended, squinting around at the unfamiliar varieties of trees and bushes.

"Let's get unloaded, then we can explore a little." That was Zina, behind them on the ramp.

Ross realized he had stopped at the base of the ramp, and was holding up the line. He quickly bent and picked up his box, and the line proceeded with the unloading.

They kept moving until the base camp items were all stacked up and waiting against Misha and Viktor finding a good location. Then they retreated back to the ship, with Gregori and Vera standing guard against the little blue flyers showing up and pilfering souvenirs.

Ross was glad to get back to the sterile ship's air. His sinuses cleared almost immediately—making his nose run. He noticed the others having the same problem.

Gordon was ahead of him in line for the midday meal. "Remember getting the sniffles last time?" Ross asked.

Gordon gave a one-shoulder shrug. "Nope. Maybe it's old age setting in."

Ross laughed, but he wondered if their anti-allergen medication was maybe a tad too vigorous. Last flight—when they'd had, perforce, no protection beyond the alien suits—had produced no such problems.

They each got some food, and Ross hunkered down with his back to a wall, glad to get his weight off his feet.

Zina waited until everyone had food, then she nodded to Gordon, who said, "Listen up, people. We've got to start wearing our communications gear right now. If we set foot off the ship, even for ten feet, we wear it." He gave them an ironic grin. "I don't know about the First Team's visit, but when Ross and Renfry and I were here last, it was me who found himself making an unexpected trip to the local flyers. No problem—that time—but we need to be prepared until we know if there have been any changes."

Ross nodded, and the others made various signs of agreement. It was clear that Gordon and Zina had been talking about general strategy.

Ross was nearly done with his meal when Viktor and Misha appeared in the doorway. "We found a good one," Misha began.

Zina addressed him in rapid-fire Russian, and Misha's mouth tightened. He nodded his head, and spread his hands.

Ross looked at Misha's belt, which was bare, and knew that the maverick agent had left his own com gear behind. Why? Showing off, Ross thought sourly.

Ross also noticed that though the silent Viktor came in for a share of the lecture, it was Misha who caught the full load. Of course it had been his idea to skip off the ship the second the ramp was down, and go out ranging around before the com gear had even been broken out.

Misha kept his head bowed, his lips curved in the merest ghost of a smile, and when Zina finished he said something short and mild in Russian. Then he looked up. "We must get moving now if we wish to get a camp set up before dark," he stated in English.

Ross shoveled his last bite of food into his mouth and stood up. At once his shoulders and arms protested, but he ignored it. "So let's move," he said.

Everyone helped. They formed a long pack train, leaving only Boris and Renfry behind to guard the ship. Each person carried as much as he or she could handle.

Misha and Viktor had done an excellent job of trailblazing, Ross noted as he trudged along behind. Of course.

But—despite his distrust of the blond agent—he was just as glad that Misha and Viktor were as good as reputed. He hadn't really thought about laying camp until he stepped out and looked at this wild land once again. But this was no easy matter. They had to position themselves not just within range of both ship and library tower, but well away from any known weasel or wild-humanoid dens. But that wasn't all. They also had to be in a good position for the transfer equipment—because the time agents would be appearing in the same spot many years earlier. So they didn't want to be where spaceport (if it was being used at all) or city action might be congested, for example.

He knew that Viktor, in particular, had spent a great deal of time with the meticulous recordings of measurement and location reported on the incomplete tape made by the First Team. It was he who had mapped out the probable location of buildings and pathways they might find in the earlier time, and he had to overlay it with the present.

The camp turned out to be in a protected grotto next to a waterfall, with a natural spy-spot on the hillocks above the falls.

Misha stepped into the little clearing first, waving a hand about with the air of a prince offering his palace.

Zina looked around, nodded slowly, glanced at Elizaveta and Gordon, who both made approving sounds.

"We shall set up camp here," Zina pronounced.

And then it was time to really get to work.

"Biomass converters here—" The most bulky machinery they'd brought, squatty olive-green cylinders, took two people to wrestle out of the ship.

"Want the transfer equipment there, or what?"

"Water samples are ready, Zina…"

"No, the housing must be here—"

Everyone talked at once. As he worked under Valentin's direction, stacking supplies and equipment whose purpose he could only guess at, Ross listened to the melange of voices. It sounded like some kind of surreal dream—the bits of English and Russian, many of them interspersed with whistles and drones of the Yilayil language. These latter referred to local sights and conditions—it was actually quicker now to think of the world in native terms.

The science team would sleep aboard the ship, but they set up a defensible hut, just in case. Once he'd finished his grunt work, Ross was ordered by a distracted Zina to aid Misha, Viktor, Gordon, Irina, and Gregori in camouflaging the hut.

By the time they'd finished, Ross's body felt like one big ache. His muscles burned, and his lungs labored for breath. Gravity seemed to have converted his body to the weight of granite.

But when he looked around wearily, expecting further orders, it was to see Renfry and Zina—both looking pale and sweaty—standing in the middle of the camp. Renfry finished explaining something, and Zina gave a nod of satisfaction.

"Good," she said. "It is done."

Ross followed her gaze. Now the clearing looked much like it did before. Nothing was immediately obvious unless you stepped close. And the sonic barriers that the science team would set up would discourage roaming predators.

"Were we spotted?" Ross asked.

Vera, atop the hill with her field glasses, nodded. "Six or seven of the little blue flyers."

"Can't be helped," Renfry said, working his neck from side to side. "We'll be contacting the flying people anyway—and they seem to be the only ones the blues communicate with."

Ross dropped onto the ground, wiping his brow. The humid air made him feel hotter and sweatier than a heat wave in the Midwest.

The Midwest. He closed his eyes, all of a sudden feeling a familiar sickening knot in the pit of his stomach. He realized, just as he had on the last journey, how very far they were from home.

A movement beside him caused him to look up, and Eveleen smiled at him as she wiped back a strand of damp hair from her clear brow. "Homesick?" she asked softly.

"Mind reader." He tried a laugh. It was almost convincing.

"Ah, we'll be in action soon, and no time for homesickness," she said with a chuckle.

"At least these guys are all excited." He nodded at Renfy and Valentin. The entire science team seemed to have been infused with some kind of mysterious energy. While all the time agents sat around, either waving broad leaves like fans or just sitting still, the scientists were busy wiring their equipment together, and getting their various systems online, while chattering at high speed.

"Excited—and worried," Eveleen murmured softly.

"Worried?" Ross frowned. "What's this? Something new come up?"

"Nothing new," Eveleen said. "Something I guess the big brains all thought of, but no one has said out loud. You know, those feral human creatures..."

Ross remembered the desperate fight during his first visit here. He frowned as an idea occurred. "I didn't think of that. You mean, they're afraid that those things might be descendants of the Russian First Team, somehow mutated?"

Eveleen's eyes were sad. "Exactly."

Ross shuddered. "Hell. Hadn't thought of that, but even if it's been centuries—hell." It seemed inadequate, but at the same time appropriate. No one wanted to think their descendants—or their friends' descendants—would be savage monsters. "Let's hope not."

Elizaveta worked at the generator, making sure the biomass converters were functioning smoothly. Ross sniffed; a faint whiff of alcohol seemed to tickle his nose, but maybe that was his imagination. He knew in general how the converters worked—converting organic matter into alcohol, which then burned pure, to power the generator.

As he watched, Elizaveta adjusted something, and that faint whiff was gone, buried in the astonishing variety of scents carried on the heavy air.

"Well, we'll start finding out tomorrow," Eveleen whispered, staring through the open door of the hut, where Gregori worked with steady care on the time-transfer apparatus.

"Maybe we'd better head back and start preparing," Ross said.

He looked up. It seemed the others had had the same idea.

In silence they returned to the ship, a good meal, and a night's sleep.

❧ ❧ ❧

Early the next morning, when it was Ross's turn to step into the strange sonic shower, he shut his eyes and let the frothy bubbles work deeply into his skin. Who knew how long it would be until he stood here again? At the back of his mind a voice whispered, "*If* you come back—" but that only succeeded in making him angry, and he closed off the shower controls and got into his transfer clothing.

Eveleen was waiting in the galley, along with the rest of the team. He went to her side. Next to her was his pack of equipment.

The others chattered quietly; when Zina appeared in the hatchway and looked around, they all fell silent.

"The time-transfer apparatus is set up, and runs successfully, Gregori reports," she said. "I suggest we waste no further time."

The others responded with gestures or murmurs of agreement.

Zina added, "I wish that I could be with you on this mission. But my place is here, in the present. And I know that Professor Ashe will carry out command as I would have done." She nodded at Gordon.

The sudden formality underscored the tension in them all—all except, perhaps, Misha. He only grinned. Ross wondered if that mention of command was a reminder to the Russian time agents, Misha especially.

Misha's grin widened slightly, but all he said was, "Let us go. We want to be there at dawn, do we not?"

As they stepped down the ramp into the soft predawn air, Renfry and Boris appeared behind them. "Good luck," Renfry called in a low voice. "See you soon."

Boris added something in Russian, and Vera turned and gave him a cheery wave. Both Boris and Renfry stood on the ramp; their job right now was to guard the ship.

There was little talk as the rest of the team marched through the dark forest to the campsite. The faint light of dawn painted the wild growth around them with splendorous color; the sun was just rising.

When they reached the campsite, Elizaveta, Gregori, and Valentin were waiting.

Zina turned to face the time agents. "I have said what is needful." Her eyes were steady in the pale light. "We will await your signal. Good hunting."

The rest of the science team stepped forward to say quick, subdued good-byes, and then Gordon and Saba walked into the hut.

Moments later the ground seemed to shake slightly: an illusion, Ross knew, a response of the mind to the distorted probability waves sweeping out from the apparatus as it catapulted the two agents into the distant past. Other than the slightly acrid scent of ozone, there was no other indication of the time machine's operation.

Misha and Viktor went next.

Then it was his and Eveleen's turn.

She said nothing, only picked up her pack. Ross did as well. They stepped inside the hut. There were the bars, the familiar but weird opaque material for them to step on. He looked down at his feet, thinking about the many jaunts to the past he'd made. Last time, on Dominium, he and Eveleen had come back as heroes. He hoped this time would be as successful but less traumatic.

The platform suddenly seemed to drop out from under him as a million voices shouted inside his head. White light filled him, squeezing out his identity for a moment that seemed endless...

Then reality collapsed back around him, a cocoon of certainty, and he opened his eyes. Next to him, Eveleen's breathing was harsh but controlled. She looked at him, her own eyes dark, her lips pressed together.

"We're here," he murmured, and leaned down to kiss her.

For a moment their lips met. Hers were dry, but warm and sweet.

"One more. For the road."

"For the century," she retorted, and gave him a smacking kiss. Then she said, "They're waiting for us." And she opened the swinging metal door of the shed.

They stepped out.

The grotto was surprisingly like the one in the present, but the smells were different. Ross sniffed, finding the air cleaner somehow. He kept sniffing as they rounded a huge shrub, to find Misha and Viktor gazing silently upward, one face puzzled, the other grim.

The Russians turned to face the new arrivals.

"The First Team had reported no flyers," Misha said without preamble, his gray eyes sardonic.

Why state the obvious? Eveleen looked aside, rolling her eyes. They'd known that since the first briefing.

"Right." Ross decided to humor him. "So your job is to search for them as well as for remains. So?"

"So look, American." He raised his hand skyward.

They were looking east at the rising sun. Against the reddish ball, a flight of huge winged shapes flapped with grace—humanoid shapes.

Flyers.

CHAPTER TWELVE

Ross said, "Where's Gordon? Saba?"

Misha pointed up the hill, which was considerably higher than the one up the timeline. Eveleen couldn't see either time agent, but then she knew she wouldn't. They'd be scanning the area under as much cover as possible.

She turned her eyes eastward, and watched the flyers disappear on the horizon. No one spoke. No one moved until the soundless shock repeated, and Vera and Irina stepped out of the shed containing the time machine. Eveleen's mind shied away reflexively from the knowledge of how fragile their link to their own time was: the shed and the machinery it contained were but projections of the apparatus in their own time.

Gordon and Saba appeared a moment later, walking quickly down the steep hillock.

"The perimeter of the port seems to be roughly the same as up the timeline," Gordon said quickly. "And completely quiet. Nothing in sight except robotic maintenance devices of various sorts, either shutdown or quiescent. As for this area, our guess was right. It's a kind of park. There's nothing but vegetation in view. But I can see buildings over that way." He pointed to the southeast.

"No spaceships at the port?" Ross asked.

"Not that I can see," Gordon replied, hefting his field scanners. He turned to Viktor. "And the landing area is full of cracks and brush—indicating nothing has either come down or taken off for many years. So let's get the second phase of this mission complete."

Viktor gave a quick nod. "We are ready. We return as quick as possible."

He and Misha vanished into the undergrowth.

Eveleen exchanged a glance with Ross. He looked grim, and she didn't blame him. Misha and Viktor's first order had been to check the burial site of the Russian biologist to make sure the bones were still there. They would not disturb the body in any way, merely make certain it was just as it would be found up the timeline in the present—to double-check that time had not been altered at this end of the timeline.

Already they had one anomaly: the flying creatures.

As if his mind had been following the same track, Gordon said, "There might be landing sites elsewhere, on another island. We're hampered by our use of the globe ships and the autopilot wire in that we can't go on a scouting trip around the planet."

"That would explain the flying people," Saba murmured. "We know we'll be finding other species who have already assimilated. It could be that the flyers landed and figured out how to assimilate some time during the century since the First Team appeared here."

Eveleen nodded her agreement. "In a hundred years, it's certainly not unreasonable."

Vera frowned. "This could include other humanoids."

Eveleen thought immediately of the feral human creatures in the present timeline—their tentacled bodies and utter lack of any form of civilization. If the Russians had disappeared, how could those feral humans be their descendants? It would mean that either other human-type beings had appeared—or that she and her team would be trapped in this time and place, and those were their descendants. Not the Russians, but hers. Ross's. Gordon's and Misha's and Vera's and the others'.

She turned to Ross, biting her lip. If…if it were true, could she bear to have children?

Don't think about it now, she told herself. Keep your mind on the mission.

"Viktor will be fast," Irina said softly. "He and Mikhail Petrovich have been to the burial site twice since we landed, in the present timeline. They will know where to go."

Mikhail Petrovich. Irina never called Misha by his nickname.

Eveleen pursed her lips. When did the men sleep? She had to admit that Misha, despite his attitudes, was a dedicated agent.

Either dedicated, she temporized—or driven.

"Let's grab some eats, shall we?" Ross suggested. "The tough stuff will be starting soon enough—why start it on an empty stomach?"

Vera grinned, and she and Irina cautiously began exploring in the immediate vicinity. Eveleen watched them go. Their job would be food traders, and as such they had mastered all the details about food experiments recorded by the First Team.

Just as the air was breathable, so was most of the food edible. Within a short time the two women returned laden with fruits and some large nutty gourds that turned out to be delicious. Irina had done a scan on a stream just meters away, and the water had nothing dangerous in it, so they each took a turn drinking after the meal.

They'd just finished when Viktor and Misha returned, appearing silently, without disturbing any of the undergrowth. Eveleen privately awarded them points for superior woodcraft.

"He's there," Misha said, his mouth tight at the corners. "We found the body, buried at the Field-of-Vagabonds. It's been left just as the First Team described."

"Then we will assume the timeline is intact," Gordon replied. "All right, ground rules again. Emergency pulses only, at least until we've had a chance to settle in and know that we're not being overheard. Relay everything through me."

He paused, his blue eyes narrowed. Everyone assented. Gordon lifted a hand. "Then let's go."

Viktor took over, leading them down a pathway. They all knew, in general, the layout of the Yilayil city as described by the First Team. Viktor had memorized every bit of data available—and he would be mapping the areas that the First Team had not reported on, as he and Misha made their methodical search for forensic evidence of the other First Team members.

"The only thing that gives me hope," Ross murmured to Eveleen as they marched single file through the thick jungle undergrowth, "is that the abrupt disappearance of the First Team might just mean that we did rescue them."

Eveleen said, "Except why don't we find anything left by our future selves, to tell us how to do it? I know I'd do that for myself, if I could. There are no signs of any of us—that we've found."

"Not up the timeline, but there might be here. Right?" Ross asked.

"But if there is, we'd have to have left it from the past, not here—because we just got here. And the apparatus doesn't permit microjumps, so we can assume we don't skip back to this day and hide out to leave us little notes to wherever we're going now."

"Unh," Ross grunted, shaking his head. "This time stuff really makes my brain ache."

On the other side of Ross, Saba was smiling. "It's almost easier to discuss in Yilayil. I need to untangle those odd tense constructions."

"Doesn't matter," Ashe said tersely. "From now on, if you speak, speak Yilayil," he ordered. And he added a quick comment in that language that Eveleen translated to herself; leaving out the identifiers and the false origin they'd developed from the First Team's personae, it meant: *We are on their ground, we do as they do.*

No further reminder of the fate of the Russian biologist needed to be made.

Eveleen toiled along, her knapsack on her back. The humid air made her feel damp and hot before long, and the scents of the millions of herbs and blossoms around them were overpowering. She knew they'd eventually be coming to a cleared area; maybe her sinuses would unclog.

As she walked, she heard Saba half suppress a sneeze, followed almost immediately by Irina. Viktor and Gordon began breathing through their mouths. But no one spoke again as they kept walking.

Once they stopped. Viktor lifted a hand, then dashed down the trail aways, followed by Misha. Eveleen watched them move silently and swiftly. She thought she heard a low thrumming, but it was soon gone, and she wondered if it was just the pounding of her own heartbeat in her skull.

Then Misha and Viktor reappeared, and waved them on.

They had to emerge from the jungle within the borders for the foreign enclaves, or *Nurayil.* Yilayil meant "People of the People"; this designation was only for the nocturnal weasel folk. All other races were Nurayil—"People of the Stars."

They descended a hill, and Eveleen glimpsed buildings through the thinning trees.

At once they halted, and Misha and Viktor withdrew into the trees. Ashe nodded at Eveleen, Ross, and Saba, and the four started down the trail, Eveleen walking with Ross, and the other two just behind.

Eveleen felt her palms sweating. She knew her story, she felt comfortable in the simple forms of the question-rituals, but still, her adrenaline was spiking.

A series of round, low buildings were the first things they saw. Each had a round opening, into which beings of several kinds moved in and out. Eveleen felt slightly reassured when she saw those who met one another on the trail make the expected ritual gestures before one or the other stepped aside. The heavy air did not carry the sounds of the ritual responses, at least not at first. As they neared the first building, she could hear the tweets, whistles, and drones of many beings communicating.

It was all much quicker and noisier than she had ever imagined. She saw Ross staring around, his forehead tense. Ashe focused directly ahead of him; Saba, however, gazed around, her eyes narrowed.

Almost at once they encountered three short, heavy-looking bipeds with tough, bumpy hides. Their whistles were so high and quick Eveleen almost couldn't follow, but she recognized familiar notes among them.

Saba whistled in return, and stepped aside. The other three followed. The beings continued on their way without another glance.

Beside Eveleen, Ross let out a long, slow sigh.

It worked! It worked! Etiquette declared that the stranger defer to all; when one met acquaintances, the one who performed a service the more recently took precedence.

If they just deferred to everyone, at least now, they'd manage.

Four buildings in, they found the Transport Center, and Ashe gave Eveleen and Ross a quick nod.

"Here we go," Ross murmured under his breath.

Eveleen watched Ashe and Saba move on. They were going to try to get to the House of Knowledge, and at least see it, even if they couldn't get Saba in as a worker right away. Some time spent in its proximity ought to provide a sense of what was going on there.

In the meantime, Ross and Eveleen had to establish themselves as transportation workers. In private they'd called themselves cabbies, as they memorized the data provided by the First Team on the rail-skimmers the Yilayil and Nurayil used for transport.

The big building was full of beings, the warm, heavy air shrill with whistling, the droning sounding like an orchestra of out-of-tune bagpipes. Ross and Eveleen made their way to one side, where functionaries sat at a complicated console. Eveleen felt Ross walking tensely at her side, as he scanned the crowds for the familiar shapes of Baldies. Eveleen did not see anyone that remotely matched that description. She did see at the console two of the tall, spidery beings that the First Team had identified as being involved in all aspects of Nurayil tech.

They made their way up the line, and found themselves abruptly addressed not by the spidery beings, but by a tall, imposing creature with six arms. Related to the weasel folk?

116

Eveleen desperately banished speculation as the being addressed them: "I, Fargag of Nurayil Transport, this morning see strangers here?"

Eveleen wet her lips, and responded with slow care, "I, Eveleen of Fire Mountain Enclave, come to learn ti[*trill*]kee and to work as I learn."

Fargag fired at them a question of challenge: "Fire Mountain Enclave—unknown to me!"

"I, Ross of Fire Mountain, say that our Enclave is known to us," Ross whistled. "Known many generations to us, but we now travel to learn ti[*trill*]kee."

Fargag whistled a liquid phrase that made Eveleen's knees tremble with relief. It was a kind of cautious acceptance of temporary status. Beings who were anxious to learn "proper deportment" (ti[*trill*]kee) were provisionally accepted. At least, so it seemed, Eveleen thought. She could never forget that the First Team had been provisionally accepted—but they had disappeared.

Fargag instructed them to pass on to Virigu, one of the spidery beings.

They deferred as Fargag passed to the next newcomers, and Eveleen heard his challenging whistle/drone as they waited to address Virigu.

Within a short time they were tested in maintenance of the transport vehicles. They both had studied until they knew the mechanics of the rail-skimmers in their sleep; in fact, Eveleen reflected, as she swiftly disassembled, cleaned, then assembled a series of parts, that she had done this several times during her strange jumble of dreams aboard the globe ship.

They were accepted as maintenance workers—which meant pressing their palm on a square silver measure—and when questioned about their domicile, their second delicate moment came. They admitted that no one from Fire Mountain Enclave was currently in residence among the Nurayil, but they wished to establish a domicile, and once again they were accepted at face value. Virigu put them to work at once, for the turnover was apparently high at this job.

The day's work lasted until the light outside began to fade. At that time, all Nurayil but those formally accepted for service to the Yilayil were expected to withdraw to their domiciles.

Ross and Eveleen followed a number of other beings who didn't have family or clan domiciles. The housing for all the unconnected beings was inconveniently located at the far edge of the Nurayil enclave, but Eveleen and Ross were grateful that it was still there at all. They found that things had changed little in the hundred years since the First Team discovered the place—small round chambers, like cells in a beehive, lined a large round building that Ross and Ashe had found empty and hollow in the present timeline.

No one organized it. Eveleen and Ross poked their heads in at the doors of any unmarked or open rooms as they wound their way slowly up a ramp, until at last they found one—an inner cell, with no window—that had apparently been recently vacated.

No belongings were in it, and the little identity console on the opposite wall from the access gleamed purple, indicating that no one currently claimed the place.

In haste Ross slapped his palm on the metal plate below the light, and Eveleen followed suit, for they could hear feet shuffling out in the corridor, and it was possible that some tired, grumpy being might want to try to claim their place if they weren't formally "in." No one protected Nurayil, unless their families or clans did. This meant that those without either were at the bottom of all hierarchies, and must look out for themselves.

The light gleamed yellow—it was theirs.

Ross hit the door control, and the door slid shut. They were alone.

Eveleen looked around. The cell was just that, smaller even than the cabins aboard the globe ship. A storage compartment opened next to the door, and she shoved her knapsack into it. There were no furnishings; they'd have to scout those out. At least the flooring had some give, and Eveleen felt tired enough to sleep on brick. But she made herself look in the little alcove in one corner of the room. There was a waste recycle unit, and next to it an adjustable frame that vibrated slightly; it was cleaning the air that moved through it. Remembering the instructions from the First Team, she activated it, took off her clothes, then stepped through. It felt a little like pushing one's way through some kind of invisible gelatinous mass, but when she stepped out the other side, all the grit and dead skin was gone from her body. It wasn't refreshing like a good hot shower, or even like the sonic bath on the globe ship, but she did feel clean.

She passed her clothes through the field, and watched the grime in them patter down to the gutter at the bottom of the frame, and slurp away to the recycler.

Dressed again, and feeling slightly better, she went out to find Ross digging in his pack.

"Let's get the sticker on the door," Ross said.

"Oh. Right. Here, I'll do it." Eveleen held out her hand.

Ross handed her a plastic-backed sticker that they'd brought from Earth. The cells of the domicile were all marked in some way by their owners, for there was no other way to tell them apart, unless you counted—and they were at sixty or seventy cells up the ramp.

Irina and Vera and the others also had stickers; this was the only way they'd be able to find one another at night, at least until they had assimilated and could trust using the radios freely.

Eveleen opened the door, affixed the sticker to the outside of it, and closed it again. When she turned around, Ross had gone into the fresher alcove. She squatted down to dig in his pack for food, but before her hand closed on a container a soft tapping came at the door: three short, three long.

She bounced up and hit the control. Vera stood out in the hall, looking tired and sweaty but triumphant.

"Come in," Eveleen said. "Have you found a room yet?"

"Irina is there. She will be here in a moment." The redhead sat down cross-legged, and pulled a substantial packet from her knapsack. "So! We are successful—we are now food gatherers. Here is a meal!" She unwrapped her packet with a triumphant air. "Is good, all of it," she added.

"Shall we divide it into six portions?"

Vera shook her head. "We ate. Save out four only."

Eveleen said, "Have you seen Gordon and Saba?"

Vera shook her head just as another tapping came at the door, the same code.

Ross opened it, and Irina walked in, graceful and quiet as always. She frowned slightly. "No Gordon? Saba?" she asked directly. "It is very dark without."

Ross looked grim, and Eveleen felt her adrenaline spiking once again. No one was supposed to be out at night but the Yilayil and those who had gained their sanction. It had been dangerous a hundred years before, and there was no evidence that it was any safer now.

"Maybe we'd better wait on the food," Ross said, unclipping his radio transmitter from his belt. "I'll zap them once, and see if we get an answer." He looked around.

Eveleen and the two Russians all nodded agreement.

Part of Zina's orders had been to keep actual communications to a minimum, until they knew that it was safe. Various sonic codes were to be used, and those sparingly.

Ross tapped out the "Check in!" code, then sat down—and a tapping came at the door, the usual pattern, but somehow more urgent.

Ross moved fast, opening the door.

Gordon stood there alone, his face tired and grim.

"Saba?" Eveleen asked. "Don't tell me they already took her in?"

Gordon did not speak until the door was shut behind him. "As soon as we crossed into the zone of the House of Knowledge, I knew something was wrong. Everyone we met ignored me, nor did they challenge Saba. They didn't even address her."

"What?" Irina asked. "No questions? No demands for proper Nurayil deference?"

"What happened?" Eveleen began.

Gordon turned to her. "As soon as we got there, she was taken right in, and I was left outside staring at faces carved on giant poles—twenty feet high at least. A different face on each, from various races."

He paused.

"Is this bad?" Vera prompted.

"I don't know," Gordon replied. "I can only tell you this: the one at the very front was absolutely, obviously Saba."

CHAPTER THIRTEEN

Ross had seen that expression on Gordon's face before—when Travis Fox was finally listed officially as "missing in action," and given up by the officials at the Project.

"You tried her on the transmitter?" Ross asked, indicating his belt com.

"I pulsed her," Gordon said. "She did pulse me back. But when I tried voice, all I got was noise. There must be some kind of sophisticated digital jammer operating, forbidding communication above a certain level of complexity."

Ross said nothing for a moment, considering the level of technology needed to jam a spread-spectrum com system, something impossible to Terran science.

"A statue of Saba... in *this time*," Eveleen said slowly.

Ross turned to his wife, who paced back and forth along the wall of the tiny room. She looked up. "It must mean that we're going to be making another jump, only farther back."

"To when First Team disappears," Vera said, nodding. "We were all hoping we'd be going back to rescue them, weren't we?"

"If it is safe to do so," Irina said in her precise voice. "We do not go back until we are assured that it will not destroy the timeline."

"Well, I hope to," Eveleen said, then grimaced. "That is, to make it plain, I hope that it transpires that we've already been back there and rescued them and that's why they disappeared. Does that make sense?" She made a face, rubbing her forehead. "Sheesh! I do hate thinking in possible timelines, it scrambles my brain!"

Ross nodded, appreciating his wife's attempt to lighten the tension, but Gordon's expression did not change.

"We're not going backward or forward in time without Saba," Gordon said. "I won't leave her in there."

"You can't get in?" Ross asked.

"Tried." Gordon shook his head. "Tried offers, questions, and even a challenge—and it almost got me lynched. So I beat a retreat, figuring if I pushed it any harder, it might only jeopardize Saba. Came back here, found a room at the top of this Nurayil dorm. It's a long walk up the ramp, but from its window I can see the House of Knowledge."

"Now that was a good idea," Ross said, his mind rapidly developing—and then discarding—possible plans. They simply didn't know enough. But one thing was for certain: being able to watch the House of Knowledge had to be an advantage. "Didn't you and Saba work out some codes on the com, for just in case?"

"We did," Gordon said. "Mostly voice codes, but some pulse ones as well."

Irina sat silently, frowning, her mouth in a straight line. Next to her, Vera smiled and shook her curly head. "It might not be so bad come morning. We know she's alive, at least."

Gordon nodded slowly. "We'll give it a few days. Say, a week, unless there's an emergency. Settle in, gather data. Then meet—all of us, including Misha and Viktor, if we can get them—to review our strategy."

"Sounds like a plan," Ross said. "Come on, let's chow down. No one can rest, or think, with an empty gut. And I don't know about you, but we put in a day of hard work."

He pushed a portion of the food toward Gordon, and was relieved when the professor took it and began methodically to eat.

Eveleen gave them a cheery smile. "Hard labor indeed. You can tell those rail-skimmers are old. Unless today was a real gift from Murphy, they must break down all the time."

Gordon swung his head toward the Russian women. "And you?"

"We are now gatherers," Irina said. "It appears that eating establishments will hire on their preferred gatherers, and one can then get prepared food as well as work credit."

Vera said, "We'll find out which places make the sorts of things we can eat, and zero in on them. No one has noticed our field analyzers, and we're going to be careful to do it when no one else is around. In the meantime, we walk about with our gatherers' tools and listen. A few challenges, but no one took any interest in beings from Fire Mountain Enclave."

"None in us either," Eveleen said.

"Good." Gordon finished his share and got to his feet. "Let's meet tomorrow night and compare notes."

Everyone agreed, and very soon Gordon and the Russians departed, leaving Ross and Eveleen together in the tiny cell.

They looked at each other.

"Alone at last," she said with a tired grin as she held her arms out. "It's not the Yilayil honeymoon suite—"

"Privacy," Ross murmured into her soft hair, "ranks it up there over any luxury penthouse on Earth."

"Privacy," Eveleen said, laughing.

124

⚜ ⚜ ⚜

Cold shock numbed Saba as she thought of those tall, carved wood statues before the House of Knowledge—and her face on the foremost one.

"This means I've been here."

It was the only possible explanation. She sat in the room that the guardians of the House of Knowledge had brought her to, trying to clear her mind and plan. Except her mind refused to work. So she looked around. The walls were plain, except for paintings that looked very old; she sat on a low couch made of some woven material that felt like flax.

How long had she been here? She glanced at her chrono. An hour and a half.

She sat back, closing her eyes—but then the door opened, one of the green beings, who seemed to be the guardians of the House, entered and beckoned to her.

She said nothing as she rose and walked out of the room.

Fast Yilayil voices exchanged ritual greetings around her—vying, apparently, for the honor of escorting her inside. She knew she ought to be listening, and she caught a few words. Someone trilled something about making a place in readiness, but she lost track of the rest of the statement. Her mind could not veer from that image of her own face, in a time when she supposedly had never been.

When? What had happened?

Someone addressed her: "Saba-music-maker of Far Star is welcome at last to the Yil."

To "the people." Not to any specific ones—Nurayil or Yilayil. They definitely knew who she was. That meant she had already accomplished something.

125

The first realization banished that earlier image of women from some distant planet that happened to resemble her. The second realization made her heart pound.

If I have been here, she thought, then I know I will have left myself some kind of message. I know it as well as I know myself. Somehow, I must find it, so that I can accomplish what must be done, and protect the integrity of time.

So deciding, she felt inner conviction at last, and with it the ability to think—to assess.

She turned her attention to her surroundings.

Cool, dry air was her first awareness. The second was the glare-free light, from some hidden source. The walls were plain, as had been that parlor to which she'd initially been brought.

Before her stood two robed beings, one tall and spidery, the other feline, with sleek black fur everywhere except the face. The latter spoke.

"We, Rilla and Virigu, teachers of the House of Knowledge, now welcome Saba of the Far Star. We are teachers of deportment."

Saba knew the response to that. "I, Saba of the Far Star, am ready to learn deportment." If nothing else, this would buy her time.

"Saba now come with us." Rilla's voice was scratchy, her whistles weak, but she was understandable.

The Virigu had not yet spoken. Saba gave the spidery being a glance, remembering what the First Team had said about these creatures; they all bore the name Virigu, and they were the highest-ranking Nurayil in that they were involved with all levels of technology.

Saba was led up a curving ramp. "We are females," Rilla went on. "We wear robes which symbolize our dedication to Knowledge."

Saba said nothing. She felt her belt communicator buzzing against her hip, but she did not move her hands to it to acknowledge Gordon's call, not with these two beings watching her. Though so far Rilla and Virigu had behaved with respect, the fact that she had been taken here without being asked indicated she might in fact be in danger.

"We protect you," Virigu trilled, an uncanny parallel to Saba's thoughts. "We teach you."

They paused at a landing, and Saba paused as well. She glanced down, saw a splendid mosaic far below, on the ground floor. It depicted the night sky, and constellations not even remotely familiar.

Rilla moved again, leading the way. Saba was distracted momentarily by the swaying of a long, luxurious black tail among the draperies of Rilla's robe.

They paused before a door. Saba noted that it was alone on a corridor, with a blank wall adjacent. Virigu pointed to her hand with a long, chitinous digit. She then indicated a silver plate next to the door, and Saba pressed her hand against it.

A series of tiny lights rippled, and the door slid open.

All three passed inside a small room furnished with a low couch. On one wall faded paintings made a complicated scene; on the other lines promised some kind of furnishings now folded away.

"You domicile here," Rilla said. She touched a control panel on the blank wall, and a kind of storage enclosure slid out. Saba saw what looked like a stepladder of boxes, each with a tiny light gleaming above a control button at one corner. "Robes," Rilla added, pressing the control on the topmost box. It folded silently out, showing two of the flaxen robes neatly folded.

Saba nodded, unmoving. She was not going to change in front of these others unless she could not avoid it. She did not want to risk exposing, and then losing, her belt com, which she wore inside her overalls.

"We leave, you come to us for eat, we begin to learn," Rilla said, and with a swish of robes, the two left.

Before she did anything, Saba looked around the room. Was she being monitored? She realized that there was nothing obvious—nothing she could identify, so she might as well dismiss that worry for now.

Instead, she explored the room, first touching the controls on each of the storage boxes. Some of the implements she could only guess at; others seemed to be universal—a hairbrush. A toothbrush, though shaped differently. There was a box with a plate and Yilayil instructions. She puzzled out the script, then took off her boot and placed her foot on it. Lights rippled, and a moment later a slipper appeared from a slot in the back of the box, twin in color and material to those she'd seen on Rilla's feet.

She pressed the master control and the boxes all folded neatly away into the wall, leaving only faint lines to indicate where they were. She moved to a control near the corner; this one seemed to control something that extended from floor to ceiling.

She positioned herself directly before the control, touched it, and this time the wall slid back and a tiny alcove appeared, encompassing the corner of the room. She saw a recycle unit, a large frame that reminded her somewhat of the globe ship's sonic "shower," and a sink with a water faucet.

When that slid away, she tried the last control, and found herself with a desk and wall monitor. The keypads were utterly different than Terran keyboards.

But it was unmistakably a computer. Was it her own? Was there protected space on it? This would take exploring—theentire room required careful examination. She knew that if she had any opportunity whatsoever, she would leave herself some kind of message, no matter how brief or crude. Something.

But that would have to wait. They apparently expected her to rejoin them in the House.

First she took out her belt com, and tried to raise Ashe. Nothing but static—inconvenient, but not unexpected. She tried the pulse—and a few moments later she got a return pulse.

So. She tapped out the code for "I'm well" and "I'm investigating." A moment later she got the expected answer: "I received your message."

Communication! For a moment she felt a strong urge to sit down and fumble her way through the other codes they'd developed—except she still did not know who might be listening, by whatever means. The whole idea behind the codes was quick exchanges, fast enough not to trip some kind of high-tech monitoring system.

Likewise she did not know how long Rilla and Virigu would wait for her without coming back to investigate.

So she changed into the robe, used the alcove to freshen up, and passed her clothing through the "shower" experimentally. It seemed to work on clothes as well as on people. She checked the water with a tool that Zina had issued to each team member; it registered as pure $H20$. She tasted a sip from a cup that she found waiting—handleless, but unmistakably a drinking cup—and found that the water reminded her of pure, almost tasteless distilled water.

Did all the beings here, then, need light, water, and... And harmony?

It was time to find out.

She dressed again in her overalls, but put one of the robes on over them. Her belt com went right back on her belt under the robe, but she stowed her pack—with her laptop—in the lowest of the closet boxes, as she'd mentally named them.

Then it was time to go to work.

CHAPTER FOURTEEN

The next few days were so much alike that they later blurred in memory.

Each morning Ross and Eveleen left their little cell and walked across the Nurayil district of the port city. Sometime during that first night, a heavy cloud bank had moved in, and a light but steady rain began to fall—without, apparently, surcease.

Ross felt at first that this was a blessing. The rain cooled the humid air slightly, but more importantly it drenched the overpowering scents emanating from the vast jungle bordering the Nurayil area. His sinuses cleared; the heavy smell of wet pavement was preferable to the millions of sweet perfumes.

At the Transport facility, he and Eveleen worked hard, almost continually, alongside numerous other beings descended from a variety of races. Virigu seldom spoke to anyone, but watched continually. Some beings did very little, and no one said anything. Ross and Eveleen kept at their jobs—and by the second day, they saw that good workers would be promoted to other sections.

Their goal was to pilot the rail-skimmers so that they could enable the team to be able to move about undetected, should movement be needed. If they could only become drivers through promotion, then they would continue to work hard.

Most of their fellow workers kept to themselves, or stayed strictly with those of their own kind, but not all. At the one break officially designated, at midday, there was some chatter among a few beings—while little gray Moova circulated through with vending carts, selling an astonishing variety of foods.

Ross noted that the Moova had palm plates on their vending machines: there did not seem to be any kind of coinage or money in other forms. Just the unknown credit as registered by the palm plates.

The mealtime conversation was seldom interesting, but it was good practice in following the language—especially as used by a variety of beings with different types of mouths and vocal structures. Some of the whistles were thin and piercing, others curiously liquid. One set of beings sounded like oboes; lacking a name for them, Eveleen and Ross in private referred to them as the music people.

They both noticed that even among those beings who stayed close to their own kind, no one spoke anything but Yilayil. Ross and Eveleen were careful to do the same, if there was any remote chance of being overheard. It was sometimes frustrating, but at least he was with Eveleen, whose spirits were irrepressibly high. She attacked the work with vigor and interest, and she seemed to regard the world without fear.

As Ross once had. He tried to regain that carefree sense of adventure, but Eveleen's presence triggered that protective instinct. He was always on the watch for danger—something he was careful to hide.

Each evening, Irina, Vera, and Gordon joined them in Ross and Eveleen's room—theirs being the first one of the Terrans along that ramp.

At first, no one had much of anything to report. Gordon had exchanged some brief communications with Saba, who—not surprisingly—seemed to be "learning deportment" as well. He had not heard from Misha and his partner. The two Russian women were at least as busy as Ross and Eveleen at their jobs. The rest of their time they spent trying to listen to the conversations around them, without trespassing against "proper deportment." Vera did her best to get the beings she encountered talking; Irina listened, and took copious notes on her laptop. She did that at the nightly sessions as well, something that bothered Ross slightly at first, but then he decided it was her way of approaching her own part of the mission, and so he tuned her out. Eveleen didn't seem to mind. She kept up her martial-arts practice every night, whether the others were around or not.

"They all talk so fast," Ross said one night. "And there's so much we hadn't been able to learn about this language. We're still having a tough time at Transport."

"It reminds me of English lessons," Vera said with a grin. "Four years in school, and I thought I was so good with this tongue. But then my schoolmates and I were taken on a trip to England, and—ha! Everyone talked so quick, and with slang, it made my head spin! So much I found that I didn't know."

"A good time, then, to compare notes," Gordon put in. "Here is a challenge I heard today between the guardians of the House of Knowledge and a pair of those gray-skinned beings who look a little like tree stumps with extra eyes—"

"Moova," Irina said. "We found out today. The Moova all take a very great interest in foods."

"Moova," Gordon repeated. "I'll remember. Here's the exchange."

And he whistle/droned, in quick fashion, a long pattern to which they all listened intently.

"What's that tense?" Vera asked. "'Time-as-was ...'"

"Sounds like a mixture of time-as-was/to come."

"Conditional?" Ross asked, trying to concentrate.

"No." Gordon shook his head. "Conditional goes like this—" He demonstrated, and Ross remembered the lesson.

"Then what is this new tense?" Irina asked. "Or is it merely some kind of shortcut?"

"We'll have to be on the listen for more of these short-cuts," Eveleen suggested in a grim voice as she moved through a kata. "In case they have a third meaning that the First Team never caught onto."

"Hmmm." Gordon frowned, and Irina looked up, her eyes narrowed.

After they'd thoroughly discussed possible meanings for all the words in the exchange, the group parted to sleep. Ross found himself reluctant to see them go.

As soon as the door was shut, Eveleen yawned, then said, "Weird, how isolation will make a small society into a very intense society."

"What do you mean?" Ross pulled out their single furnishing, gotten the day before. It was a kind of futon that functioned as a couch and as a sleeping mat. The air never seemed to get cool, so they hadn't any need of blankets. At least the sonic shower kept the air filtered.

"Well, we all know how—if one were to try to define a social butterfly—Gordon would be the last person ever named. Irina and Vera are nice, but I never would have picked them as buddies. Yet I look forward all day to seeing them, and I find every word they say interesting. Then, when the evening ends, I'm sorry to see them go. Was it the same when you were stuck in the past with other men, or is this a female thing?"

"No, it was more or less the same," Ross admitted. "Travis, Gordon, Renfry, and I talked a lot about home when we first came here. Those cubes that showed what you valued most had to be hidden for a while, there—it hurt too much to look at them, but we couldn't stay away."

Eveleen nodded slowly. "That was real isolation," she said with sympathy. "You four didn't have any idea if you'd ever go home again."

"Exactly. But it was the same on Earth. I remember hunkering around the fire with some of the other time agents, back in prehistoric times. There was a sense of companionship, though I don't think any of us would have named ourselves particularly social men."

"It's this weird isolation within a crowd. I felt a bit like that when I went with my high school team to Japan to attend a special martial-arts camp," Eveleen admitted, yawning again. "Though there, everyone I encountered was really nice, but I couldn't speak the language, and not everyone spoke English."

"At least you were all humans," Ross commented.

Eveleen grinned. "Yes. At least we were all humans. Here, they don't care, which is a good thing, since too much notice might be dangerous. I can't get it out of my head. Though we're being so careful to follow all the rules reported by the First Team, we still don't know which rule they broke—what caused their disappearance."

"It's been on my mind as well," Ross admitted, feeling that instinct flare again. But he repressed it, just as he repressed the urge to sneak out of the Nurayil dorm and nose around—see just what it was the mysterious Yilayil didn't want the underlings seeing.

This urge hadn't been so bad the first night or so. Then, everything was so new, and he was tired and ready for sleep as soon as the nightly talk session was over. But now, especially when there was no kind of distraction in the little cell—no books, television, music, even—he wished to be out exploring. If he were alone...

No. Don't even think that. Not for a moment, he told himself.

He turned to look at his wife, who was seated on the ground, working a complicated yoga step, her face serene. She was content, and he ought to be happy it was so.

As for exploring, that was Misha's job. And if Ross had that guy figured right, he wouldn't appreciate anyone horning in on his turf.

"Ross?"

He looked up, saw Eveleen watching him.

"Anything wrong?" she asked.

"No," he said. "Just thinking—about the mission. You know, those other races. That kind of thing. As for our not being noticed, I'm just as happy to be ignored."

Eveleen smiled, shrugged, and went back to her yoga.

CHAPTER FIFTEEN

The very next morning the Transport Maintenance Virigu assigned Ross and Eveleen to a new area of the maintenance facility. Virigu seemed to assume that they worked as a pair—an impression that they did nothing to dispel.

They were greeted by a small scaled being who had hands and tentacles, again reminding them of the modern-day savage humanoids. Otherwise there was no resemblance; the creature had a beaklike snout, deepset eyes, and a tail.

"I, Bock of Nurayil Transport Design, this day must accept two Nurayil of unknown enclave and ability. Virigu of Nurayil Transport maligns the Jecc of Harbeast Teeth Islands!"

As Bock spoke, several more Jecc gathered round, their tails twitching. Ross looked them over, noted that they all wore identical garments rather like overalls, but with no pockets. The arms and tentacles were free; front flap of the garments covered the creatures' bulky midsections.

"I, Ross of Fire Mountain Enclave, this day am told by Virigu that our job is here, and so it is," Ross hum/whistled. Annoyance sharpened his tones, but he didn't think that so bad a thing—this groundless challenge was too blatant.

137

Chirps and whistles went up from all the assembled Jecc. Two or three of them crowded close to Ross; one nudged Eveleen, and she almost stumbled. But she recovered her step, planted her feet, and the next push caused the small creature to squeak and back up a step or two, to the dismay of the others pressing in. Eveleen didn't budge.

Bock riposted with a rapid series of whistle/drones, meaning: "We'll test your knowledge, interloper."

And Ross fired right back the equivalent of: "Be my guest."

The rest of the day, the Jecc did just that. They pestered Ross and Eveleen constantly with questions, demanding to know if they were aware of the functions of various rail-skimmer parts.

The department, Ross discovered, was intended to repair salvaged parts of old rail-skimmers so that new ones could be assembled. The department was not comprised entirely of Jecc, but they were the majority, and they kept Ross and Eveleen away from the others.

Ross had to bite down hard on his temper at least twenty times that day. Each time some Jecc cruised by and pinched a part he was reaching for, or knocked into him from behind just as he was assembling a delicate piece, he was ready to haul off and smack the little beggars across the room.

But he looked over at Eveleen, who was getting the same treatment. Each time she calmly picked up her pieces—taking care that they stayed right on her, or under a knee—and continued as though nothing had interrupted her.

Parts salvaged from rail-skimmers deemed unusable were available to all, but for some reason the Jecc seemed to like to take parts already selected—by someone else. Ross's temper abated just slightly when he saw while walking across the floor to get more parts that they also did this to each other.

One Jecc snagged a connector, stashed it underneath the front flap of its coverall in a movement so quick it was almost a blur. Then the Jecc scuttled away noiselessly, just as the one who'd been robbed started groping around for the connector. That Jecc jerked its head this way and that in weird birdlike movements, whistling a high tweeting sound that Ross couldn't interpret.

At the day's end, Ross felt the grip of tension on his neck as he and Eveleen walked out of the building. Hard rain drummed on the ground and splashed in gouting falls at corners and overhangs. A rail-skimmer whirred by, and Ross looked at it with regret; they had not worked enough, apparently, to earn credit for that kind of luxury. So far the futon, their lunches, and their housing took up their days' accumulated credit, according to the console on the wall of their cell.

Neither spoke until they were safely in their cell. Then Ross went to the wall console and touched the plate. Above it, the flat screen lit with several buttons. Below that was a number, in Yilayil script: they had apparently moved into the black again, though just barely.

"Strange," Eveleen said, looking tiredly at the console as she swung her arms back and forth to work out kinks from her muscles. "We never agreed to a pay rate, or to rent for this place. How does anyone get ahead? Is everything at Virigu's discretion, or is there some big boss over Virigu who sets the prices on work and goods?"

"Maybe we'll find out," Ross said. "Me, I just wish we could kick back with a pot of fresh-brewed coffee, a newspaper—in English—and maybe a good action flick."

"While you're at it, let's have a Jacuzzi and a stereo," Eveleen added, laughing.

Tapping at the door caused them both to fall silent. It was the familiar pattern, and something about the quick sound made Ross think immediately of Gordon.

A moment later he saw he was right. "Saba?" Ross asked as soon as the door was closed.

Gordon shook his head, his blue eyes tired but alert. "Same. She's alive, has a room of her own, and her day is filled with deportment lessons. Nothing more yet—all we have are our codes." His hair was dotted with droplets, indicating he'd just come from outside.

"How's the delivery boy business?" Ross asked as Gordon hunkered down on the floor with his back to a wall.

Eveleen continued doing her kata warm-ups.

Ashe shrugged. "I'm not that high yet. Until I either come up with some prestigious favor I can do for someone, or some seniority, I'm still hauling trash to the recycler."

Ross jerked his thumb over his shoulder at the wall console. "Your pay rate as lousy as ours?"

"I have the same furniture," Gordon said, indicating the futon. "I calculate I owe another day's pay on it."

"How does anyone else without family or connections manage to eat?" Eveleen asked, her voice only slightly husky as her arms arced and snapped through a complicated exercise.

"Probably the same way we do: they scrounge, they get or make friends, they go into debt to someone a little higher," Gordon said. "The current society is not designed to easily accommodate newcomers."

"Conformity," Eveleen said, and finished up her kata with a "Whoosh! This humidity is tough to work in."

"Probably why the Yilayil built underground," Ashe commented. "Think of it—furred beings. Heavy fur like those creatures we saw up the timeline, anyway, would have evolved in cold weather, one would think." He got to his feet and moved to the console. "But you're right, Eveleen. This culture selects for conformity, and does its best to guarantee it. Yet the technical systems all over this city," he tapped the little wall console with a finger, "are predicated on the fact that each individual is unique."

Ross grunted. "Hadn't thought about that, but of course you're right."

Ashe gave a nod. "Whether by finger, tentacle, tongue, or whatever means one wishes to be identified, apparently one of the few things these beings have in common with us is this one fact: we are all individuals, differing subtly from every other being, or this kind of measure would not work."

Ross looked up at the console, and nodded. It was true. He hadn't been asked his name, or age, or anything else; he was registered in some unknown computer somewhere just by his palm print. And wherever he went in the starport city, if he wished to buy something, or use a transport, or change his residence, he would have to press his hand on a similar silver plate.

"It's also a damn good way to keep track of people," Ross pointed out, wondering if the system had some sinister use.

Eveleen nodded. "I was thinking about that today. Misha and Viktor are existing outside this mysterious registry—but that's because they are not here in the city. How long would they make it in this city without having to sign in? Are some beings trying to exist outside the system in a similar way?"

"And for what reason?" Gordon asked. "We can't be the only ones here with plans of our own."

"Now that's a grim thought," Ross said, just as tapping sounded at the door again, and he went to let in the Russian women.

"News about Saba?" Irina asked, her dark eyes narrowed, as soon as she entered.

"No change," Ashe replied.

Irina grunted a response in Russian, which Ross had learned meant, more or less, *Is good enough for now.* Then she said in English, "She is alive. This bodes well."

"Anything new to report?" Gordon asked them.

"The pollen count is way up," Vera said. "This despite the rain."

Irina sat down, graceful and neat as always. "Nothing new for me to report."

Ross said, "You two pick up anything about some feisty little guys called Jecc?"

Vera and Irina exchanged grimaces.

"Uh oh," Eveleen said, grinning wryly. "Bad news on the horizon, right?"

Vera snorted. "All we know is that they just love to surround a person and rob you blind, unless you can get to a group bigger and tougher than they are."

"They seem to think it a game," Irina added as she passed around some fresh tubers and another dish that looked like chopped carrots, but tasted more like peppered zucchini. "Luckily they tweet these weird little songs when they run about in packs, so you can hear them coming. The first couple times, when we didn't know what the sound was, we got pretty much everything taken. Everything small— luckily none of our important equipment, which we keep zipped up."

"But now we hear that noise and we run like rabbits," Vera put in. "We asked one of the Moova about them, and found out their name—and that everyone avoids them. They don't like anyone—yet they seem to be pretending to learn deportment. I take it you have also encountered the Jecc?"

"They run the department we got assigned to today," Eveleen said. "And if we want to get us a transport vehicle, we're going to have to figure out a way around them."

Gordon said musingly, "Pretending to learn deportment...Interesting. Interesting," he repeated, tapping absently at the side of his dish. "You'd think something would happen to them if they are that antisocial. That behavior pattern doesn't fit the conformity paradigm, does it?"

"Not the way I see it," Ross said, setting aside his dish. He felt full—and the food didn't taste bad—but the craving was so strong for a good cup of coffee and something *normal* to eat. He ignored it impatiently, focusing on the problem. "You know what this smells like? Politics. Of some sort. And I am here to tell you I really, really hate that stink."

"Politics would be a problem," Gordon conceded. "At least insofar as we might cross some powermonger or other all unawares." He turned to the Russian women.

"Yes," Vera said. "I know what comes next: more listening. We are doing what we can."

Gordon said, "I know. But the more we can find out, the quicker we can act. I'm limited in what I have access to—but I feel I have to stay close to the House of Knowledge, until I know for certain that Saba is not in danger."

"Right," Eveleen said. "Well, we'll do our bit. We'll work like doggies, and see if those Jecc will back down. We simply have to get a rail-skimmer."

"I suppose there is no opportunity to conceal the parts, build one, and conceal that?" Irina asked. She smiled slightly. "This is what Mikhail Petrovich would do."

Ross hid his annoyance at the mention of the guy's name—and the implication that he wasn't as innovative, if not as smart. "Everything is registered, locked down, and otherwise accounted for—" he began, and then he frowned. "No, that's not really an option. We might manage to build one, but since they follow buried rails, it would have to be registered with the central dispatcher, or whatever the equivalent is, to avoid collisions. At least, that's what we were told. And what we thought. But the Jecc and their stealing..."

"Could they be building their own transports? For whatever purpose?" Eveleen asked, her gaze considering.

"And ought we to discuss this with Virigu and let them take their chances?" Ross added. "I have to say, much as I hate squealing in a general sense, after today's fun and games it would give me a hell of a lot of satisfaction."

"It's too easy," Gordon said. "Unless your Virigu is a total fool, surely this has been noticed before."

Ross sighed. "Yeah, as usual you're right. I guess what I need to do is watch these Jecc and see if they actually remove the parts they steal, or if they all get put back again. Which would be crazy."

Gordon got to his feet. "What's crazy to one might be tradition to another. You know that. One of our first lessons as time agents. Meantime, I'm dead tired, and want some rest before another day of trash hauling. It'll be a week tomorrow, so I'm planning to put out the call to Misha and Viktor." He paused at the door, and turned to Vera. "Have either of you heard from them?"

"No," Vera said, looking down at her feet.

"No." Irina's voice was flat.

Ross wondered if it was true, then quashed the thought. Enough problems faced them with possible conspiracies among the Nurayil; he wasn't even going to entertain such thoughts about his fellow humans unless forced into it.

"I'll report on their response—if any—tomorrow. Good night, all."

Gordon nodded at them, and left.

Irina said quietly, "We shall endeavor to discover more about these Jecc, if we can."

"And anything else," Vera added, getting up slowly and stretching. A huge yawn seized her, then she grinned. "A difficult business, this collecting of gossip. If only it were so arduous at home!"

Everyone laughed, and the women departed.

Ross's mind was full of conflicting thoughts—and from the look of Eveleen, who rubbed her thumbnail absently back and forth over her lower lip, she felt the same.

If only he could get out and—

"Come on," he said. "Let's call it a day."

CHAPTER SIXTEEN

"For an archaeologist," Gordon Ashe said to himself as he finished loading the recycler-bound wagon, "being a trash man is a golden opportunity."

His tone was somewhat grim, and certainly ironic, but he did believe there was a great deal of truth in what he'd said just the same.

The grimness came of the fact that the recycle transport system had obviously been breaking down for many years, and it was apparently easier to get some unfortunate Nurayil to see to it than to bother with replacement parts or a new system.

The wagon worked, like the rail-skimmers, on the mag-lev principle: super-conductive magnets floating above buried rails. But it was obviously much older, slow, and it was up to Gordon to pick out the little plants that insisted on taking root all along the track. His unknown predecessor had not bothered.

The loader system had long since ceased to function, leaving the trash to be loaded by hand.

This way, at least, Gordon got a good look at the House of Knowledge's castoffs—everything they did not run through the plumbing recycler. Even if he had had an automated loader, he still would have sorted the trash, partly to examine it, and partly in case there was some way that Saba could get a message to him.

Paper and pen seemed to be out. But he knew she had at least one data disk in her laptop; if her machine had not been confiscated, perhaps she would slip a disk into the waste, which he could then read in his own machine.

Except how to get it back to her? Well, no need to think that out. She probably had already dismissed the idea; at least no disk had appeared. He hoped because there was no need yet for such a drastic move.

As he grunted a bulky, heavy lump of metal into the wagon, he distracted himself momentarily with speculating what it might have been used for. Nothing came to mind. It looked like an old internal combustion engine block crushed by a four-dimensional waffle iron.

And it weighed a ton.

Clang! Klunk! He paused, breathing heavily, thinking over what really concerned him: the code messages he'd received the night before.

They were all repeats: "searching," "deportment lessons," "well-being," "no danger."

Frustrating. He wanted a real status report—he also wanted to find out what she was learning, and to learn it as well.

He sighed, and stared at the jumble of material on the loading platform. What were these things, and what had they been used for? Among the detritus were what looked like a steel umbrella, half inside-out; an exploded plastic xylophone; and a half-dozen foamed alloy shoe trees made for someone twenty-five feet tall with feet that had toes at both ends. Alien trash.

"Any sufficiently advanced technology is indistinguishable from magic," he muttered. If Arthur C. Clarke had had this job, Gordon thought, he might well have added that such a technology's discards are indistinguishable from art.

Well, bad art, anyway. Most of the discards looked like the kind of incomprehensible sculptures that often showed up in public places back home on Earth.

He wondered what the other Nurayil thought of it, or how much awareness they had of the technology that sustained this odd civilization. One thing seemed sure: it was slowly winding down, for down the timeline, the civilization definitely had crumbled.

How long, he wondered, could the ancient Inca, for instance, have kept a twentieth-century city running? Would they have mastered the technology, destroyed themselves with it, or merely ridden it down into ruin as the machines decayed for lack of knowledge? Was that what had happened here?

He sighed as the last of the stuff slid into the wagon.

Already he was wet from the misting rain that never seemed to stop, but at least it kept him somewhat cool. Shaking the rain from his eyes, he slid onto the control seat and activated the wagon.

It shuddered, whining on an excruciating note, then slid forward at a snail's pace. Once he was well out of sight of any of the guardians, he slid up his sleeve and glanced at his watch. Good. He'd calculated well; he'd arrive at the recycle building in plenty of time, then.

The wagon lumbered shudderingly along its route. Occasionally it lurched and almost stopped. Gordon jumped out each time and used a flat tool he'd found to wedge up growing plants whose roots were already fouling the rails. The wagon moved so slowly that he'd only have to run a few steps to catch up.

Back to communication—and the next problem. From Saba there was not enough, but from the Russians there was too much.

He thought over what he'd say to the two Russian men, and how he'd say it. He'd decided against taking the women to task. He wouldn't heed to, if Misha was cooperative.

And he did believe the women when they'd said they hadn't communicated with Misha or Viktor. For Vera, though, it wasn't for lack of trying, for she'd been pulsing Misha just about every night. Was she trying to get him to talk real-time? Apparently he hadn't responded—but he'd been pulsing Irina in turn. And she'd been obeying the command to keep silence.

Gordon did not want to have to say anything to Vera. The mission was too important. He did not want to risk bad blood with any of the Russians. Perhaps she didn't intend to talk to Misha, only to get that return pulse—just as Gordon himself did each evening with Saba—but still, he needed to make sure that the orders were kept, at least until they knew they were safe. And it was always easier to remonstrate with men.

He grimaced at the thought, and shook his head.

Slowly the wagon trundled through a tunnel of green growth. He'd be at the recycling building very soon.

His thoughts were abruptly splintered when he heard what sounded like voices—human voices. Children's voices?

He looked around. Nothing.

He forced himself to scan more slowly, each tree and fern. Still nothing. Once the light shafting weakly through the thin rain clouds overhead seemed to darken for a moment, and he looked up, but of course only saw the canopy of jungle growth, and beyond it the gray of clouds.

Now there was silence, except for the quiet *tick* and *plop* of raindrops on broad leaves.

He breathed deeply, wondering if he'd possibly imagined the voices. The heavy scents of the jungle tickled the back of his sinuses.

He was still listening, and watching, when the wagon abruptly emerged into a cemented area. Around the perimeter there were cracks, with rootlings and little plants thriving; it was strange to think that this would all be utterly overgrown down the timeline in the present. Was the science team walking around this very area right now?

He shrugged away the fancy. The wagon slid smoothly now toward the building. Lights rippled above an access door, which then slid up.

Gordon jumped off the wagon, which would finish its job automatically within the building, and emerge empty through the adjacent access.

He started walking around the cement apron, looking for the Russians—or anyone else who might be about.

No one else seemed to be lurking, which was good. He'd deliberately picked noon, having discovered that most of the other beings in the Nurayil part of the city preferred dawn for their recycling, and of course the mysterious Yilayil did their disposal during the night.

He slowed his steps, walking closer to the jungle. No one in sight.

He'd nearly completed a full circle when he heard a quick whistle—not a Yilayil whistle, but a familiar melody, an old jazz tune.

He stopped, his head jerking up, and he saw Misha lounging against a tree, his long blond hair backlit by the weak sunlight. Like a shadow, Viktor loomed at his shoulder, still and quiet as the trees around them.

Gordon finished his circuit, stepped off the cement apron, and joined them. "Is there a reason why we're hiding?' he asked.

"Yes," Misha said, smiling slightly.

In surprise Gordon waited for an explanation.

Instead, Viktor jerked his head toward the shadowy undergrowth behind him, and took off down the trail. In silence Gordon followed, Misha behind him.

They walked for a short time, emerging on a mossy outcropping just beneath the spreading canopy of a tree whose fringed leaves were a deep blue-green. A natural fence of rocks blocked one end, beyond which the cliff fell away three or four meters to a swift-moving stream.

Gordon entered the little area, saw packs and equipment neatly stored, and realized that this was the men's current campsite.

"Welcome home," Misha said. "At least, home for two days. We're almost finished at this end of the district. Coffee?"

Gordon did not know how the insouciant Russian had managed to smuggle it in, but he knew an extravagant gesture when he saw one. "Love some," he said, matching Misha's casual tone—as if they had it every day.

Of course, maybe the Russians did.

Misha snorted a laugh. Even Viktor smiled slightly before he scanned the sky with quick thoroughness, then ran down to the stream to scoop up a pan of water.

When he returned Misha had a small fire going—almost smokeless, Gordon noted. How much experimentation had gone into finding out which deadwood was safe to burn?

No one spoke until the pan was set on a tripod over the fire, then Misha looked up at Gordon. "Questions?"

"How about a report?"

The Russian shrugged, an elegant movement. "In essentials, we have nothing. We have been over the Nurayil burial site twice, sounding for these." He touched his jaw, and Gordon thought of the implants the Russians all had in their teeth. "Nothing."

Gordon nodded grimly. In their first briefing, Zina had told him about the implants, stating that even if the bodies were cremated by normal means, the implants would still give off a signal. This was how the First Team had found their biologist in the first place; scanning for the signal was a part of their regular routine.

"Go on," he said.

"We've been working out in a circle—but our speed has been impeded by these damn flyers we saw on Day One."

Now Gordon understood the cover, and the scanning. "Flyers," he repeated.

Misha and Viktor both nodded.

"They spotted us the morning of Day Two. The rain had started, and there were no shadows. We didn't think to look up," Misha said.

Viktor added, in heavily accented English, "Make no noise."

"Heard nothing, saw nothing. They must have spotted us from above, and they swooped down." Misha demonstrated. "Screaming."

"Words," Viktor added that in Russian.

"We took off for the thickest cover, and outran 'em. They've been circling the entire area ever since. Slow flights. Have to assume they're looking for us," Misha said. "We hid out entirely the second day, and most of the third. By the fourth we saw a pattern: crepuscular hours preferred."

Gordon nodded. "Dawn and dusk. Well, that makes sense, doesn't it? Can't be out at night, not if they aren't sanctioned by the Yilayil, and noontime flying would be hot work when the sun's out."

Misha gave his elegant shrug again. "I do not know. So anyway, we work then, and keep under cover at dawn and dusk."

"And ping Irina," Gordon added drily.

Misha grinned. "Boredom. What is the danger of a single ping? I see you are pinging Saba every night."

Gordon said, "She's locked up in the House of Knowledge. They took her on sight." And he went on to give the Russians a full report, starting with the statue of Saba awaiting them, and ending with an outline of everyone's activities to date.

Misha listened closely, his challenging smile fading. At the end, he said, "Much to be discovered, then. Your suggestions with regard to these flyers? We know they're searching for us, but not why. Could be that roasted Russki is their favorite appetizer."

"I haven't seen any in the Nurayil district," Gordon said. "But I'm limited in my movements. I can ask the others. If the flyers are not trying to integrate themselves into the society, it could be for a number of reasons, but we'll have to assume for now that their reasons won't advance our goals any. I'd say play least-in-sight for now."

Viktor gave a short, sharp nod.

Misha spread his hands. "You're the boss."

Gordon, looking from one to the other, suspected that some arguing had taken place—Viktor pleading caution, and Misha wanting action.

"Keep searching," Gordon said. "There has to be a sign of them somewhere. I can't believe the First Team was taken off the island, not without leaving some sort of clue."

"Ah." Misha looked down at the water, which was just beginning to boil.

He carefully measured out a small portion of brown powder from an airtight bag, and cast it into the bottom of the pan. A rough-and-ready way to make coffee, but as the delicious aroma rose up, Gordon found himself breathing deeply.

They shared a cup each of the coffee. Gordon drank his right down to the bitter residue.

"Thanks," he said at last. "I needed that."

"We'll escort you back," Misha said with an airy wave of his hand. "Time to get to work."

Viktor had already broken down the firepit and cleaned the pan. Their gear was stowed; they could pick up and move fast at a moment's notice.

The return trip was accomplished in silence. The two men disappeared into the jungle shortly after Gordon stepped onto the apron and found his empty wagon waiting.

He activated the control, got aboard for the slow ride back. For once he was not impatient of the long trip, for he had much to think about.

Saba walked down the ramp to the translation room. If she turned her head too fast, a faint headache throbbed at her temples. She concentrated on breathing slowly, in and out, as she walked the rest of the way.

Everything seemed a little too bright, a little too loud this morning. Yet there was nothing loud, or glaring, in her surroundings. Her slippers whispered on the cool flooring, and her robe swayed gently against her body, one side, the other. The muted lighting seemed exactly the same as it had for the past week; there were no shadows anywhere, no bright lances of light, so it could not have been intensified. But her eyes seemed overly sensitive. All her senses, in fact, seemed heightened, she realized as she listened to the rhythmic swishing of her flaxen robe.

Has to be just stress, she thought as she entered the huge viewing room. I'm fragmenting my focus too much—it has to be that.

As she passed down the long rows of working people, she performed a quick mental assessment.

Her first priority, she still believed, was to find whatever message she'd left herself from the past—if it could be found. That had meant a lot of furtive, desperate searching. Then she had her deportment lessons, which required a desperate mental shift; just the day before she'd found herself utterly lost as they used references to time that the First Team had not even hinted at. And threaded through all this were her doubts about the other beings here, their motivations, their intentions toward her. And of course she had the mission to think about.

On top of it all, the frustration of being limited to pulse code communication once a day.

I have some important task to perform, she thought, trying to gather her strength. I know that I do, or that statue of me would not be out front.

That was another goal: to find out who the other statues depicted, and why they were so honored. But when she asked Virigo or Rilla, they gave her meaningless names, and whistled the traditional phrase for "Nurayil honored as Yil"—which told her exactly nothing.

Perhaps she would find out more in the records. As yet the terminal in her room had not been activated. Just as well; she could barely read Yilayil script. The First Team had only given them the basic consonant sounds, assuming a phonetic alphabet. And superficialy it was; foreign languages were diligently reproduced phonetically.

Thinking this, she glanced down at the nearest person, a weedy young Virigu—a male. They were very rare, for some reason; most of the Virigu were female.

He watched a tape on a terminal, his spidery fingers blurring across pads on his console as he translated what he saw.

She paused and looked around.

That's what they were all doing—translating into Yilayil tapes taken from chips. They listened to. the voices on the tapes and translated; Rilla had told her that when she had mastered deportment (a term that also included mastery of language, apparently) she would translate tapes as well.

That had both excited and frightened her. Were there tapes from the First Team somewhere? Or would she be trained in some other language, to translate tapes from some unknown world?

Or had other humans come, before or after the First Team?

Her headache throbbed, and she tried to dismiss the thoughts. Instead, she went back to considering the Yilayil script: phonetic for Nurayil, but for the Yilayil it was apparently ideographic—each symbol standing for a concept, and not just a sound.

"Saba of Far Star."

She had reached the far end; Zhot awaited her.

He vanished into the chamber beyond the viewing room, and Saba found that the rest of her "class" was there—both Nurayil, which she found reassuring, and both trying to master the language.

Zhot was an ancient male of a species the name of which had not been mentioned to her. He was shaped rather like a tall, supple seal, but he moved like a reptile. His round body was covered with nubbly sandy-colored scales, except for his face, which was whiskery with tiny antenae constantly waving and vibrating. She had not seen his legs beneath his robe, but when he walked, the motion was sudden and noiseless. The first few times she'd seen him, it had unnerved her.

His voice, though, was like liquid music.

"We begin today our discourse upon the experience of [dis-order-resulting in matter-energy inert/uniform] and its expression."

Dis-order... Saba struggled desperately between Yilayil and Terran language. Entropy? she thought, confused.

Zhot gave her no time to consider as he emitted a long trill, most of which escaped Saba at first, and then looked at the class expectantly.

Both the others were silent, Saba noted. Were they as confused as she?

She turned her mind to the trill, as Zhot repeated it more slowly. Grateful, she pounced mentally on each phrase. There was very little information on the concrete layers used in everyday discourse, and the higher-level modulations all concerned the strange tenses and temporalities that they had discussed the day before.

Saba forced herself to relax. It was impossible to translate those levels into any language she knew; they had to be experienced, in the same fashion as music. But the rational part of her mind insisted on scattering phrases across her consciousness.

Consequence-of-act... as is-was... echo back from will-be... conditional termination-of-volition...

Her mind refused the rest. She shook her head.

"It is not true for servants of knowledge," a Virigu stated at last.

Zhot nodded.

The second being added, in slow, careful Yilayil, "We speak of what we know/experience."

Zhot turned expectantly to Saba.

She finally felt forced to say, "I don't understand."

He paused for what seemed a very long time.

"Your people tell stories, yes?"

She nodded, but he did not respond, and she suddenly realized that the gesture perhaps had no meaning for him. Hastily she wet her dry mouth, and whistled, "Yes, we tell stories."

"Contrary to fact, and true?"

"Yes."

"Teller of stories sees those-who-live in story all-at-once." Then he fluted another phrase with upper-level modulations, similar to the first. "If story not satisfactory at end, lives of those-within changed at beginning. They will differently, act differently." Another trill, again with the same bizarre tenses.

Was this mode of discourse for storytelling, then?

"We/you live in entropy, struggle against entropy, but not in stories. There we live outside entropy."

"Yes," she said, hesitantly.

"So, too, we/you know entropy on two levels, more. So, too, servants of knowledge speak of entropy on two levels, more."

"But we do not experience it that other way."

"No," said Zhot. "We," and here she heard the emphasis, "do not. We are servants." Again a complex fluting.

Subject is-was-will-be servant to those who choosing-choices-made dance above decay.

"The Yilayil?"

Zhot emitted the choking snort she had guessed meant laughter in his race. Another trill.

Choices made-making termination-of-volition for subjects.

A thrill shot through her. Down the timeline the Yilayil were savages.

"Then Yilayil..." She hesitated, not wanting to give away the fact that she knew anything about time further on. "Decay?"

Zhot trilled again.

Improper transition in mode of discourse.

Saba stifled the urge to groan and hold her head. Instead, she listened as the other two took up the conversation and labored through a painstaking discussion of tenses. Saba had tremendous difficulty following it—her headache was considerably worse at the conclusion of the lesson—but at least she was fairly sure of one thing. The Virigu and the other being were exactly as confused as she was.

Chapter Seventeen

Eveleen looked at the Jecc swarming about her, all at waist height, and thought, They are like children. They moved fast like children, rammed each other and exchanged buffets and shoves, and their squeaky whistles and drones all reminded her of children. Unpleasant, nightmarish children, to be sure. There was nothing cute or appealing in the stares from those deepset eyes, or the rows of needle-sharp teeth in the coldly grinning beaklike snouts. Or in the little hands—or tentacles—that tried to steal parts from Eveleen's pile if she didn't watch them constantly.

She twisted her head, working her neck as she looked about the cavernous assembly chamber. It smelled of hot alloys and lubricant and a little like burned toast. That was the Jecc. They all smelled a little like burned toast sprinkled with rosemary.

How long would she and Ross have to work among them? As her fingers operated automatically at disassembling a cooling unit and replacing the worn-out parts, she considered the other beings in the department.

No one seemed to make any rules. The Virigu in charge certainly didn't. They merely oversaw, ordering people about when there was apparently a need. People reported for work when they wished to, apparently, and took days off when they wanted.

In this department, as yet no one among the few other species had been promoted—or transferred—which gave her nothing by which to calculate the duration of their probable stay. As for the Jecc, any number of them might have been transferred or promoted, but they looked so much alike that it was difficult to tell.

Not that they were interchangeable. They were all more or less the same size and mass, and they all wore identical plain coveralls, but their gray-green skin was mottled and stippled with iridescent blue dots. She'd realized one morning that the dots made subtle patterns, when a couple of them actually sat still enough for her to scrutinize them. And she memorized the pattern, endeavoring to watch these particular Jecc.

So she did—that day. She saw the one with the snail-shell whorls clip at least three connectors from other Jecc; the one with the braided whorls seemed to concentrate on stealing from other beings.

The next day, though, neither of them was present—at least, as far as she could tell. After she finished reconstructing one directional unit she moved about, on the pretext of getting more parts, and scrutinized as many stationary Jecc as she could—and though she did see that snail-whorl pattern again, it seemed tighter, smaller, with more dots. *Different.*

All new Jecc?

Or was the blue stuff paint?

She asked Vera that night, "Have you found out any more data on the Jecc?"

"No," Vera said, pausing in the act of wolfing down some food. She grinned briefly. "All the others do is curse them. No one likes them. Apparently they don't even live in the city, though how that works is beyond me. But the Moova, everyone else, call them pests." She swallowed, and sighed. "Sorry—no chance to eat today."

Irina nodded her sleek head. She ate daintily, as though she sat in a duchess's formal dining room. "I begin a new labor today." She frowned, massaging her forehead with her fingertips. "Excuse me—my English seems to be regressing. I began a new job today. I work now for Lootignef of the Moova."

"And I for Toofiha," Vera added.

"Moova?" Ross asked.

Both Russians nodded.

"And they don't let you eat on the job?"

Both heads shook decisively.

"They are rivals," Vera said. "We did this on purpose, hoping to find out more information that way. The Moova are very jealous of data, and of their foods."

"Sure is good, though," Ross said, holding up a thin roll of some kind of rice-bread mixed with seasoned vegetables. "Big change from the raw stuff, healthy as it might be."

Vera sighed. "How I dream of coffee! And ice cream. And torte..."

Eveleen saw Irina glance over at Vera, her black eyes narrowed. Irina's refined face was largely serene, but that could very well be a facade. Right now, if Eveleen was any judge of character, it seemed that the ex-ballerina was thoroughly tired of her partner.

Of course Eveleen said nothing. She just continued to watch as she worked through her katas. Her stomach was hungry, but her joints were achy and her neck tight. The only remedy, she felt, was to work out, which she couldn't do while full. Her share of the food sat on a napkin next to Ross.

Ross was frowning. "They say bad things about the Jecc? Isn't that anti-deportment? Anti-harmony?"

"Not," Irina said precisely, "if what you say is to point out ways in which the Jecc are anti-harmonious."

Eveleen snorted. "I guess they aren't going to get promoted to the next level anytime soon, eh?"

Vera said, "The Moova say they don't try to harmonize, but I don't know how much of that is just talk. No one has much real data about them, this I can say with certainty. To bring up the subject is to hear, over and over, that they are thieves and pests—stealing things that don't even matter."

Just then Gordon's familiar tap sounded at the door, and Ross moved to open it.

Gordon came in, bringing a swirl of rain-scented air with him. "Big storm out there," he commented.

"Must be," Eveleen said, sniffing for that rain scent. It was already gone, filtered out. The ubiquitous clean, sterile air smelled just as always—and of course there were no windows to look out of. Eveleen fought a sudden surge of claustrophobia and forced up the pace of her kata. "Any news?" she asked over her shoulder.

Gordon shook his head. "Status quo." He sat down and Vera handed him his food. "Pollen count still up?" he asked.

Vera said, "It is. Very high." She smacked her lips as she finished her food.

Eveleen watched Irina, who worked studiously through her food as if the room were silent. Was there another reason why the two had not taken jobs at the same place? Not necessarily, Eveleen thought. Irina, at least, was too dedicated to the mission. She wondered if Vera even knew how irritating she was to her partner.

With a snap and whirl, she finished her last move, then she sank down next to Ross. Gratitude for his presence suffused her. She might be feeling claustrophobic—restless—but at least she had him. And wasn't it better to let the others do their jobs than to think about going out and exploring during the long evenings?

Ross sat back. "Bringing me to what's been bothering me since the first briefing, and that is: who decides? Are the Yilayil watching us when we work? Or do the various Virigu spy on us and send in reports? Or what?"

"Another thing for us to discover," Gordon said equably.

Eveleen noted the tense postures and tight faces in the others. "What I wish," she said, "was that we had TV. I'd even watch alien TV. These nights sitting in this room get a little old."

And she saw an immediate reaction in the two women. Sympathy now flooded her, but she tried to hide it; though the authorities on Earth had been worried about married agents in the field together, they probably hadn't considered what a relief it would be to be penned up with someone you love, rather than someone else with whom you might have little in common outside of the job at hand.

Ross, however, was frowning. "That's another thing," he said. "Deportment—conformity. The Nurayil are kept utterly in the dark, far as I can see. We don't know what our labor is worth. We don't have access to what passes for news, or any kind of data. We don't even get local entertainment."

"I can address that," Gordon said as he worked his neck by twisting his head slowly back and forth. His expression was calm, as always, but his blue eyes were tired. "Every race has its own entertainment—I see it as I pass through the city on my rounds. The Yilayil don't seem to care what beings do in their own space, just as no one has interfered with our laptops or our brief spurts of signal. And someone, at least, has to know. The technology here is sufficiently advanced that it seems safer to assume that they do, rather than the opposite."

Irina nodded. "This is so. I have seen the Moova gathered round their *gyoon*—" And, gesturing with her long hands, she described a round flat plate on a table that projected holographic images. "It looked to me like Moova writhing underwater, but they were very intent."

"Sounds like gargling," Vera put in with a grin. "I have seen this as well." Her round face was briefly serious. "But it is only in private—not when they interact with the rest of Nurayil."

Good spy work, Eveleen thought, and her appreciation for the Russian women increased. They've seen more than we have. Again—stronger—she felt that intense urge to be out and exploring, but she repressed it. If she went, Ross would go—Ross, who always took chances. Thinking about what had happened to the First Team's biologist always cooled her wish to see Ross out taking risks.

She stole a look at Ross—just in time to catch a glance from his narrowed eyes, his dark brows quirked. What was he thinking? For once she couldn't guess at his thoughts.

"I am tired," Irina said suddenly. "I think it is time to sleep."

Vera yawned. "I must admit I have had a headache most of the day. I need sleep as well."

Gordon smiled, said, "Maybe it's something in the air— I've had that headache as well."

Vera said, "The pollens I can measure for we are supposedly immune to. But we have to accept that there might be others that we cannot measure for."

Gordon nodded. "Maybe that's it. Allergies! What a planet! Well, on that note, I think I'll call it a night." He stood, and followed the two women out, everyone wishing one another good night and good rest.

As Ross turned away from the closed door, he said, "Get the feeling everyone is sick of everyone else?"

Eveleen gave her head a shake. "I get the feeling that everyone feels lousy, and no one wants to complain." She decided not to mention that glance she'd caught from Irina—not until she knew she was right. To speculate without facts felt too much like gossip, and even though it was only Ross, what she said might affect how he responded to the others. And Irina, at least, Eveleen thought with sudden conviction, was very, very observant.

"They're not the only ones," Ross said, surprising her. "I have to admit it's hard to think with this headache on me."

"You didn't mention it," Eveleen said, instantly concerned.

He shrugged, an abrupt motion that made it clear how much he loathed any kind of personal weakness. "What can I do about it? Complaining would bore us both."

"Mentioning a headache isn't exactly complaining," Eveleen said wryly. "As it happens, I've been feeling achy all day. Not so much my head as my joints. Neck."

Ross looked up, frowning. "Gordon said allergies, but maybe it's something more than that. Think we're getting sick? Not just us, but the whole team?"

"Oh, lord, I hope not," Eveleen exclaimed. "I don't want to even think about what kind of alien microbes we might be fighting..." Horrible scenarios reeled through her mind— the Jecc carrying some kind of dangerous virus, Ross and Eveleen exposed, and exposing the others. Or was it the Moova, through their food?

She shook her head firmly, wincing against a pang in her temples. "No," she said out loud. "I *won't* think about it—not until I have evidence."

"In that case," Ross said with a twisted grin, "let's do what Gordon and the Russians are probably doing right now: let's break some pain reliever out of our packs and get some rest."

A week later, they still felt much the same.

Ross had stopped taking anything but the anti-allergens. He'd already run through half his allotment of pain killers, and though he didn't say anything, his grim thought was if they felt any worse, they'd need them.

They certainly hadn't gotten better. After a couple nights, Gordon got everyone to state their symptoms so he could keep a record, just as the First Team had reported, in detail, their malaise a month or so into their stay.

"I thought the medical brains had decided it was allergies," Eveleen said to Ross one day when they were walking to work. "Didn't they say that at our first briefing?"

"I can't remember what anyone said," Ross admitted, grinning.

The rain was very heavy, and most beings were under the awnings to avoid it. Ross and Eveleen had donned their rain ponchos and walked right through the deluge.

"Ahhh," Eveleen said, taking a deep breath. "It might just be psychological trickery, but I feel like the air is cleaner."

"So you do think it's allergens making us sick?" Ross asked her.

She shrugged, giving him a wry look. Her face was slightly tense, and her eyes shadowed from broken sleep, but she didn't look dangerously sick. She'd better not, he thought. If she did get seriously ill, mission or not, they were going back down the timeline to the sterile air of the ship.

"I don't know," she said. "How could I? I just imagine the air being full of guck that our immune systems don't like. And when it rains like this, I convince myself the air is purified, and I hope this stupid headache will vanish."

Ross said nothing. He'd begun to wonder if he'd live with a headache all his life. Even with the meds, it was never really gone.

"Well, we got every damn anti-allergen in us they could concoct," he reminded her. "And the science team did do an allergen check when we landed, remember?"

Her thin brows furrowed. "Hard to remember anything, except how to build cooling units," she said with a soft laugh. "So you think what's hit us is viral?"

"I don't know," it was his turn to say. "It can't be just exposure to the Jecc or the Moova or one of the other races because Misha and Viktor are apparently sick as well."

Eveleen sighed. "I'd forgotten that. Not that Gordon was exactly gabby with the details."

Ross shrugged. "What's to detail? They feel much like we do, and they haven't seen anyone—despite those flyers chasing them whenever they catch sight of them."

They neared the big building housing Transport, and slipped back into Yilayil. Ross could feel Eveleen's reluctance as strong as his own. It was hard to think in any language when your head continuously ached—and double that for an alien tongue.

Eveleen trilled the equivalent for: "I'll want something hot for midday meal."

"A good idea," he responded, and they both fell silent.

Three or four weird purple-greenish beings moved in ahead of them, reminding Ross of seven-foot-tall crosses between teddy bears and sharks. They disappeared in the direction of the rail-skimmer body shop. Apparently they were so strong they could lift most of the big alloy plates that most other beings needed cranes for.

They were quiet, they worked hard, and they didn't give anyone any trouble. Yet here they were, among the Nurayil.

Ross felt a surge of impatience. He hadn't voiced a growing conviction even to Eveleen, but he was wondering if the whole deportment thing was a myth in order to get free—or almost free—labor from all the other races.

The idea of his working so hard, while sick, in what might be a royal scam put him in a thoroughly rotten mood.

The Jecc didn't help. When he and Eveleen got to their workstation, it seemed like there were more of them than ever. He sniffed the gritty, oily smells, and looked at the worn parts they were supposed to retool. When a Jecc rammed against his hip as it scurried down an adjacent corridor, the sudden jar sent a pang through his already aching head.

Annoyance crystallized into the need for action. He watched Eveleen square her shoulders and march off to collect parts for her portion of the day's work—wrapping them tightly in her rain poncho and holding it with both hands. Then she disappeared in the direction of the assembly benches.

Ross smiled to himself.

It was time, he decided, to do a little consciousness raising by showing the Jecc just how it felt to be hassled.

So he shifted a big part into one hand, keeping the other lightly resting against the cool alloy as he paced along a row of Jecc busily retooling connectors and exhaust valves.

And when one reached to alter what Ross called the buffing machine (though it didn't look remotely like any buffing machine you'd find in a mechanic's shop on Earth), he whipped his fingers out and snagged a fine set of data chips from where they stuck out of the Jecc's overall.

The creature didn't even notice, and Ross laughed silently to himself. So his old skills hadn't left him, eh?

He'd given up that kind of life when he was recruited to the time agents—but on this occasion, he was glad he remembered how to pick pockets.

He watched the Jecc at intervals while finishing a piece of work. The one he'd robbed discovered the missing chip, its head moving back and forth, but then it got right back to work. No further reaction.

Ross went walking again, close behind a row of Jecc busy working away. Two of them didn't bother glancing up, and both of them within seconds were lighter of a filter and a measure tool respectively.

And so the day went.

Ross nearly laughed out loud a few times when he watched, from the vantage of his workstation, his victims discover their losses. Ross was careful to put his stolen booty in another location, usually in the parts section, after he got it. He still didn't know why the Jecc stole and hoarded parts that were readily available to everyone, but in case there was some kind of mysterious personal bond with these bits of machinery, he didn't want them to feel deprived. Just...warned? Startled?

He examined his own motivations as he finished a last buffing job. At lunch he forebore telling Eveleen about his private game. He wasn't sure she would agree, and she looked so headachy he didn't want to risk making it worse for her.

Maybe it was stupid, but it felt right.

And so he decided to make a couple more five-finger discounts before the day ended—and he'd try it again the next. In fact, the idea of it made him look forward to another day for the very first time since his arrival.

His first pinch was a bigger part, and the victim immediately turned on a neighbor and exclaimed in an excited tongue that was definitely not Yilayil. The neighbor touched the victim's muzzle, and it fell silent. Both looked around in a manner that reminded Ross forcibly of guilty children. He almost regretted his action, but not quite.

No, not quite. One more pinch, he'd promised himself. He could see that Eveleen needed to quit for the day. Her hands moved slowly, and the angle of her head was expressive of weariness. He realized that he too was tired—only the adrenaline of his secret game kept him going.

One more.

He saw a Jecc just turning away from a partially disassembled drive unit. He reached, his fingers closed on the main component—

The Jecc's reaction was a blur: A fraction of a second later Ross found his finger pinned to the workbench by a small hand as he gazed down into yellowish-gray unblinking eyes.

CHAPTER EIGHTEEN

Saba pressed her fingertips to her cheeks.

Hot.

It was no longer a matter of tiredness, she was definitely sick. And with something she couldn't sleep off; Virigu had left her alone the day before after twice trying to summon her to work. Did the Yilayil never actully get sick? Or worse, was there some terrible taboo against illness? Saba had realized she did not have the vocabulary to tell her tutors that she did not feel well. She'd only said, repeating it several times, that she had to sleep more. But it had sufficed—they left her alone.

And so she'd slept soundlessly for hours and hours.

Today she'd woken up feeling slept out—yet her body felt no better. She was decidedly feverish, and weak.

She shook her head. Time to stop being stoic and break out the pain relievers in her pack. She had a mission, she was the only one in this particular position, and she was not going to allow some stupid virus or flu to stop the work. Everyone else was doing their jobs, or Gordon would have sent her the signal indicating an emergency.

Well, then. She could do hers as well.

So she rose, walked through the weird glue-field shower, dressed, and took some medication, waiting long enough for it to start taking effect before she left her room.

What I need, she thought as she moved slowly toward the tutorial chamber, is to comprehend the gestalt of this place. Her attention was fragmented, and her perception of the others was fragmented as well.

On Earth, this had always been her initial approach to any new situation, to listen for patterns, for the music of the place. Though sometimes that "music" was hard to hear, it had to be there.

That had been the most important lesson her mother had taught her. From her father, a doctor, she had acquired intellectual curiosity and ambition; from her mother, a wise woman of the Dorze, she had learned that *yets*, vocal music, was in fact a part of human life.

Certainly it was among the Dorze, but her mother had convinced her that all peoples made music, even when they were not necessarily aware of it. To deliberately distort or deny music, as some modern cultures seemed to do, was to dehumanize one, and the healthy person merely sought music in other forms.

These beings are not human, Saba thought. But this language is music. I think, therefore, that among those who can speak and hear, music must be a universal.

And I must find the musical pattern here before I can try to understand these people—and find out what it is I am here for.

When she arrived in the usual place, a breeze of cool, rainy-smelling air drifted across her fever-heated face. She breathed slowly, her eyes closing. It was wonderful, but it only lasted seconds.

When she opened her eyes, Virigu was before her.

"I, Virigu," she began, "take you now to the place where we store knowledge."

Saba wondered if her day of sleep had been misinterpreted, but unless someone said something threatening, she refused to worry. It was going to take all her energy just to follow this new lesson—and to work on the task she had set herself.

The new lesson proved to be with the Yilayil computers. Her delight and curiosity, however, were soon quenched by the stressful task of learning what each keypad meant. They did not correspond with the phonetic letters that the First Team had taught them; instead, they bore idealized keystrokes that were pressed in combination to build up the Yilayil ideographics, which Virigu now made clear it was time to learn.

That meant thinking in Yilayil, and distilling symbols—alien symbols—into meaning for a human being.

Virigu sat next to her at another keyboard, pressing one key at a time, while complicated symbols assembled themselves on the terminal. Patiently, calmly, she described each, then had Saba run through the definitions after which she practiced five over and over, one for each digit on her hand. The groups of five seemed a considerate way of teaching, but Saba wished she could learn this in twos. Or one at a time.

Time sped by. She had the first grouping down and was superficially acquainted with the second group when subtle bell tones, just barely heard, indicated it was time for a change.

They moved down to the refectory and Saba forced herself to drink some of the soup that all the others were taking. She knew that hers was—somehow—deemed appropriate for her biochemistry, for a quick glance in all the bowls showed different colors and consistencies for various races.

But a tiny portion of her mind was afraid that the food might be part of her illness; at any rate she had no appetite. Still, she forced herself to eat the soup.

Afterward it was time for another session with Zhot.

This time the subject was knowledge.

The other two tutorees were not present, only Saba, Virigu, and Rilla.

Again—as it had been for the... her head panged as she tried to count up the days, all so alike. Three weeks? Four? As it had been all along, the higher-level modulations all incorporated strange tenses and conditional temporalities that seemed to confuse even Rilla and Virigu, it seemed.

Yet Zhot persisted. After he had asked each to define knowledge, he turned to Saba, his whiskers stiff, his eyes intent.

As always when confronted by differing paradigms, Saba opted for the simple.

"Knowledge," she trilled, "is that which is known."

Zhot droned/whistled a fast, complicated response.

Consequence-of-knowing... as is-was... unfolding from actions-will-be...

Her mind refused the rest. She shook her head, saying, "What I am perceiving is that knowledge stands outside of time."

"What is time?" was the immediate response.

"The... artificial measure we apply to the progression of events," she said, again opting for the simple.

"Has time meaning for those who exist all-at-once?"

Saba bit her lip, fighting the urge to retort: Ask those who exist all-at-once, when you find them.

She would not get angry. Conditional tenses—hypothetical states of being—the tutoring sessions with Zhot always seemed to involve these discussions. They hadn't yet touched on the other oddity in the language, the bizarre sensory correlations. She wondered what they portended.

No wonder I'm not learning any faster, she thought with a bleak inner laugh. What happened to teaching language by talking about things beings actually do—like eating, sleeping, reading, working?

But again she forced her fragmenting thoughts to clear, and concentrated.

"I cannot answer that," she finally said. "But I would surmise that it does not."

Zhot whirled around, his reptilian speed startling.

"Beings outside of time experience those-who-live-in-time all-at-once." Then he fluted another phrase with upper-level modulations, similar to the first. "If beings-in-time not satisfactory at end-of-time, lives of those-within, altered at beginning-of-time. Knowledge is—" He trilled the impossible tenses yet again.

Saba fought the urge to hold her head in her hands, and abruptly Zhot whirled to Virigu and Rilla, this time demanding the purpose of knowledge with these givens.

Rilla's answer was almost as difficult to follow as Zhot's, but not quite. From it Saba gathered that the purpose of knowledge was to avert entropy.

When she heard the term, she remembered the discussion during which entropy had been the" subject. Was there a connection after all? She'd assumed that the discussion topics were random, formed around various language lessons.

Nothing is accidental, she thought, feeling a visceral sense of warning.

Swiftly she reviewed the topics of discourse before her long sleep. One day the growth of trees and the seeding of new. Another day, the measure of celestial bodies moving through space. Before that...

"...dance-above-decay," Zhot's voice interrupted her thoughts, and again she felt that inner zap.

There was something going on here—something she simply wasn't getting. But she knew it was important.

She forced her mind to clear—but Zhot had apparently finished.

When Saba was back in her room, she found that the terminal had been turned on, and it extended from her wall, with a little bench below it.

She drank some water, then sat down slowly. She traced the key-groupings she'd learned, and watched the symbols flow across the terminal. Then she tried two of the keys, just to see what happened—and the original meaning did not compound. Instead, a third meaning flowed on the terminal, something totally incomprehensible.

She sighed and went to lie down.

Time...no, don't think about their time. Her time. Time to stop fragmenting.

Her message to self, Gordon, the mission, sickness, music, gestalt.

Everything must be dismissed except gestalt.

Gestalt outside-of-time?

Don't even think about it. First just gestalt.

She closed her eyes and slept.

Rain slashed through the jungle growth, a steady roar that covered the sounds of humans making their way at top speed. Gordon followed Viktor and Misha, his mouth open to ease his breathing, his head aching with every step.

Though the two Russians had readily admitted feeling the same symptoms suffered by everyone else on the team, their speed seemed undiminished. Could it be they felt less ill—that maybe living in the city had a deleterious effect beyond whatever it was that had affected them all?

Gordon listened to Viktor's rasping cough, which intermittently punctuated the rain sounds, and decided he'd withhold judgment on relative intensities of illness.

Instead, he concentrated on moving with the same speed, an effort that became increasingly difficult.

Then, just when Gordon was thinking he'd be forced to call a halt, Misha whirled around and said, "Here it is."

Gordon bent over, his hands on his knees, and fought to catch his breath. He noticed that both Viktor and Misha were breathing through their mouths; Viktor had dropped to the spongy moss covering the ground, but Misha leaned against a tree with a deceptively casual air. Gordon watched, amused, as he said, "Here what is?"

"The last camp," Misha said, waving a hand as though producing a magical scene.

Silently Viktor rose, digging in the tangled growth beneath a huge tree, and pulled out a pack—fungus-encrusted, discolored—but still recognizable as the type all the Russians carried.

Misha rummaged around under a semicircle of bright flowers, revealing a ring of stones that had to have been deliberately set. Gordon nodded, impressed with the detective work that had gone into this finding.

Misha dug into one of the packs and pulled out a warped notebook. He carefully opened it, and almost reverently held it out for Gordon's perusal, his manner so far removed from his usual that Gordon knew before he looked at it that this was a major find.

He looked down at the close Russian writing, and puzzled out a few words.

This was definitely from the First Team—one of the agents. Gordon recognized her name.

He looked up at Misha. "Svetlana."

Misha's face was uncharacteristically blank as he took the notebook from Gordon's hands, but before the archaeologist could speak, he gestured to Viktor, who handed him another notebook—and this time neither of them made a move to take it back.

"We find nearby," Viktor said. "I show you his camp as well."

Gordon looked down at the notebook, then up. "This one is Pavel's."

Misha nodded once. "I knew Pavel. I knew them all," he added, his accent very strong.

"Have you read Pavel's notebook?"

Again Misha nodded. "Skimmed it only, soon as we found it. He was the last. Svetlana here," he indicated the notebook still gripped in his own hand, "disappeared before Pavel did."

"'Disappeared'?"

Once again Misha nodded, his mouth grim. "We shall have to read these records more carefully, for much is not clear, but this I know. There are no bodies here. And Pavel saw no one die, beyond that first death. They just vanished. One by one."

CHAPTER NINETEEN

Ross looked down into the Jecc's eyes, watching the pupils narrow like a cat's, then widen again.

The Jecc chattered in a hissing language, then altered swiftly to Yilayil: "My progeny will be swift!"

It grabbed for the tool, then scuttled away with a flick of its long tail.

Ross stared after the creature in blank surprise. He'd expected any kind of reaction—anger, fight, outrage—anything but that. And why the comment about progeny, or had he gotten the words wrong?

He'd scarcely had those thoughts when he felt the light touch of fingers against his hip, and he looked down to see another Jecc scurrying off, carrying the calibrating tool he had stuck in his pocket.

Ross gave a laugh, and turned back to his job—for now.

The war was on.

No, not a war. It was a *game*.

All the rest of the workday, Ross and the Jecc carried on this quick, strange interaction. No longer did he find them shoving him out of the way, or bumping him when he was busy—but all his small tools, especially those he tried to hide in his pockets, disappeared. He marked each Jecc who robbed him, and he made certain to get the tools right back again. The calibrating tool must have exchanged hands six times—mostly between Ross and two specific Jecc, one with a star made of purple dots over one eye, and another who was distinguishable by the braided pattern of dots down the back of its skull.

Ross began to see a pattern to the theft game. His calibrating tool, which was in no way remarkable from any other tool supplied by the Transport Department, would be nipped from him, and slid into a Jecc's pouch beneath its coveralls. If he watched closely—without being obvious about it—he could just see the edges of the pouch, though the Jecc kept this portion of their bodies covered. These pouches reminded him of a kangaroo pouch—or of a frog's mouth. After a time, the Jecc would reach in again, with a furtive movement, remove the tool, and use it, or set it nearby—and bingo! It would be stolen again.

That was the pattern: in the pouch, out—steal, pouch, out—disappear, take back.

In the meantime the work progressed steadily. Faster than before. Ross was aware of a change in atmosphere. No one disturbed him, though he saw the Jecc bump up against Eveleen and the other non-Jecc beings, exactly as they always had.

Ross found his job much easier, despite the game.

So he played it right until darkness—perceived through the big hangar at the end of their workstation—began to fall. No more disabled rail-skimmers had been brought in. The outside workers had already left their jobs.

Ross was so bemused by the day's activities he was scarcely aware of the usual headache and scratchy throat. It wasn't until Eveleen fell in beside him, her eyes marked with tiredness, and her lovely voice sounding slightly hoarse, that he remembered he'd meant to quit much earlier.

Sickness had become a part of life, it seemed.

Since there wasn't anything he could do, there was always distraction. "The Jecc have pouches like kangaroos," he said to his wife as they walked out hand in hand.

"Yilayil," she whistled.

Ross grimaced, and repeated his statement in Yilayil. Truth was, he'd been thinking in English all day—not good for the mission, he realized. But so much easier!

The word for pouch he didn't know—he created a compound, which was often done in Yilayil. Eveleen nodded, brushing raindrops from her face as she considered his words.

Ross went on to explain the theft game, and the unexpected results. Eveleen's interest sharpened—he felt it, despite the steady rain pelting against their rain gear. The tale took until they reached the building that looked to him like a giant muffin—home.

Eveleen pushed her hood back from her face. Ross looked both ways; a small, greenish being was just disappearing up the ramp, tentacles swinging rhythmically. He waited until it was gone and bent to kiss the raindrops from Eveleen's eyelashes.

She smiled, but nudged him silently to move on.

They did not talk until they were safely in their cell, and clean and dry. Then she said, "I think it was dangerous to try that—"

"I know," he said, feeling a twinge of guilt.

Eveleen shook her head. "I'm not pointing fingers. It's not like I've done anything for the cause."

Her back was to him. Was that bitterness he heard in her soft voice? She couldn't be angry with herself for not having made any discoveries—how could she?

Unbidden came his wish from the very first week—that he could get out and poke around during the nights. Not get into trouble, of course, just do some listening on his own. He shook his head, as if to banish the thought.

Eveleen took in a deep breath, turned around and smiled. "I was thinking that your instincts have always been good. Maybe there's something for us to learn in this weird Jecc game, with the tools and the pouches and all."

Ross shrugged, fighting a huge yawn. "I don't see how. But one thing for sure: they didn't get in my way. If anything, it seemed easier to do my work. I used to have to wait for what I needed, but after that Jecc caught me everything seemed to be there when I wanted it, and no one rammed against me or upset my balance so I'd have to reconstruct."

"Maybe I ought to try stealing," Eveleen said with a wry smile. "It was business as usual for me."

"I saw that too," Ross said. "And for all those other non – Jecc, stuck way off in the corner."

"I think it's for self-protection," Eveleen said. "I'd been thinking we ought to try to join them, if we can. At least the Jecc don't go there—much. Don't bother them nearly as much as they do anyone directly in their space."

"Maybe, but not yet—"

Ross stopped talking when the familiar tattoo sounded at their door.

"It's Gordon," he said, frowning. "He never arrives before Irina and Vera."

"Uh oh," Eveleen said softly.

Ross sprang to the door and opened it.

Gordon came in, his bright blue eyes looking tired, but his mouth was set in a hard line that reminded Ross of the old days—of impending action.

"A find," Ashe said abruptly, running a hand impatiently through his white hair to shake the raindrops off.

Eveleen pursed her lips. "The bodies—?"

"No." Ashe turned to her. "But new records. Misha and Viktor stumbled onto a camp used by a couple of the First Team." He pulled a warped notebook from his parka, its pages reminding Ross of lettuces. A hundred years buried in a moist environment would do that, even in a supposedly airtight pack; they were probably lucky the books hadn't rotted all through.

"I'll be going through this more closely, comparing it with what records we already have, but Misha and Viktor skimmed it and summarized its contents."

"And the gist is—?" Ross prompted.

"The First Team disappeared one by one. They got sick beforehand, just as we are now. They didn't get sick as early in their mission."

Eveleen and Ross both nodded, remembering the records they'd studied.

"Apparently the illness worsened rapidly for them all, at least according to one of these records. The other one is more cryptic."

Ashe paused. "Thirsty."

Ross moved to the other room. "I'll get you some water."

"Thanks." A few moments later, Gordon took the cup from Ross, drank down the water, then leaned his head back against the wall.

"There's worse to come," Eveleen said wryly, "isn't there."

It wasn't even a question.

Ashe nodded once. "Worse—better, I don't know. It doesn't give us any answers, only more questions. The short version is this: the team members were not together, as we'd surmised."

"But that was orders," Ross protested. "If dangerous conditions existed—"

"Those were orders, and they did apparently pull together, as we have recorded by the records we found at the contact site. However, it must have been after that person had disappeared—"

"'Disappeared'?" Eveleen repeated. "Not died?"

A knock at the door interrupted them, and Ross moved to let in the two Russian women.

Quickly, while Vera passed out the evening's food, Ashe rapidly brought the women up-to-date on the discussion so far.

Neither spoke until he was done. Then Irina said, in her slow, accented voice, "They have disappeared one by one? What means this for us?"

"That's what I'm trying to figure out," Gordon said. "Misha and Viktor have found no human remains, and they have just about covered the entire island. Misha wants to jump back to one of these campsites and watch, of course."

Vera looked up sharply, her lips parted.

Irina shook her head, her fine brows creased slightly. "No. Is not a good idea, not if they sickened rapidly. This disease we all share, it might be more virulent a century ago."

"But if they just got sick and died," Eveleen protested, "then we'd find bodies, right?"

"So we would think," Gordon answered. "Of course, it could be that roving Yilayil or Nurayil scooped them up and obliterated them, although we don't have any indication of this kind of burial custom. But maybe death by illness is treated differently than death by execution, or death by more natural causes."

Vera said softly, "Misha. He had friends with First Team..."

Gordon said in a gentle voice, "I know that. He explained—a little. Misha is not exactly gabby with personal details." He smiled wryly, and Vera smiled back, but her eyes remained troubled. "I made him promise to do nothing until Zina is consulted."

Ross felt relief zing through him. "Good thinking. Throw this one in their laps—let the scientists hash out what this sickness is, and all the rest of it."

Gordon nodded. "I'm going to ask you to help me copy Pavel's notebook out—I don't trust it not to disappear," he said to the women. "And Svetlana's, which Misha insisted on keeping and translating himself, will also be copied. He says he has the time when they're hiding from the flyers. As soon as we have copies, I'll send Viktor forward to report, and we'll wait on Zina's decision before we act."

Irina's brow cleared.

"Is good," she said in Russian, and then in English, "very good."

CHAPTER TWENTY

Saba's discovery of the terminal in her room having been activated was a signal to her that she must devote herself to this aspect of the mission.

For two days she forced herself to sit at that terminal in her room, alternately shivering with chills and panting from what seemed stifling heat. She worked at mastering the Yilayil keypads.

Alternating between that and the records of the First Team on her own laptop, her fevered mind constructed dream fantasies that seemed real. When she did not work, she set the audio to play Yilayil music of the Great Dance, the rising and falling voices reminding her somehow of the music of the Dorze, at home in Ethiopia; music that was embedded in daily life, and was heard continually during not just the little customs of each day—waking, sleeping, meals—but during weddings and funerals, and in the festivities occurring throughout the year.

She did not understand the music, not as she did that of the Dorze. She had spent her childhood with Dorze music. As she listened to this music she sensed a kind of kinship, a need—shared by two vastly different peoples—to celebrate the dance of life and death in music.

But true understanding still eluded her. All her goals were still pieces. Shards. It hurt to think, and though she fought the image, her mind persisted in seeing her goals as jagged pieces of glass—or mirror—that must be fit together. But she did not have to touch them, and bleed, for willing ghost hands had appeared to do that: Katarina, the First Team linguist, whose words Saba had perused so deeply for meaning that she had committed them to memory—and began perceiving traces of the personality who had spoken them.

When Saba's tired body forced her to lie down, she began holding conversations with Katarina. She'd seen a photo of the Russian linguist during one of the briefings back in the United States, and now she envisioned that face, broad across the cheeks, wide-set dark eyes, dark gray-streaked hair short and glossy. Katarina's Mongolian antecedents looked out from the shape of her skull, strong and imperturbable and brave.

Saba, from utterly different people, still felt a kinship with Katarina.

The ghost of the Russian woman sometimes seemed real, so strong was Saba's dream state. "Listen," Katarina said, over and over. "Listen outside of time."

More of the strange tenses.

Baffled by the bizarre temporalities of the language, Saba began instead to explore the sensory contradictions. She discovered that one set of keystrokes set up the modulation into the sensory mode, modifying straightforward ideographs into strange little contradictory nuggets of meaning. They were almost like Zen koans. Certainly the feel of a green taste was just as ungraspable as the sound of one hand clapping. Somehow, she began to sense, there was some connection between the strange tenses and the contradictory sensory modalities. But she could not grasp its wholeness.

"Gestalt," she said to her ghost. "I think this is what you were sensing, was it not? You laid out the shards of this mirror."

"It is not a mirror," Katarina said. "It is a window." Katarina smiled, her eyes narrowing to half-moons. "Find the gestalt, Saba Mariam. Find the gestalt—set me free." .

Saba dragged herself up from her bed, drank some water, then sat down at her terminal. "Pieces," she murmured. "Pieces."

But again she ran into the mental wall of her own ignorance.

Finally she forced herself to rise, leaning against the real wall until the waves of darkness throbbed through her brain and then died away. Then she donned her robe and walked out in the direction of the translation chamber.

She realized when she reached it that she had lost track of time. It was late.

In fact, it was night, and only the Yilayil were about.

She began to retreat, for she knew the etiquette: not until she had been invited could she interact with the Yilayil.

The sleek weasel-shaped beings ignored her, and she stood uncertainly, until the *wisp-wisp* of a robe upon the floor brought her attention round.

Zhot stood there, still, his eyes unblinking.

"Come. Train," he droned.

Unquestioning, Saba followed him into the chamber beyond, where she saw a terminal. She sank down onto the bench, resolutely dismissing the ache of head and neck, and spread her hands lightly over the keypads.

They were too far apart for true comfort. Vividly she saw the long, furred, double-knuckled digits of the four-armed Yilayil.

"Now," Zhot said. "Begin."

She tapped out the combinations she had learned, and then, when Zhot said nothing, she went on to those she'd managed to puzzle out.

Moving with his accustomed fluidity, Zhot reached down to tap out a new combination, which caused symbols to flow across the screen.

"See," he commanded. "And let go of the connections you impose..."

Again time streamed by, uncounted, as Saba worked under Zhot's direction. Saba's fever slowly increased, noticed only on the periphery of her attention: chills, heat, ache. She dismissed them all. She was aware only that Katarina seemed to stand at her other shoulder, watching in approval.

She remembered a brief discussion of synesthesia from her neurology studies, how some people perceived shapes to have tastes, or colors sounds. The instructor had said that no one really understood the phenomenon, but that it was thought to emerge from the limbic system, where symbols and emotions were correlated.

Where symbols and emotions dance, she thought suddenly. The thought moved her hands, and a new combination of ideographs popped up on the screen.

"You begin to perceive," said Zhot. She started. She had not realized he was still standing there.

Saba did not understand what she had done, so she returned her attention to her hands, and to the symbols scrolling across the screen. Slowly, slowly, she was beginning to make sense of them; or rather, to stop trying to force sense on them and let them speak—dance?—for themselves.

The organization was indeed akin to Chinese writing, something she understood the guiding principles of, though she did not speak or read Chinese.

But finding a familiar structure accentuated the kinship of beings otherwise so far from one another in temporal reality. The miracle of similar structure—of hands, and brain, and mouth to talk and eyes to look—produced similarities in language. It was a bond, a universal bond. It was exciting to penetrate it.

"I will find you, Katarina," she said to her ghost when, abruptly, Zhot departed and she was left to find her way back to her room.

She collapsed in gratitude onto her bed, dropping immediately into a deep sleep.

Thirst and chills forced her awake again. Groggy and cold, she rose to draw water. The room lights came on as soon as she left the bed. She reached to fill her water glass—then paused, activated the sonic screen, and passed it through a couple times.

The water had registered as pure. She was sure the sonic screen killed microbes... so why was she sick?

She sighed, filled the cup, drank thirstily. Then she reluctantly helped herself to another precious dose of her medicine. She'd feel the fever drop soon, and then she could work.

Restlessness brought her to her feet. She tabbed on the computer, blinked at the blurry screen, then decided to wait until the medicine dose had restored her equilibrium.

Instead, the restlessness distilled into a single, strong urge: for fresh air, for light.

Was it morning? She would find out.

She passed her flaxen robe through the, cleaner, then pulled it on, sighing with relief as its folds draped softly down her body to the floor. Then she tabbed her door open, and slid out, moving silently.

Not down. That way led only to the grand mosaic—suns and stars—and the chambers of knowledge, more and more of them the farther down one went.

Instead, for the first time, she turned her steps upward.

As she walked, she thought about the Yilayil metaphors and images. One shard was the fact that human and Yilayil idiom evoked opposites: for humans, upward and light meant freedom, oppprtunity, beauty. Dancing—free—in the sun. How many earth cultures carried just such a potent image?

For the Yilayil, harmony, the Great Dance, meant darkness. Downward and dark were the preferred directions. Saba had unconsciously fallen into the same thought pattern; that was inevitable when one focused one's attention on achieving ti[*trill*]kee.

Upward was undesirable, upward was...danger?

She frowned, thinking over the little gestures, the modes of expression she'd unconsciously assimilated while trying to reach for greater understanding.

Was there danger? Her steps up the ramp did not falter. The desire for light, for stillness and air, was too strong.

No one had forbidden her to go upward. Yet she had never seen anyone go there. Still, this space was here, she thought, looking around. There were even rooms.

She paused, laying a hand on a door. The rooms were far apart, but they were there. Rooms—or passages?

She touched the silver control, and to her surprise, the door slid open.

She looked out—not in. This was not a room, it was a kind of balcony, looking out at the morning sun above the tops of the buildings. In the distance she could see the solid green line of the jungle, pressing up against the city borders. And at one end, the edge of the long-abandoned spaceport.

She stepped out onto the balcony, then stopped. Now visible from the door was more space—and on it several still figures.

She saw three beings she did not recognize, but the fourth was Zhot.

He was not wearing his flaxen robe. Saba glanced down his body, seeing the supple seallike muscle structure, the scaled skin. In the strong, clear sunlight his skin had a greenish flush, almost a glow, overlaying the sandy coloration she was used to seeing.

The urge to fling off her clothing—which suddenly felt heavy and confining—seized her. How wonderful just to stand, breathing the fresh air, and feeling the sunlight on face, skin, limbs!

She took a deep breath, then forced herself away.

She had work to do.

The urge stayed with her as she retreated back down the ramp to her room. But duty steadied her, as always. It was morning, almost time for her daily signal to Gordon, Now that she was away from the allure of the sunlight, her eyes ached with the need for sleep, and her mouth was dry, but duty had become habit, and habit steadied her mind. Anchored her to reality.

What to do until the time for the signal?

She turned to her terminal, and touched the control. The screen lit. Sitting down, Saba worked her fingers into one of the patterns she'd recently learned. Without really considering what she was doing, she tested her ability to tranliterate, and traced out Zhot's name.

To her surprise, a new screen flickered into place, offering her choices. On her keypad, several keys lit with subtle color.

She touched the control that she recognized as indicating world-of-origin.

And once again the screen rippled, this time showing a rapidly moving vid of Zhot's people. Two voices whispered from the terminal's audio system: one language she couldn't recognize at all, but the other was Yilayil—someone's translation!

Curious, she watched what seemed rather like one of those travel vids she used to view in school: *Welcome to Kenya!* or *Welcome to Australia!* only this was more like the equivalent of *Welcome to Earth!* because it featured the world's primary in a schematic, and an unfamiliar system, zeroing in on the fourth body out.

Zhot's world was, like the Yilayil world, primarily water, only it seemed to have two very long continents straddling either side of the equator. On it Zhot's people seemed to be the most numerous beings, along with some undersea creatures that might have been sentient, but after the brief introduction, the screen paused and offered choices, this time showing different beings.

History of races?

Saba touched the control that corresponded to Zhot's seal-people, and watched in fascination. This time she listened to the Yilayil, not trying to translate any single words, but letting the whole flow through her.

Zhot's people, the Valeafeh, seemed to have had technology for a very long time. A matriarchy of loosely intersecting tribal families, they fostered young of other races and in turn sent out their young males to learn before coming back to settle down to service; the females stayed in order to learn government.

Opposite from the Virigu? Saba thought, making a mental note to look them up in their turn.

She found lots more information—including data on daily life. But nowhere did she see a glimpse of any of the

Valeafeh behaving as she'd just witnessed Zhot behaving. Nor did any of them look green.

Strange! Had she inadvertently stumbled onto a custom that was taboo, or at least forbidden witnesses? Saba decided that must be it, knowing that any travelogue vid made about Earth would not include acts considered private and intimate.

Well, at least Zhot had not woken from his meditation, or nap, or whatever he'd been doing, and Saba decided she would not bring it up. No harm done.

She glanced at the chrono. At last, time for her daily signal to Gordon.

She clicked the communicator on, and her thumb hovered over the little plastic key she had used for so long to send the pulse codes.

For a moment she looked down uncomprehendingly at the walkie-talkie's little display screen. Her vision, though blurry, was clear enough to warn her that the usual pattern of green lights had altered.

She frowned, and held the device up to the light to reread the displays.

Then she identified the single button that had been blank for so long—the frequency for speaking was now clear.

"Gordon?"

"Saba!"

When Eveleen and Ross reached the Nurayil dorms, she gratefully wiped her forehead as they passed inside, and let her breath out in a whoosh.

"I don't know whether to be glad it stopped raining or not," she said to Ross as they started up the ramp.

Ross grinned at her. "I'd wanted to see the sun for the past week or three—but now I think I've had enough of it." He squinted upward. "Okay, hear that? You can go back to rain now."

Eveleen laughed. "At least abate the humidity."

"With a jungle a stone's throw away?" Ross retorted. "Not a chance."

"Well, I wish there was a way to get a weather report— either that or to get air-conditioning in the—" Eveleen stopped when she saw Gordon standing outside their room.

She felt Ross tense up beside her. Something had happened.

Nobody spoke until they'd passed inside. Then Gordon said, "The frequency cleared. I don't know why, or what it means, but at least I can talk to Saba."

"And?" Ross prompted in a sharp voice.

Gordon gave his head a shake. "She's sick. Tried to downplay it, but I suspect she's much sicker than we are."

"Damn," Ross breathed. "What do we do? Pull her out?"

Gordon said, "Even if we could—which I doubt—she won't come. Insists she's close to some kind of breakthrough. When I tried to get her to explain, I'm afraid she scared me. Made little sense. Yet it's apparent she's gotten much further than we have in her investigations. She has access to the Yilayil computer system, and she has even been permitted to walk around the House of Knowledge at night."

"Ti *[trill]*kee?" Eveleen asked, amazed.

Gordon shook his head again. "No; the Yilayil ignored her. But she wasn't shooed back by her tutor. She got more lessons."

"How sick is she?" Ross asked.

"That's what I was trying to determine." Gordon looked from one of them to the other, clearly hesitating.

Eveleen felt her heart hammer a warning tattoo. "Oh, no ..."

Gordon's dark brows furrowed. "You're in her confidence?"

Eveleen nodded soberly, then turned to Ross. "I guess, considering the circumstances, it would be fair to tell you: she was told many years ago that she carries a recessive gene for sickle-cell anemia. Definitely recessive, they said—she probably wouldn't get it, but might pass it on, especially if she ever married someone who carried the same gene."

Ross grimaced.

Eveleen said in a low voice, "It's why she decided she would never marry. Have kids. Didn't want to risk passing on a tragedy."

Gordon looked up sharply, and Eveleen knew that he hadn't heard about that. He'd probably read about the recessive gene in Saba's file, but he hadn't considered what effect it could have on her life decisions.

They're so much alike, Eveleen thought. Each reclusive, solitary, by choice. Only what is in Gordon's past? She would never ask, of course.

Ross said, "So maybe this has weakened her immune system in some way? Made her sicker than we are—if she has the same disease? She's been isolated from us, so it could be something totally different."

"Or it could be something we were all exposed to on arrival," Gordon said. "We're not going to know—at least, not unless Viktor finds out something down the timeline." He glanced at his watch.

"He signaled this morning, then?" Ross asked.

"Yes," Gordon said.

Eveleen bit her lip. Viktor had had his long walk to the transport, and he and Gordon had agreed that he'd spend a maximum of one day and one night there, taking care to arrive in the morning so that the long walk back to the meetpoint would not bring anyone out after dark.

Gordon lived with his walkie-talkie clipped to his belt. Misha's orders had been to signal as soon as Viktor emerged from the transport. If Viktor had to go back down the timeline for more conferences, at least they'd know.

So he was back. Gordon awaited only the second signal, meaning he should get to the meetpoint, wherever that was.

All, of course, before darkness fell. Which would be very soon.

Eveleen opened her mouth to ask how he'd managed to juggle his job so he could accommodate all this moving around, but was prevented by a quick knock at the door.

Ross opened it—and all four came in, Irina, Vera, Misha, and Viktor.

For a moment they all stood there, a silent tableau. Eveleen scanned them, noting the posture of each: Irina graceful and aloof; Misha standing near her, one fist propped on a hip, an ironic smile on his handsome face; Vera standing very close to Misha, unnoticed; Viktor leaning against the wall, looking exhausted, his dark hair lying in sweat-damp strands across his broad forehead.

So many people crowded into a tiny room made the walls close in, and Eveleen was aware of the sharp smell of stale sweat.

Almost at the same time, Misha grimaced and said, "It is very hot today, and in the jungle there are no amenities—"

"Come on," Ross said, gesturing toward the fresher alcove. "It's not palatial, but it's better than what you've been stuck with."

They disappeared inside. Eveleen heard Ross's voice explaining how everything worked as, in silence, Vera passed out the evening's ration of food.

Her eyes were lowered, her generous mouth, almost always smiling, was uncharacteristically somber. Eveleen guessed that Vera had discovered the open frequency and had broken the silence rule—and Misha had taken advantage of it to meet and make his report in person.

Gordon—wisely, Eveleen thought—said nothing. It was apparent from Irina's posture that she had already spoken her mind to her colleague.

The two Russian men emerged then, and everyone sat in a circle to eat.

"Viktor?" Gordon said, once Viktor had taken the edge off his appetite. "You did not report to them ill—"

"I did what you ordered: wrote out a letter stating our symptoms, copied it onto a disk. Sent it forward. Valentin came back to say come forward to report in person."

"They are sick as well," Misha said, saving Viktor from having to frame his report in English. "Same symptoms, came on about the same time."

Viktor then spoke. "Zina. She wants to end the mission."

Chapter Twenty-One

Ross reached for the makeshift calendar that he and Eveleen had begun.

Rapidly he totted up the days, then he looked up at Eveleen and nodded.

Everyone's count was the same: they were on Day 46, and had fifteen days until they reached the same number the First Team had stayed before Katarina disappeared.

Viktor said, "Zina makes order to us. Despite how we know that First Team did not all vanish that day, still, we must be gone by same day. Our time." He frowned, said something swiftly in Russian, then he rubbed his eyes tiredly.

Misha continued for Viktor: "Even if one of us disappears, as did Katarina, it is still too much. We either solve the problems we face in fourteen days—without courting extra risks—or we must just leave, return home, and give our bosses the problem."

Viktor added. "They will withdraw to the ship on Day Sixty, and get ready for takeoff. We must be there by sunset, Day Sixty." He looked up and met Irina's eyes.

Ross, watching idly, felt a spurt of surprise when he saw the man's jaw tighten. He shifted his own gaze to Irina, in time to see a tiny nod, but then she turned her attention down to her laptop—on which her fingers had been steadily typing.

Gordon said, "As long as we have Saba, I agree. But I do not leave without her."

Irina said, "We will not plan to leave without Saba." She spoke in the same kind of calm, flat voice as Gordon used.

Vera said quickly, "Why not right now? We can get her out, and leave now."

Misha struck his hand against the wall, a sharp sound that made everyone jump.

Ross hadn't realized until then how tense they all were. Tired, sick, yes, also tense.

"This mission is not failed," he stated, his accent strong. He gave Irina a cold-eyed stare. "We have time. I *will* find Svetlana."

Irina just stared back without speaking.

Ross slid a glance at his wife. Eveleen watched the two Russians, a sober expression in her eyes.

Misha said, "I have translated all her writings. I can retrace her steps, and if we go back to the day she disappeared—"

Viktor spoke in Russian, gesturing with his hands. Irina also spoke, and Misha produced a disk from his pocket. He handed it to Irina, who took it without comment.

Ross saw Gordon following this action. He said nothing.

When Irina had finished putting away the disk, Gordon said in a quiet voice, "Zina is right. We don't know what this disease is. The fact that we all have it, at both ends of the time line, makes a strong case for the First Team having been afflicted with the same thing. And though we haven't found bodies, we don't know if the First Team died before they vanished—there are too many anomalies. Until we solve at least one, we cannot go back and risk the same thing happening to us."

"Then we find out," Misha said. "You get Saba out, I solve this, my own way."

He turned to the door, hit the control. He went out without speaking another word, and Viktor, with an expressive shrug, followed.

The door closed, its sound loud in the sudden silence.

"Let's go over the facts," Eveleen said in a voice of compromise. "We know we're all sick—but our scientists don't know the cause, or the disease. We know that the First Team were not together, and that they did in fact disappear on different days, but no one earlier than Katarina, the archivist."

Vera said, "Misha won't rest until he finds some kind of evidence. He..." She paused, rolling her eyes.

"Mikhail Petrovich," Irina enunciated in her clear, emotionless voice, "is a romantic." Her tone equated *romantic* with *fool*.

Gordon said diplomatically, "He's determined to make the jump up to the First Team's time, and perhaps that is a way to find out what happened." His voice sharpened subtly. "But it might just endanger us without solving anything at all. Until we collect enough evidence to know for sure, let's not end up with the same mysterious fate. And so we're back to our original problem: we must determine, if we can, exactly what happened to them, and why."

Ross nodded, without speaking. Vera made a noise of agreement. Irina shrugged.

Gordon went on, "So let's split up, and do whatever we can to put together the few puzzle pieces we have. See if we can get some sort of picture, something to act on safely. In the meantime, nothing seems to have happened to us—" He gestured to the walkie-talkie clipped to Vera's belt. "So

I rescind the silence rule. But let's use good judgment. We still have to assume that someone who can jam can listen in."

"We speak in English," Vera said. "Russian, someone might know, or have on record from a hundred years ago. English would still be new."

Gordon nodded.

Vera gave Irina a questioning look. Irina nodded politely at Gordon, Ross, and Eveleen, then went out, her footfalls noiseless.

Ross thought about that cold, angry glance as he and Eveleen got ready to sleep. Eveleen seemed troubled; Ross glanced over at her a couple times as he rolled out their futon. She was sitting cross-legged on the floor, typing rapidly into her laptop.

When she finished, she closed the laptop and sat back with a sigh.

Ross said, "Any intuition about what's going on in Irina's head?"

Eveleen looked up, slightly startled. "You too, huh?"

Ross shrugged. "I have to admit I'm having trouble figuring these Russkis. I don't know if it's me, or them, or I'm just not a sensitive kind of a guy—"

Eveleen laughed. "Meaning you scent personal gossip behind all the angry looks and so forth. Well, so do I. We do know that Misha has romanced most of the women in the Russian service. We also know he pulled strings to be sent on this mission. I suspect that his relationship with Svetlana wasn't just lighthearted flirtation. How Irina fits into this is anybody's guess."

Ross grimaced. You didn't get this kind of talk on a mission with all men—and, he reflected, you probably didn't get it on missions with all women. Put 'em together, and what do you get?

"Chemistry," he said out loud.

"Hmm?" Eveleen asked, blinking. "Oh! Misha and Irina? Well, either that or politics. I can't pretend to understand them all. Irina especially. All I know is—or rather, all I *sense* is that Irina and Misha are going to be competing in some way, he to solve the mission, and she to get us back to Earth before we end up like the rest."

"So you don't think she wants to solve the mystery."

Eveleen paused in the act of brushing out her hair, and shook her head. "I think Irina has decided it's impossible, and she wants to wrap it up and move on."

Ross sighed as he dropped down beside her on the futon. His thoughts ranged from Misha and Irina to Saba, hidden in the House, and from there to his own situation— the Jecc game. He hadn't mentioned it to Gordon; it seemed so unimportant beside all the other crises.

But as he laid there, his mind drifting, his thoughts came back to that word *chemistry*.

After a little while, the light sensors, detecting no movement, turned the lights off. Eveleen's breathing had already become deep and even; she was asleep. Ross closed his eyes and tried to clear his mind.

Dawn the next morning was again clear, they discovered when they left the Nurayil dorm. Clear, hot, and humid.

"Ugh," Eveleen said, then she cleared her throat and somewhat breathlessly made a comment about the weather.

Ross obligingly forced his mind to switch from the quicksilver ease of his native English to the heavy freight train of Yilayil. Weird, how his brain refused to get used to this language, a problem he'd not had on previous assignments.

He asked, in Yilayil, "Have you trouble with speech in the Yilayil?" He chose the word for thought/mind/speech, realizing as he whistled and hummed the words that this was his problem, the words weren't one-for-one exchanges.

"I concur," Eveleen trilled. "To think/speak..." She hesitated, then said quickly in English, "Every word is a paragraph." She looked guiltily at Ross, then went back to Yilayil. "Practice perhaps would take a year."

Ross didn't answer. He knew they were both thinking that they didn't have a year.

They reached their workplace then, and the cool, shadowy building was a distinct relief after the early morning heat.

As Ross took up his station, he considered their performance so far. Back on Earth—what had seemed a thousand years ago—everyone had blithely assumed that he and Eveleen would be able to attain driver status without any problem, thus being able to sneak rail-skimmers out and move the teammates around as needed. At least so long as their destinations matched with the hidden rail system. They'd assumed that Misha and Viktor would of course find the bodies of the First Team, all located in the same place, having been buried on the same day, They'd assumed—

His attention splintered when he felt a dry, scaly hand at his side.

The Jecc!

The game was on.

He'd almost forgotten them. Quick as light he imprisoned the small fingers working at the communicator attached to his belt. The Jecc went very still, its pupils contracting as it stared up at him.

Ross spoke without thinking, repeating the same phrase used by the Jecc that caught him stealing, all those days ago: "My progeny will be swift."

The Jecc's gaze seemed to intensify, then fast as lightning it scuttled away.

Ross turned to his work, picking up where he'd left off in a complicated assembly the day before. The Jecc encounter was momentarily forgotten.

It didn't stay forgotten long. Within a very short time he became aware of a change in the behaviors of the Jecc. He'd become the center of their focus—not just the stealing, but they seemed to move about him in busy circles, humming a kind of shorthand Yilayil.

The only time they faded away was at midday break, when Ross went to find Eveleen. As soon as he addressed her, his Jecc followers vanished like a tide receding.

"Something weird's going on," he murmured in an undertone.

"Danger?" She used the Yilayil word.

He replied in the same tongue. "No, I believe not. A change, a transition..." Again he felt that the words carried too many meanings, and choosing them was like carrying a mental backpack up a hill, whereas English was like light tiles, easily chosen, enabling him to sprint tirelessly. Frustrating.

He changed the subject to something innocuous as they forced down something to eat. The midday sun was blisteringly hot, and the air outside the transport area was almost overpowering with heavy scents.

When he was done he peered against the sunny glare off walls and roofs, and made out the dark green line of the jungle in the near distance. Weird. It felt as if it encroached menacingly.

"No appetite either?" Eveleen asked—in Yilayil.

He shook his head.

She sighed. "I noticed we are all thinner."

Ross thought back to the night before, and nodded. He hadn't been aware of it, but when he considered the Russians and Gordon—Eveleen was right. Of course, that was to be expected, since they were all sick.

But he didn't *feel* thinner. He felt, if anything, too heavy. That had to be the heat—and the illness.

He dismissed the thought, and drank some water.

Then it was time to return to work.

As soon as he was alone, the Jecc returned, circling around closer than ever. So it went for the rest of the shift. No one stole anything, but the Jecc stayed close, as if watching him, though they did not stop their work either.

It was when he shut down his workstation that the same Jecc came forward who had addressed him so aggressively on the first day in this department.

"I, Bock of Harbeast Teeth Islands, take Ross of Fire Mountain Enclave to nest for Day of Lamentation."

Ross stared down at the little being. A threat? Or an invitation?

He looked about for Eveleen, then realized that to do so meant that the Jecc would once again disappear.

He hesitated, knowing he should report in. But he also knew what Gordon would say: "Sit tight. Zina's orders."

But they didn't know about the Jecc. And Ross had a hunch that—somehow—this was going to fit into the overall puzzle.

He turned his head, watching Eveleen slowly shutting down her own workstation.

Better she went safely back to their room. If he was doing something stupid, at least he was the only one endangered.

"Yes," he said to Bock. "I come."

Chapter Twenty-Two

"It's been two hours," Eveleen said, trying hard not to snarl into the communicator.

It wasn't Gordon's fault. It wasn't anyone's fault—except Ross's.

Dammit!

"He's signaled the safety code?" Gordon asked.

"Yes," Eveleen said. "Twice. I know he's alive, but I don't know where."

"Exactly what happened?" Gordon asked.

"Nothing. That is, at the end of the workday, I saw him shutting down his work area. He had about six Jecc with him. All of them were quiet, which was unusual for Jecc."

"I don't know any Jecc," Gordon said.

"You're lucky," Eveleen commented, then she sighed. At least their room was cool, but to be in it alone—she shut her eyes against its unwelcoming alienness. "Anyway, I was glad to shut my work down because the heat made my head ache worse than ever. But when I finished and started over to find him, I realized he was gone. At first I thought I might have missed him, and so I walked all over the Transport. Nothing. So I came back here along our usual route. Nothing. So I took out my com. We'd traded off wearing ours, since we work together and could share news. Save energy. He had his on today. I tried to raise him—no answer."

"But you said you got the code for safety," Gordon cut in.

"That was after I raced back to the Transport." Eveleen bit back a comment about the enjoyment of running in the fierce heat. Gordon knew how hot it was. Everyone knew. "He wasn't there, so I tried to raise him by voice, and when that didn't work, I tried the pulse. I got an answer back then—the safety code."

"Could someone have taken it from him?"

"That was my first thought," Eveleen said, reaching for a cup of water. She drank thirstily, then said, "Pardon."

Gordon laughed a little. "I've been drinking gallons myself. Saba as well."

"You've been talking to Saba?" Eveleen asked, diverted for a moment.

"Long conversations," Gordon said, his tone curious. "Back to Ross. You don't think someone took his com?"

"Oh. No. Not unless they also can read minds. You see, back on the ship, we'd also worked out a couple of personal codes. Just in case. Well, he pulsed one of those, too. And an hour ago, when he sent the next safety code, he sent another one—this one meaning 'Can't talk now but I'm okay.' "

She didn't mention that the first one he'd sent was the "I love you" code—not that Gordon probably couldn't guess.

Too bad we didn't work one out for "I love you, but what you did is so stupid I'm going to throttle you!" Eveleen thought grimly.

"This sounds rather like the Ross I've always known," Gordon said next, and Eveleen—though nothing could abate her exasperation—was a little comforted. "Here's my guess. He's following a hunch, something so harebrained he knew we'd all be against it. But his instincts have always been good, so far."

So far. Eveleen sighed. "Right."

"Keep in contact if anything changes," Gordon said.

Eveleen wanted to talk more—for reassurance if for nothing else—but she forced herself to sign off. She knew Gordon couldn't really help. He knew even less than she did about the situation, and it wasn't as if he didn't have plenty to worry about on his own.

He knew less than she did about—

She jumped up, ignoring the pang in her temples. Idiot! Once again she tabbed her com, but this time—for the first time—she punched in the code for Misha.

His answer came almost immediately. "Nikulin here."

Nikulin? Oh, yes, Misha's last name. Eveleen said, "Misha, have you come across any Jecc on your investigations?"

"Jecc? Yes. They have a, a lair, you must say in English, in a series of caves directly south, near the peninsula."

Eveleen let out her breath in a whoosh. "Any chance you could take me there?"

Misha gave a soft laugh. "Yes, I can. Is there a reason?"

Swiftly Eveleen outlined the situation.

Misha said nothing until she'd reached the end, only, "I will come to you." And the com went dead.

She figured Misha had to be several hours' walk away, and she repressed a wince of guilt at making him walk in the heat. This was too important.

The main thing was to get rest. Until he arrived, she might as well try to catch some sleep.

So she unrolled the futon, trying not to think about lying on it alone, laid out her equipment, and composed herself for sleep. Yet it seemed she'd only just closed her eyes when a rapid tap came at the door.

She opened it to find Misha standing there, alone. She grabbed her canteen and her com, and walked out.

He smiled down at her, his eyes impossible to read.

"Is there a problem?" he asked.

His tone suggested a problem between Ross and herself. She fought annoyance, realizing that it was a legitimate question—that the success of the mission was at stake, and so she answered in an even voice, "No. Opposite, really—" And as she spoke, she *had* it. "He's being chivalrous, I'm afraid. And..." The truth almost made her dizzy. "It's stupid, but I think I would have done the same thing."

She had a sudden, vivid mental picture of Ross stumping alongside Misha, cursing at each step as they chased after her, and she laughed out loud, then caught herself up short, choking the laughs back.

Misha gave her a quizzical glance.

Forestalling any more personal questions, she asked, "How long is the walk? All night?"

Misha shook his head. "You will see."

They reached the bottom of the ramp, then, and Eveleen realized it was quite dark outside. This was against the rules—only the Yilayil could be out. Yet Misha had gotten in successfully.

Her heart pounded as she followed him around the side of the building. They walked in a direction she'd never explored. Why not? she asked herself. And the answer came immediately, because she and Ross had spent every waking moment with each other, keeping each other safe. Alone, they probably both would have been a lot more adventurous.

And neither of them had ever spoken a word about this.

She grimaced at the ground as she walked. Well, they were going to make up for lost time, she promised.

But first—a big first—she and Misha had to find Ross, and get him back, all without anyone being caught abroad at night.

Misha raised a hand, and Eveleen stopped: He leaned out, looking in all directions, then he unfolded a small lorgnettelike device and peered through it: an infrared scanner. He did a slow circle, then folded it back up.

"No one," he murmured. "We are at the border of the city. Few come this way."

In silence she followed him at a jogging pace down a curving pathway—a skimmer rail, she realized. They ran past several small, circular buildings, almost none of which had windows. In the distance loomed the black line of the jungle.

Before they reached it, though, Misha made an abrupt diagonal. Eveleen followed, taking care to match the long strides of the Russian agent. He led the way unerringly into what seemed at first to be an overgrown garden, lit with a ghostly glow from the tower of the House of Knowledge.

They passed between two vine-covered walls, then Misha unclipped a flashlight from his belt. A quick look behind, a scan on the infrared, and he motioned Eveleen to follow.

Misha clicked the flash on, revealing a moss-covered ramp leading down in a sharp spiral.

"Careful. One can easily slip," Misha murmured.

Eveleen walked carefully, picking her way over cracked stone and jumbles of small plants that had wedged themselves in the cracks.

They walked down rapidly, passing from the hot, still air into a breezy passageway that smelled faintly like the Transport Eveleen worked at every day. At once she felt alarm, for the rail-skimmers were usually crowded—and at night, of course, they would belong exclusively to the Yilayil.

But Misha seemed to read her thoughts, for he said, "Be easy. This has been closed for centuries."

Attesting to the truth of what he said, the flashlight played over mossy walls and fungus-covered surfaces as she became aware of the musical drip of water seeping down from somewhere overhead.

Down, down they walked, into a dim-lit tunnel. Drier air whooshed softly in their faces, smelling faintly of machinery. An air circulation system?

Misha spoke now in a normal voice: "We found this by accident, when trying to escape one of the recent storms. Apparently one transport was built directly atop the older one."

He pointed down the narrow tunnel, and they walked a short distance along a meter-wide curb.

"This is the very south end of the old spaceport, which must have been abandoned several centuries before the First Team's time. We think this predates the Yilayil. Runs on different principles than those buckets you and Ross repair every day."

"Why didn't they just use this? Why build something new?" Eveleen asked.

Misha shrugged, and then motioned for her to stop, then he reached high over his head and passed his hand in front of something; Eveleen caught a faint flicker, as of lights nearly off the human-perceptible spectrum, and within seconds a hissing noise heralded the arrival of a long, peculiar-looking vehicle, not at all like the rail-skimmers. This looked more like the low, fast cars found in modern mines, only narrow, and it did not run on wheels.

They climbed in, Eveleen behind Misha. The vehicle was damp to the touch, but not full of water. Eveleen sat down carefully.

"Lie back," Misha warned. "Hands and feet together."

Eveleen obeyed. Misha did something. Without warning the car moved forward, at first slowly, then effortlessly gathering speed. The tightening in her stomach gave her the sense of diving down deep underground at a rapid clip; otherwise the tunnel indicated nothing, neither depth nor direction.

Once or twice it swerved, or dove farther, then Misha did something up front. Intersections arrived—brief flashes of light and slight impacts on her ears—then vanished again. At last the craft drove upward again, pressing her back against a hard, ridged seat, then it slowed smoothly to a stop.

"We are at the south end of the island," Misha said as they climbed out.

"Have you been all over, then?" Eveleen asked.

Misha nodded, smoothing back ruffled blond hair from his brow. "There's nothing to be found—nothing for us. But these early engineers were a damned sight better than the weasel folk. No sign of what happened to them, of course."

Eveleen bit back a comment, thinking: If I'd been alone, I would have spent all my free time looking for just this kind of thing. Her head even seemed to ache less. Was it impending action? Or maybe just the clean, filtered air of the deep transport system?

Whatever it was, they were out of it soon, for Misha motioned her into a kind of escalator, which whizzled them to another overgrown tunnel. Now the familiar flowery, warm, humid air clogged her sinuses.

They stepped out into starlit darkness.

"Do the Jecc use these transports, then?" Eveleen asked.

"Yes. We found out purely by accident. They all crowd in at dawn and dusk, and sometimes in between, but never at night. We nearly were discovered by them one morning when we were asleep at the other end."

"Huh." So the Jecc, thieves of everything small and inconsequential, had a secret transport? Eveleen wondered how many other secrets were held by the various races of this world. She shook her head. "We need a year here, not days."

"This I know," Misha said, sounding amused.

Neither spoke for the remainder of the walk, which was up a steep trail. Eveleen was glad that there was no rain—though halfway up, she would have welcomed the moisture, just to cool her off. She was very glad not to be making this journey in the middle of the day.

Once she started to ask a question, but Misha reached, putting a hand to her lips.

She shrugged him off, and nodded. His face, scarcely discernible in the starlight, was unreadable, but she sensed his amusement at her reaction.

Presently he stopped, and motioned for her to drop to her knees. He did also, and they crawled slowly along a narrow cliff, then stopped. Misha pointed over a rocky edge, and she lay flat and stretched slowly out, looking down.

She found herself staring directly down a wide vent. The familiar burned-toast smell of the Jecc was very pronounced, along with a not-unpleasant, slightly astringent scent rather like the herb rosemary.

She inched farther out, looking down into the yellowish light, and caught sight of muted colors. Blinking the sweat out of her eyes, she scrunched forward on her elbows until she had a full view down the vent shaft, into a chamber whose walls were covered with some kind of mural. She saw stars, plants, cavorting figures that, at the steep angle at which she was forced to view, were hard to make out. They seemed to be Jecc, only they didn't look quite right. She wriggled around, trying different angles, but she couldn't really see well; the angle was still too sharp.

The swift rise and fall of voices came then, faint, carried on the currents of soft air.

In silence she waited, listening to the voices, wondering what to do next, when she heard another voice, a lone voice, human.

It belonged to Ross.

Eveleen listened to the familiar timbre of his voice. He was whistle/humming something in Yilayil, but the distance, the soft whooshing of the air passing up the vent, made words difficult to discern.

One thing, though, for certain: his voice made it clear that he was not in any danger.

She pressed her cheek against a rock, trying to assess the maelstrom of emotions crashing through her mind.

He was safe.

But he hadn't told her.

And they hadn't done any exploring...

Once he returned unharmed she knew she had a right to get really angry with him. It was inexcusable, to just take off without warning. Dangerous, *rock-headed*, and inexcusable. Yet she knew she would probably have done the same thing, and for the same reason: she couldn't bear the thought of him going willingly into danger.

They'd guarded each other, without speaking of it, keeping one another from exploring, from taking risks. Eveleen thought of that secret transport so close to the Nurayil dorm. She and Ross should have found it, weeks ago. But they'd guarded each other from doing anything daring— anything they probably would have done were they single.

Single. Now, suddenly, she understood Milliard's real concern about newlyweds on a mission together.

She sighed, listening to Ross's voice among the high chatters of the Jecc. Oh, Ross! She knew she could make a scene. She was his wife, his helpmeet. She had a right to communication! Then she thought of Saba, who had chosen, with intellectual forbearance, never to have a mate. To close herself off from the possibility of this kind of sharing, because of the possibility of genetic-borne tragedy. Oh, sure, there were ways to make certain one didn't have children—and likewise there were plenty of successful relationships that did not include offspring. Eveleen considered for the first time the possibility that Saba's policy was actually the result of a specific relationship. In other words, she had found the right person, but her circumstances and that person's own wishes could not be made to compromise.

That was real tragedy. Next to it, fussing about "rights" seemed just petty.

She looked over at Misha, who watched her in silence.

"Thanks," she said softly. "Let's go back."

Neither spoke as they made the return journey.

CHAPTER TWENTY-THREE

"Zina has set a limit." Gordon's voice sounded quiet and reassuring. "We lift ship before Blossom Day. I'm working on plans for repatriation."

Saba closed her eyes, listening to the calm voice.

"Blossom Day" was their old code for the day of disappearance. If she was reading his oblique words right, the First Team had not all disappeared on the same day, only Katarina. But apparently Zina wanted them to move forward in time well before that day, and it had something to do with the illness they all shared.

"I am learning," she said. "I learn slowly, and there is much to be learned. I think...I know there is something important here."

"Continue to learn," Gordon replied. Then he paused, and she heard him drinking water. They were evidently all thirsty, and their appetites had diminished.

Then he went on to talk about his college days, and how much he'd enjoyed discovering archaeology. They buried their real communication in long innocuous talks, but Saba found that she enjoyed these talks just the same.

At first he'd talked generalities, but gradually, as they found similar areas of interest, he'd become more personal.

"It was the discovery of paradigm that hooked me in," he said. "Oh, I'd heard about worldview and 'Weltanschauung' and so forth all during high school, but it was that visceral understanding that other cultures saw the universe through utterly different metaphors that fascinated me."

"Yes," Saba said. "I was lucky—I saw it early, because my parents came from such vastly different backgrounds." She described riding across the plains of Ethiopia with her father, a doctor, to visit the different peoples. And then there came a new culture to learn, when she moved to the capital city to begin her advanced education. "But that is what brought me to my studies, the expression of paradigm through music."

"Music," Gordon mused. "It was on the periphery of my attention when I was growing up."

"It was a part of life for me," Saba said. "Music stitched together the ..." Inadvertently a Yilayil word came to mind, along with image—color—but she reverted to English. "The fabrics of meaning." As she said it, she frowned. "Fabric"— so inadequate! And so she whistle/hummed her idea, using the outside-time tense she'd been struggling to comprehend, and it came closer to expressing the image.

Gordon drew in a deep breath—she could hear it. "I'm not sure I understand," he said finally. "I perceive each word separately, but the verb—"

"It's part of my lessons," Saba said, thinking that— even if they were overheard, which they must assume to be the case—this conversation could not possibly endanger anyone.

Then she remembered the time, and sat up suddenly, dizzily, staring at her watch. "Ah, I am late," she said. "But I enjoyed our discussion."

"Until later, then," Gordon responded, and clicked off.

Saba rose slowly, testing her strength, her sense of gravity. At Gordon's insistence, she was now using full doses of medication. She worked to time the hours of their strongest effect with her lessons, so she could be as clearheaded as possible when she was trying to learn the alien language in all its nuances.

She pulled on her robe, and stepped outside her room. Pausing, she looked at the blank wall adjacent. Why did they have her alone on a corridor? The wall, a dead end, intrigued her subconscious mind. In her dreams, Katarina often came through it, like a ghost.

Sometimes Katarina sang, old chants out of Saba's childhood that the Russian probably never had even heard: the polyphonic *edho* of the Dorze; Eritrean songs, echoing two thousand years of history from the long-ago kingdom of Axum; even the songs of the mysterious Afar, who shun all foreigners.

It was the polyphonic *edho* that Saba most often heard, wreathing through the never-ceasing music of the Yilayil. So different to the ears, but the brain insisted on finding connecting points.

She sighed, and walked down to the teaching chamber, where she found Zhot—no longer green—pacing back and forth.

As always, he began without preamble.

"All peoples have part of brain where sensory organs connect, where the senses happen first," Zhot said.

Saba nodded, puzzled at the new direction the lesson was taking. So they would not work on the computer, then?

"We will talk about vision," Zhot continued—again, as if reading her mind. It was eerie, how often their thoughts paralleled—even when she was having the most difficulty comprehending him. "What do your people call the brain part where vision happens?"

That, at least, she could answer, for she had studied neurology for a time in her efforts to plumb the mysteries of music's universal effect on humans. "The visual cortex."

"And if this is destroyed, no vision, yes?"

She nodded again.

"Do you understand****?" Zhot whistle-trilled a complex phrase.

Sight denied but body affirms perception? She shook her head, confused. Her head panged, colors and even tastes flitting through her consciousness. She dismissed them as irrelevant, and grasped at the words that came with them.

"Blindsight!" she exclaimed. "They deny sight, indeed cannot see, but can sometimes grasp objects, tell their shapes."

"Yes! This is true for all sentients with this brain damage. And they do not trust what they perceive, do not believe they perceive, call it guessing," Zhot continued, more excited than she had ever seen him, "for they have no sensations to anchor perception."

Her momentary satisfaction at her understanding him ebbed as she realized she had no idea why they were discussing blindsight. A wave of weakness washed over her, and she swayed in her chair, suddenly dizzy.

"Only a little more," Zhot said, in the first concessions to her condition she had ever known from him.

"I apologize," Saba said. "I discover that I am hungry." She thought longingly of the bluish cheese pudding that was often served, and her stomach growled. She suspected, from its effect on her metabolism, that it was pure protein.

"We talk, then eat," Zhot said. "Your people have legends of those among you who see the future, yes?" he continued.

"Yes. It is very rare, and not to be depended on."

"No more than blindsight," said Zhot, his tail swishing beneath his robes. The sight made more colors flit across Saba's vision, and dizziness dissolved the edges of her vision. She closed her eyes, and concentrated on his words. "For we who live in time have no sensory organ for time, and so no sensations to anchor the perception of time. Do you understand?"

"I ... I ..." She paused, a sudden onslaught of weariness—dizziness—washing through her mind. She fought vertigo, opened her eyes. They stung. The fever was back—already.

"Think, listen, taste," Zhot said. "Now we eat."

Taste, eat. Everything seemed connected by some inner meaning. Saba tried to penetrate it, but the malaise made it impossible, and she gratefully followed Zhot to the refectory to join the other beings for the morning meal.

Dawn was graying the gathering clouds when Ross slipped out of the Jecc transport and jogged back to the Nurayil dorm. Now that the adventure was over, his emotions were mixed: excitement at action, at discovery, laced with guilt. He knew he ought to have communicated. Eveleen would be angry. As she had a right to be.

Still, this rational acceptance of his culpability didn't make the prospect of facing the music any easier.

When he reached the dorm building, some of the beings they shared it with were already descending to go off to whatever it was they did during the daylight hours. He moved quickly between them, running up the ramp. He was not even tempted to go directly to work. Better to confront her now, and get it over with.

He reached their cell, and opened the door.

He wasn't sure what he expected to find except an angry wife. What he saw was Eveleen and Gordon sitting cross-legged on the floor, each working at his or her laptop, food beside them. He saw the bluish stuff that tasted kind of like cheesecake, and swallowed a couple times. He was suddenly ravenous.

But he turned his attention from the food to his wife's assessing brown eyes. He met that gaze—and he saw her grin.

"Well," she said, "since I didn't get to share your adventure, how about a detailed report?"

"Of course," he said. "Ah, you're not mad? Not that I'd blame you."

Gordon said nothing, only smiled slightly.

Eveleen said, "Oh, I wasn't mad once I'd made sure you were all right."

"What?" Ross demanded.

Eveleen's smile sharpened a little at the corners. "Misha showed me the way to the Jecc caves. I got a good peek, but not much more."

Ross drew in a slow breath. "You—"

"Went out to make sure you were okay," Eveleen said slowly. "Just as you would have done, had I been the one to skip out. We'll have to talk about that, but later. We all have to get to work. Sit down, have some breakfast. I take it the Jecc didn't feed you?"

"Oh, they tried, but I just pretended. The stuff they like would make a squirrel happy, but it was too close to nuts and gravel for my taste. Or what looked like gravel."

Ashe sat back, his brows lifted slightly. "You thought there was something important to pursue—enough so that you avoided our orders. I'm here to follow up on whatever it was you discovered."

Ross sat down, knowing that Gordon's mild manner was deceptive. It was as much of a reprimand as Gordon was going to make—but it was enough.

"I'm not sure," Ross said, "but I think there *is* something."

"Go on," Eveleen said. "I'll type it up as you talk."

"I didn't put it all together until I got to the Jecc city. Because that's what it is, a little city. They are pretty handy with their fingers for building, and not just thieving. Hot and cold running water—and they like baths just as much as humans. Forget this ecologically sound but unsatisfying glue-field thing." Ross waved behind him.

Gordon gave a faint grin, but his attitude was still one of waiting.

"Anyway, when I got there, I saw Jecc with kids in their pouches. They don't come into the Nurayil town when they are gestating their young. I think they are biologically a lot like marsupials—the young are born helpless, and finish gestating in the pouches. But the Jecc are asexual. All that thieving comes down to the exchange of genetic material."

"That's why our tools feel like they've been dusted with pollen?" Eveleen asked.

"Exactly. And by playing what I thought was a game, I somehow made myself one of the gang. See, it works like this, far as I can figure: it's an honor to be stolen from, because it means someone else wants your genetic material for their offspring. But it's not just stealing, because you're expected to get the thing right back again. And you're not supposed to get caught, but if you do, you make some comment about progeny—though in the past, I think, they used to fight. But that fighting turned to ritualistic dueling by the time they got civilized—developed writing and reached for the stars. They are insatiably curious. I think they feel rejected by the rest of the beings on this world because no one participates in their thieving games."

"But they can't expect to be exchanging genetic material with other races, can they?" Gordon asked.

"No. I don't think it's that all the time with them, either. They also do it with new encounters, so I believe it's a kind of acceptance custom as well. A social exchange. Only no one outside of the Jecc seems to know it—or care."

"Is that why they don't try to become harmonized?" Eveleen asked.

"It might be a part, but here's where it gets weird. They are wary of ti[*trill*]kee because every generation or so, the ones here on this island seem to disappear."

Gordon let out a long whistle—not a Yilayil whistle, but a low, American expression of "Uh oh!"

"Oh, but that's not all of it. They seem to want to fit in, but they want to know what happened to their ancestors. For beings who don't have families the way we have them, they are very involved with their ancestors. They showed me those caves you saw. Each one makes a mosaic about its life, and accomplishments, naming its progeny. They used to have more, but now they only have one, maybe two, if their population drops in number."

"The mosaics looked interesting."

"Not just that," Ross said, feeling for words. "Sad, kind of. Poignant. Their ancestors didn't just stop at depicting themselves. They have special rooms that show pictures from their homeworld, and others showing their journey through space. Jecc have spread over several worlds, and they used to keep in contact—they have things not unlike those picture cubes we found on the globe ship. Remember, Gordon? That showed pictures of home?"

"Yes," Ashe said. "Go on."

225

"Well, the Jecc have these ancient message cubes, and they revere them. Play them often—I don't know what kind of energy they run off. Solar? Anyhow, here's the kicker. The Jecc in the messages are different."

"Different? How?'" Gordon asked.

"Taller. Bigger. But the real change is the tentacles. The Jecc of the past didn't have them. And all of a sudden—if the mosaics are correct—a generation or so after they arrived here, all the offspring were born with them."

"Tentacles," Eveleen said, looking up from her typing. "The Yilayil don't have them—they have four arms—but a lot of the other beings here all have those tentacles."

"Those savage human types did as well, down in our time," Ross said. "Anyway, the tentacles are new, and the Jecc mourn the fact that even if they had a spaceship, because of them they could never go home again. That's what yesterday was, their Day of Lamentation. They seem to have these about once a month."

"Mutation," Gordon said slowly, getting to his feet. "No, more than mutation. Genetic alteration. Tentacles are too much of a change to be a mutation, and on many races, at that. But alteration by whom, and to what purpose?" He frowned as he packed up his laptop. "This requires thought." He shook his head. "But later. For now, we'd better not make any overt changes in our routines, because we still don't know who is watching or listening. I'm off to work."

He left, and Eveleen slowly and thoughtfully shut down her computer.

Ross watched, trying to figure out what to say.

But Eveleen forestalled him. She got to her feet and put her hands on his shoulders. She smiled up into his face.

"How long," she asked, "do you think it would have taken for us to get thoroughly sick of each other?"

"What?" Ross gazed at her in astonishment.

Her eyes were narrowed in amusement—and understanding. "If we hadn't gotten whatever this illness is. How long would we have guarded one another against taking risks—meanwhile getting more and more frustrated?"

"I—" Ross let his breath out in a whoosh. "I don't know."

Eveleen turned away, no longer smiling. "We should have found that old transport system, Ross. You and I—weeks ago. Misha and Viktor stumbled on it only because they were looking for some kind of shelter from one of those rainstorms. That station is right near us. We should have been out, exploring, ages ago. We two are action agents, not Vera and Irina. They are communicators, analysts. But they've been finding out data, much more than we have."

Ross sighed. "I know. It's just—"

"You don't have to say it, because I felt exactly the same. You're used to taking action—taking risks. And when you were risking only yourself, it was perfectly all right. I know because I felt the same way. But when it came to considering your safety, I couldn't stand the thought that something might happen to you, and I meant to stay with you every minute. Keep you safe. Keep you out of harm's way."

Ross laughed a little raggedly. "Hell, Eveleen."

"And we didn't even *talk*. Just heroically did our duty as spouses—guarding each other from doing our duty as agents." She gave him a troubled look. "If we can't work this out, we shouldn't be partners. If we were on our own again, we'd have that old freedom of action. And we're both action people—you have to admit it. That's what brought us together in the first place."

Ross said, "Don't think that."

"But we have to," Eveleen said. "If we can't handle the emotional consequences of our jobs, then we'd be better off working separately. We have to consider it—but later. Right now, we'd better get to work. Gordon said we don't want to alter our routines any."

Ross nodded, forcing himself to grab his share of the breakfast. He would munch it on the way, though he really didn't want to eat. Didn't want to work. Truth was, he felt heartsick. Anger would have been better than that logical calmness.

The worst of it was, he knew she was right.

Outside, the air was slightly cooler, a strong breeze smelling of rain bringing some relief. Eveleen walked beside him, her profile serene, as she made light comments in Yilayil.

Ross didn't talk. He thought about his night with the Jecc—and when they got to work, and the Jecc recommenced their little game, he thought about Eveleen.

On the way back from work, he said, "You're right. And I promise. No more hiding. Half and half, share fair and square, as we used to say on the streets when I was a kid."

"Share fair and square," Eveleen repeated, her eyes steady and bright with a sheen of unshed tears. "That, my dear, is *real* trust."

Ross didn't respond. As always, his deepest emotions were impossible to express. He looked forward to their being alone at last, so that he could at least try.

But when they reached the Nurayil dorm, they found Misha waiting outside their cell, pacing like a caged cat.

A small group of Moova trundled past, but he paid them no heed. As soon as he saw them he said abruptly, "Open up."

In mute surprise, Eveleen palmed the door open.

As soon as they were inside, Misha said, "The flyers. They got Viktor."

Ross looked to Eveleen. She looked back, question in her eyes.

"What are we waiting for?" Ross said. "Let's go get him back."

CHAPTER TWENTY-FOUR

Saba spent the day drifting in and out of consciousness. Gordon called her once, and then again. His worry penetrated the strange dreaming wakefulness that she couldn't seem to escape on her own. Patiently, slowly, he bade her describe—in detail—her room, her hands, courses she'd taken in university. Anything to anchor her to reality.

But as soon as they quit conversing, she lay down again, exhausted, and the strange dreams seized her—always punctuated by Yilayil voices singing never-ending chants. Twice she rose to shut down the Yilayil computer, so that the sound would cease and she could sleep, but both times she found it dark. Was the sound coming from hidden speakers? Or—somehow—was she dreaming it, too? Except how could she dream language she only partially understood?

Her mind kept insisting on listening, and trying to parse the complicated levels of verb and modifier until she'd rise again, cram more anti-inflammatory meds into her dry mouth, and wash it down with long gulps of water.

Once she awoke suddenly, and Zhot seemed to be in her room. He demanded definitions for time and space and insisted that she learn the terms for those who stood outside temporal reality ...

She slept again, and when she woke a second time—now drenched in sweat—she wasn't sure if she'd dreamed the conversation or not.

As soon as she sat up, the sensors flicked the lights on. The lights seemed dim; she felt a sudden longing for the bright clarity of sunlight.

She looked up, about to reach for her medication—and there was Zhot, standing in the shadows of the corner.

"Are your senses one, or many?" Zhot's voice blurred in a scintillation of green-tasting rainbows—Saba knew the thought senseless, but it was the only description that fit.

"Many," she said slowly. Her lips felt dry and cracked. She reached for water, drank. When she looked up, Zhot was still there.

"Different modes of sensation, yes?" he insisted. Now she heard the *wisp-wisp* of his slippered feet on her floor, the quiet hiss of his robe as he walked back and forth in front of her door.

Her muzzy mind jumped to the musical modes, and she worried a moment at the problem of whether the taste of water was Dorian or Myxolydian.

When she looked up again, her vision had gone blurry; in Zhot's place she saw Katarina.

Katarina did not wait for an answer, or maybe it was an hour later. Saba didn't know.

"But you can imagine colors for tastes, sounds for shapes, different modes?" she continued. "Symbolically associate them?" Katarina spoke in Russian, or was it still Yilayil?

Katarina was a warm slurpy column of melted licorice emitting blue bubbles that enveloped her head, each conveying a quantum of meaning.

Now Saba tried to assign the proper color to the modes, until she suddenly, but only for a flashing moment, realized that she was below the words, below the world of symbols, in a seamless unity of sensation. Then everything wrenched back into focus, intensifying her headache, and Katarina was gone.

Synesthesis, Saba realized.

Unable to think beyond that, Saba lay down, and slept.

Urgency bled through her dreams: there was something she had to understand, to learn, to know. Now! Now!

She gasped, woke up, fumbling with trembling fingers for her water.

As she drank, she realized that the sound that had wakened her was that of movement outside her door—not footsteps, but voices. Yilayil voices, chanting.

She levered herself painfully off the bed, all her joints aching. The room spun about her for a moment, then steadied. After some experimentation she found that she could walk, albeit slowly, as long as she did not move her head quickly. It took all her strength for her to pull on her robe, but she welcomed its warmth.

She opened the door, in time to see two weasel faces look directly into her eyes before passing onward. They did not pause in the eerie whistle-punctuated chant, but passed slowly onward, their robes swaying in time to their steps

Saba turned her head—impossible that they would walk in that direction. There was nothing next to her room but a wall.

An unfamiliar glow lit the corridor. The adjacent wall was gone! In its place was an archway, its ceiling lit from beneath. Was it a stairway?

She waited, but no one appeared, and she became aware of a weird sound, almost like a heartbeat, but with strange musical overtones and harmonics. It seemed to come up through the floor, through her feet, but then she realized that some of the sound, the musical part, was more audible from the open door.

"Is this real?" she whispered, and then she reached for her com—her link to sanity. She clicked it on, and said wearily, "Is this real?"

She held it out, for a few seconds, but her arm could not bear the weight, and so she clipped it to her belt—and then forgot it as she concentrated on the difficult actions involved in standing on her feet.

She groped her way through the door, and stood in dismay. The stairs she had expected to find were apparently endless. She blinked feverish eyes. The perspective was odd, and her eyes wouldn't quite focus on the walls.

Only a few steps before her were in focus. The music crescendoed, echoing in cacophony—then it resolved, each voice, each instrument harmonious, the whole transcending melody into a form of mind-numbing beauty.

The music was more complex than any she had ever heard. It beckoned her downward.

Is this my fever? she thought. Am I really here? Only her trembling legs and pounding head and heart tied her to reality—but those too could be part of her dream.

Again the sense of urgency gripped her. She stumbled on.

Time was fragmented now; she had a vague sense that sunset had passed, that it was no longer Yilayil time. She remembered the two Yilayil faces, so briefly seen.

Sight blurred; and she knew she had to be hallucinating, for now she saw ghosts: the First Team, all lined up along the stairs in a row. And then Gordon. He reached a hand toward her, but she passed through his fingers. When she paused, swaying, on the stairs, she looked back—and he was watching her, his blue eyes mute with appeal, his sunbleached hair disarrayed as if he had been running. He's sick too, she thought, and she passed downward.

Finally she reached the bottom, and found herself in a huge cavern, glittering with the light of torches, bioluminescent spheres, electric lights, and other sources of illumination she did not recognize.

All the races of the planet were represented there, distributed about the vast space in a complex pattern whose geometry seemed to hold importance, but again the meaning escaped her.

The cavern was also full of stalactites and stalagmites, of fragile webs of rock, arrays of stone cylinders, and other forms, some natural, some obviously shaped, and some whose provenance she could not discern.

The beings danced among them, striking them with various instruments adapted to their sizes and physical nature. Big creatures held huge hammerlike strikers, little creatures carried small rods, or flexible drumsticks. Some struck the rocks, some stroked them, some tapped them. Some were on scaffolding high on the walls, some, the Jecc for instance, even swung on fragile trapezes, the length of the pendulum thus formed determining their rhythm: pulses of complex beats at long intervals.

This was but one aspect of the sound that pulsed in her head, her blood, and impelled her forward. She saw Zhot and stumbled toward him. He turned to her, welcome in his greenish face.

"We thought you too ill. Tonight we see."

"See?" Saba said weakly.

He waved one arm at the activity all around, while still stroking a stalagmite with the filelike rod in his other. It made a grating noise that made her teeth itch.

"Sensation! We anchor perception, achieve the unity of sensation that denies time, and those who dance-above-decay speak, we see, we hear."

Dance-abooe-decay. Again, he used one of those non-temporal verbs.

A tall Yilayil approached with deliberate step, its elongated body only remotely resembling an Earth weasel. The gowned creature studied her with large eyes that gleamed with intelligence and compassion; another approached on her other side.

The first Yilayil motioned for her to step forward. The second one held out a small rod, about two feet long. Her fingers closed round it. She glanced at the thing in her hand, confused.

Zhot turned back to his stalagmite, while the two Yilayil pressed her forward, gently, to a small fan of rock, so thin she could see light through it.

The first Yilayil pantomimed drawing the rod across the top of the rock-fan; she tried it, producing a melodic glissando. The Yilayil both nodded and whirled away.

For a time Saba stroked the fan at random, and then the pulse of the music penetrated her consciousness once more, sounds and voices rising and falling in a syncopation that caused her to grope for meaning within a context ingrained in memory, deep and abiding, from her earliest years.

The *edho* of the Dorze usually had five components. There was the *yetsu as*, the chorus—the chanting voices. Response, reaction, cohesion ....

The Yilayil. They were the *pile*, the highest voices, and limitless in number, at once the most important and the least important of the harmonic pattern.

The *kaletso*—who was that? Was it Zhot? The *kaletso* was the youngest, extending the melodic interventions of the *aife*—

The *ban'e*. The "belchers," the percussive voices. Those were the ones making music on the stones.

The *dombe*, those who cover. The other races, all singing sustained music to better the cohesion.

But who were the *aife*, the elder, the eyes?

Saba's mind reached, and reached again—

And the pattern changed in her mind, and she abandoned the symbol of childhood, immersing her consciousness in the alien harmonics—

And the music resolved wholly into beauty such as she had never heard, and she was part of it. Her will fled, and she became one with the music. The sound became color became touch became scent and then all of them and the cavern dissolved into pure sensation for a moment, bereft of perception, then snapped back, and she was somewhere else.

She saw men and women, dark and stern of face, in the ancient dress of the great Ethiopian kingdom of Axum, and others bearing gifts of gold and myrrh and jewels. Then violence, war, men struggling, weapons lifted, chariots sweeping across sandy wastes, the legions of Rome, men in white with scimitars uplifted, women weeping, pale men in pith helmets, swarthy men in uniforms with archaic rifles, an old man dragged from a throne and cast into darkness, the bright line of a rocket traced against a full moon huge on the horizon...

Then she gasped as the sneering, hate-filled visage of a Baldy confronted her, but just as suddenly his face became fearful, terrified, and disappeared.

Now she saw the Earth, bright and small, dwindling to a point, and the sun with it, merely another point of light in the glory of the galaxy, but from that insignificance grew a web of light, like sap refilling the veins of a dying leaf, melding with other webs from other stars widely scattered, and to her eyes was presented the destiny of humankind, glory and shame together as humanity reclaimed the ruins of the star-spanning empire that had crumbled so long ago.

Something Some*THING SOMETHING* sang in her head...

The *aife?*

...spoke in her head...

...spoke in her head.

A vast pressure surged through her mind.

It was too much to comprehend—to bear.

She swayed, dropped the rod, and fell senseless to the ground.

"As near as we can tell, they live off the island entirely," Misha said as they trotted through the darkening streets.

Rain tapped against Eveleen's face, cool and pleasant after two days of incessant heat. She ran at Ross's side, her jogging pace easily matching the taller men's strides.

Misha used his infrared scanner to detect body heat. Three times they ducked back behind shrubs or once a low wall, as beings walked by: once the tall green ones that functioned as guardians of the peace, and twice gliding Yilayil, talking swiftly in the language that was so melodic when they used it.

"All in the direction of the House of Knowledge," Ross observed, staring after the Yilayil. "Think something is happening?"

"How would we know?" Eveleen asked, thinking immediately of Saba. "We haven't been outside enough to put together any kind of pattern."

"True," Ross said, but his tone temporized—and Eveleen knew, without asking, that he felt the same sense of danger that gripped her.

"Come." Misha jerked his head, impatient to be gone.

No one spoke again until they had descended to the ancient transport station that the Russians had found.

"We spent three days riding this thing. Finding where it went. Where it still works," Misha said as they waited for one of the flat cars.

When it came up, they squeezed in, lying flat as Eveleen had the first time, and once again commenced a long ride, swooping downward. Concussions of air at intersections testified to the size and complexity of the system. It was miraculous that it still worked—that, somehow, there was still energy to run it.

Finally Misha stopped the car, which hummed beneath them. In the dim bluish light, he looked back at them. "This station here"—he gestured upward at an archway and glowing light— "is on the west coast of our island. As you see, the transport goes on. I think it crossed beneath the bay to a smaller island off to the west. We have seen the flyers retreating there when the sun sets; we think that is where they live. And I assume that this transport goes there as well, but I don't know. Want to test it, or find another way across?"

Eveleen said, "Test it."

At the same moment Ross said, "I'm not in the mood for a night swim."

Misha smiled faintly. "Then we go."

He faced forward again, leaned back—his yellow hair brushed over Eveleen's knees—and activated the car.

Again it dove downward, so fast her stomach seemed to drop. Then, quite as suddenly, it swooped up again, and she had to swallow to keep her ears from popping painfully. There were no intersection concussions this time. When the car stopped, all three climbed out.

"Here is what happened," Misha said as they walked toward the ramp leading upward. "We circled back for one last check at the Yilayil graveyard—just in case. We were careless—not enough sleep, maybe too sick." He shrugged. "It was clouding up, and we forgot to check for shadows. They came on us quite suddenly. I got under cover, Viktor did not. When I came out, I saw two of them holding him in a kind of net. They flew west, high, fast."

"So it's probable they took him here," Ross said.

Misha shrugged again. "Where else?"

And why? Eveleen thought—but she didn't speak out loud. They were here to find out why.

Cold air fingered their faces, and Eveleen pulled her rain jacket tight against her. Misha paused, checking his infrared and his flashlight.

Ross and Eveleen also had flashes clipped to their belts; in silence, Eveleen gripped hers, but she did not turn it on.

Misha led the way, scanning with the infrared. No warm bodies showed up on the screen.

Ross murmured, "Why do I think that the First Team ended up here?"

"There were no flyers in their time," Eveleen whispered back. "Not in any of the records—or were there, Misha?"

He shook his head. "No. No flyers."

Ross grunted. "Well, it was a nice solution."

"This mission has no easy solutions," Misha retorted in a sardonic voice.

"It's had no solutions at all, so far," Eveleen shot back.

Misha laughed softly, then paused again. They'd reached the entrance to the station. It was nearly overgrown with ferny plants. They tromped over thick moss and scrubby brush, then pushed through the hanging boughs.

Obviously the flyers did not know about the station, or if they did, they didn't use it: The three were the first ones in centuries to step that way; Eveleen could tell even in the darkness.

Misha had fixed his flashlight so that it emitted a thin pinhole of light. He shined it carefully, then clicked it off. Eveleen blinked in the sudden darkness, until her eyes began to adjust; whatever he'd seen was enough to orient him, but he was used to moving about in jungle at night. She was content, for now, to follow.

They found themselves on a rocky ledge that was once some kind of road. Flat portions, broken by hearty plants, made walking easier.

The road was built into the side of a cliff. They rounded a hill, and below them, quite suddenly, they saw dancing lights.

Too late they heard the *swoosh* of great wings beating; Eveleen looked up sharply, to see five long shapes dive down on them.

Misha's hand went to his side—his weapon. He didn't unclip it, though. Eveleen kept her own hands away from her sides, balancing lightly on her feet. Adrenaline flooded her system, temporarily banishing malaise, headache, tiredness.

Ross had gone still. "Wait," he said.

Misha gave a short nod; he'd decided the same.

240

The five winged creatures surrounded them, and one of them gestured below. The distant yellow light outlined a sharp face with bluish highlights; the creature looked excited.

It opened its mouth, and began to speak. Eveleen heard a stream of non-Yilayil gibberish, and wondered what was being said. It sounded hauntingly familiar.

Then she heard a sharp indrawn breath from Misha.

Ross looked up. Eveleen's heart thumped.

"What?" she croaked.

"This language," Misha said, his voice suddenly hoarse. "It—it is—Russian."

CHAPTER TWENTY-FIVE

Gordon saw Saba lying on the ground.

No one else was in the cave. His footsteps hissed and grated as he ran heedlessly down the worn stone steps to the vast floor.

There Saba lay, utterly quiescent, her body, slender and graceful the last time he had seen her, now dangerously thin and frail.

"Saba. Saba," Gordon breathed, and knelt at her side.

He placed fingers to her neck, and gratitude flooded through him when he found a pulse—rapid and light, but steady.

She sucked in a deep, shuddering breath, and opened her eyes.

In the weird glow from the multiple light sources, she stared up at him, her black eyes reflecting the harsh light.

"Saba."

"Gordon? Are you real?" The whisper was the merest ghost.

"I am." A strangled laugh escaped him. "You left your com on. That was quite a concert."

"It was real, then?"

"Well, I heard real sounds, all right—but I don't yet know what you heard that might have been different. Can I help you?"

"Yes. Please." She lifted a hand.

He bent and slid his arm round her shoulders. So light, she was!

He rose, lifting her—and realized that his strength had been sapped as well.

"I can walk. Just help me balance," she murmured.

Gordon let her feet touch ground, and together they proceeded slowly up the steps, each of them soon breathing harshly.

They stopped when Saba made a sign. Both sank down onto the steps, Saba leaning against the stone wall. Gordon unclipped his canteen and they both took deep swigs of water.

Saba leaned her head against the rough wall. Her face in the dim lighting was drawn, but her eyes were steady and alert. "How'd you get in?"

"Over the last couple weeks I marked at least three ways around those green guards," Gordon said with a grim laugh. "And I found that this building is riddled with enough tunnels to make the New York subway system look simple. I've been exploring them during the early morning hours. I even found your room. And I mean to take you there right now—unless you think my presence will endanger you."

Saba canted her head, her eyes going unfocused. Gordon watched in dismay, hoping she was not about to fade out on him—but then she blinked, and saw him again, and smiled faintly. "No. No trouble."

He didn't ask. He could be patient.

When she was ready, she nodded, and again they moved up the stairs, drunken-sailor style.

"It's not...as far...as I thought," she panted when they had neared the top—but still she had to stop and rest.

This time, though, it was a short rest. She gulped some water, drew in a deep breath, and straightened up. They continued on, straight to her room.

No one was about. Saba reached, palmed the door open, and they passed inside. Full-spectrum lighting, somehow calibrated to be comfortable for the human eye, clicked on.

Gordon helped her to the narrow bed, and she collapsed gratefully. "I have a lot to tell you," she murmured. "Let me catch my breath."

Gordon looked around the chamber. It looked comfortable; his attention was immediately drawn to the unfamiliar computer system. "Is this the Yilayil terminal? May I turn it on?"

She nodded.

He touched the keypads, noting how different they were from human keyboards. The screen lit, and some of the pads glowed faintly.

Yilayil script flowed across the screen. With difficulty he made out some of the words, then he shook his head. He'd make no sense out of this system. He closed it down again.

Saba said, "First, tell me, please. What did you hear? I mean last night."

"Voices. Whistles, trills, chants, and a lot of percussives that I could not identify. I heard you speak to someone. I only caught a few words, something about you being ill. That was the most distinct voice. Then there was just the chanting, on and on and on, until it either ended or your battery ran low: it faded suddenly into quiet, then silence. I tried to raise you, couldn't, so I reported to Irina, and moved in myself to check things out."

Saba opened her eyes. "The Yilayil are not..." She paused, then frowned slightly. "That's not true. They *are* the predominant culture, and all others are shaped to them, but the drive to conformity is not engendered by them merely for the sake of dominance. The issues behind ti[*trill*]kee are a response to yet another, greater ..." Her voice suspended, and once again her gaze went diffuse.

This time the reverie, or whatever it was, lasted far longer.

Gordon drove his teeth into his lip, fighting for patience. He sat at her side, waiting, and again she blinked and focused on him.

After a few seconds, he prompted, "There is someone else behind the Yilayil ti[*trill*]kee?"

Saba breathed in and out, her brow furrowed in perplexity. Then she said slowly, "The harmony is Yilayil, but it is an attempt to understand the incomprehensible. Almost, I wish to say, the—the ineffable, except that carries spiritual connotations, does it not? And these *are* finite beings, that is ones with corporeal existence, I am quite sure of that—though as yet I am sure of little else concerning them."

"So there is yet another race here, is that it?" Gordon said.

"Yes, but they exist outside of time."

"Impossible."

She shook her head slightly. "It's true. I don't know how, but I know this much: they knew I was coming. They gave me Zhot, and Rilla, and the Virigu I know. The carving out front was waiting for me. From each I have learned many things. Rilla has looked out for my comfort. I believe it is she who programmed my room, turned on my computer. The Virigu, I have come to realize, are in some ways empaths. They sense emotions, and perhaps—in some way—patterns of thought."

Gordon nodded. "Go on."

"As for Zhot, he seems to be the prime communicator.He kept trying to get me to 'taste color' and the like, at the same time as I had to learn to think outside temporal limitations. It's, oh, a little like Zen, I think. Koans of synesthesia, to break apart the unity of the sense that bars the time sense. Perhaps the entities even knew that music would be the metaphor, the catalyst, for understanding... It sounds egocentric, doesn't it, to surmise that music has developed here in preparation for my coming?"

"I can believe anything, if you present enough proof," Gordon said with care.

Her slim, dark fingers pressed against his wrist. "Ah, my anchor, my link to reality." She laughed soundlessly. "Here's what I can discern. These entities are not in constant communication with the House of Knowledge, or the beings in it. That would overpower them, remove their free will."

"How do you perceive them, then?"

"Voices, in the mind—through the music," Saba said.

"I heard nothing like that," Gordon said.

She looked at him. "Did you understand everything you heard? Did you taste and feel the music? Did you***?" She trilled a Yilayil term that he did not comprehend at all.

"One of the temporal verbs?" he guessed.

She nodded. "It takes all the senses to comprehend the deepest symbols, and when one is able to do that, one can— partially—hear *them*."

"And so?" he prompted.

"And there is some event nigh, something important. We are crucial to it."

Gordon thought of the disappearance of the First Team. He did not like what he was hearing. All the clues added up to something drastic—like human sacrifice. And Saba was lying, weak and enervated, in the midst of what might be the enemy.

Gordon repressed a sigh.

His communicator pulsed him then, and he clicked it on. "Ashe here."

"They are returned," Irina's voice filled the room. "All of them. They are all going to Ross and Eveleen's room."

Saba nodded. "Go. I'll be safe enough."

Gordon nodded, reaching to unclip her com. She pointed to the recharger, and he slid it in, and saw the red light come on. There were still charges left in it, he saw with relief. Not many, but enough.

Then he got to his feet, hesitating.

"I will be all right," she said.

"I'd feel better if you could contact me," he said, pointing to the recharging com. "Shall I leave you mine?"

"No," she said. "You're the leader, you must have one. I know I am safe, for now. I need sleep."

Gordon nodded, thinking that if need be he could break in again—and this time bring Ross and the other men.

Sneaking out of the House of Knowledge was strangely easy. He attributed it to the daylight hours—and once he was outside, he did not need to use care.

Once he was outside of the House boundaries, he moved rapidly across to the Nurayil dorm, taking care not to confront anyone who would demand precedence.

The rain kept him cool, though he was thoroughly soaked by the time he reached the dorm.

Inside Ross and Eveleen's chamber, he found everyone on the team—that is, everyone except Irina. They all sat against the walls, looking tired and thin. Everyone had water at hand, and he smelled the cream-cheese-and-lemon odor of the protein food they all seemed to crave.

Viktor was also there. Gordon saw him and sighed with relief.

"False alarm, then?" he asked.

Misha gave him a wry grin. "Not," he said, "even remotely true. We have much to report."

"How's Saba? Do we need to do something?" Eveleen asked, as always quick in her concern for others.

"I found her. She's still there, but she insists she's safe. I'll give you a report on what she said after you explain." He waved a hand at Misha, but he turned to survey them all.

"We think we've solved the mystery of the First Team," Ross said.

"What's this?" Gordon drew in a deep breath, trying to marshal his thoughts.

"The flyers," Eveleen spoke now, her eyes tired but alert. "They speak a kind of Russian. They were fixated on us because they recognized us, sort of, but humans have turned into mythic figures for them."

Gordon felt as if someone had hit him in the head. He sat down, took a long drink of water, then he said, "Go ahead. Talk."

"They took Viktor to *talk* to," Eveleen said. "Viktor heard it all while we were traveling to get him."

The Russian nodded, his eyes exhausted.

"They told it in stories. They live in primitive surroundings, but in recognizable tree huts. They lost technology, somehow, when they gained the wings—"

"Gained wings?" Gordon cut in. "Is that what you're trying to tell me? They all just…dropped everything and sprouted wings?"

"That's not clear," Ross said. "They told it in a form of poetry, apparently." He looked over at Viktor, who nodded again. "Their first generation is recognizable—by the names—as our First Team. We still don't know how or why they abandoned all their gear, and the mission, and ran off. How they got to the island isn't clear, and when the wings happened isn't either."

"Babies," Viktor said. "Their babies flew."

"And they stayed there, and built a new culture," Eveleen added. "They seem quite happy—exuberant, even. They really wanted us to stay with them, but when we said we had to go they were willing to let us leave."

"They're blue," Ross added. "Sky-colored. The First Team are the ancestors of our flyers down the timeline!"

"So they all—what, mutated? That's nonsense. Genetics doesn't work that way."

"Of course not," Vera cut in, her voice uncertain. "This is what Irina and I have recently discovered, and what Ross tells us about these Jecc corroborates it. From separate evidence, Irina found out that the Moova practice infanticide—culling out genetic defects. Not by choice. See, a week or two ago, her employer was desolate. The grief was the more profound because it was apparently the third one in the family in a year. At first we thought it was illness, but apparently nobody suffers illness. There are no doctors—as least among the Moova. But I don't think there are any for the other races either."

"We're sick," Gordon pointed out the obvious.

Vera nodded, her face troubled. "We will come to that. First, last week. We did not report this, as we had no real evidence, only our guesses. But we decided that desperate measures require quick action. Irina told me to decoy the Moova, and she did some excavating on their computing system, and found out that they, too, have altered from their original form, but it is more slow. They try desperately to halt the changes through this practice. What seems to be happening to the races here is genetic manipulation, on an impossible scale."

"Genetic manipulation?" Gordon repeated.

Ross laughed, a sardonic, unpleasant laugh, quite unlike his usual. "Oh, but you haven't figured out the good part yet. What it *means*."

Eveleen's brown eyes were huge now, and strained. "What it means is, this is what's happening to *us*."

Chapter Twenty-Six

Ross watched the news impact Gordon Ashe. As usual, the archaeologist showed little reaction other than the narrowing of his blue eyes and a tightening of his shoulders. Then he looked up, his mouth grim. "Where's Irina?"

Eyes turned to Vera, who shrugged. "Probably either finishing her work or else following up on something."

"Following up on what?"

Vera shrugged again. "She does not always talk about what she's working on ... She finished entering Pavel's notebook, and a couple of evenings she sneaked out—"

"Wanted Svetlana's data," Misha interrupted. "I gave her a disk containing what was pertinent to us."

"So is she preparing a report for us all, then?" Gordon prompted.

"I don't know," Vera said. "All I know is, she has been gone some evenings, verifying data was all she said. I asked her twice. More than that, she ignores the question." Vera gave a rueful smile. "As for me, I confess most evenings I am asleep within moments after we leave here. I am hungry very much, I want protein, I need sleep very much." She winced, and shrugged again, this time rolling her shoulders as if her back itched. "Do you think if we do not leave soon we're going to sprout wings?"

Misha laughed.

"No," Viktor said. "Our bones, they are losing mass."

That doused Misha's humor like water on a fire.

"None of us have much body fat left," Eveleen observed, then she turned to Vera. "You two have analyzed all our food. Is that cheesecake stuff we all seem to want made out of protein?"

"Yes," Vera said.

"Fueling molecular changes," Gordon said. "Our metabolisms are working in overdrive. Some of the malaise is probably due to just that." He frowned slightly, then turned to Viktor. "What other data did Irina need for verifying?"

"My maps," Viktor said. "Needs for final report."

Gordon looked down at his hands, then up. "The mission has been canceled. Zina is not going to authorize a trip back to the First Team's time." He did not look Misha's way.

Ross glanced at the blond Russian, who smiled derisively.

I'll bet anything he's already tried to make a jump on his own, Ross thought, and tried not to let it annoy him. He didn't know for certain, and anyway, the Russian had obviously been denied access to the machinery that set the time jumps—to the past.

"So let's end it," Gordon finished. "Let's all put in a regular day—a last data gathering—while I work on getting Saba out, and then we're all out of here."

"Sounds good to me," Ross said.

"I am ready," Vera added, rolling her eyes.

Misha said nothing.

Gordon got to his feet as he unhooked his communicator from his belt. "Saba doesn't answer," he said a moment later, then, as he started out the door, Ross heard his voice. "Irina? Listen, here's the latest…"

"Anything else?" Ross said when the others had not moved. He looked at Vera, who bit her lip, but his question was really for Misha.

"Good night," Misha said, and he went out. Viktor followed, sending a brief grin over his shoulder.

Vera left in silence.

Saba took her medicine, then went down to the refectory to eat something. When that was done, she went directly to the chamber where Zhot had given his lessons—and there she found Rilla and Virigu waiting, alone, obviously for her.

In Yilayil, Saba said, "I must talk about what I experienced last night, for I have many questions."

Rilla said, "We are here, by your desire."

Saba looked at Virigu, and Rilla forestalled her by saying, "A question about Virigu's knowledge of our motives and desires is best addressed to me, for just as your people do not go before others without garments to conceal the outer being, so the Virigu do not talk of what is not spoken aloud."

Saba parsed that, thinking: So telepathy is a taboo? A brief spark of humor lit her mind, instantly extinguished. She hoped that Virigu did not hear it, even as she acknowledged to herself that one culture's (or race's) taboos almost invariably seem funny to another that does not share them.

Saba said, "I wish to understand what I saw/sensed/experienced last night."

She paused, considering the sudden flowering of sensory images when she used the weighted verb. It had *tasted*. *Felt*. She had *seen* it as well.

"You joined the Great Dance," Rilla said. "You have found ti[*trill*]kee, and so you are a part of the dance. You must be a part of the dance," she added.

Saba said carefully, "This is why the carving of myself outside the House of Knowledge?" The verb for *carving* tasted of destruction and distortion. Strange.

"Carving?" Rilla repeated, then she made a gesture of negation. "It is always there. It grows there."

"Grows," Saba repeated. "You mean, it's a living tree? Or was?" she amended, remembering that there were no branches on it, no leaves. The carving was a tall pole, the image at the top, recalling totems of various Earth cultures—except where those were rough, this one was remarkably smooth and polished, an almost photographic representation of her own face.

Rilla glanced at Virigu, who said something in a low murmur, and then she faced Saba. "It is not done, to take the trees, kill them, and make them into semblances of something else."

Saba said, "But it was done in the past, right?"

Again Rilla made a gesture of negation. "It is there, always. For all beings to see. For you to come and find your place."

"So you are saying that it grew there, for us to find?"

Virigu and Rilla agreed.

Saba shivered. Again she felt that weird tug at her brain, as if from inside. It wasn't as if someone tried to access her mind—like a computer accessing a disk. It was as if a planet-sized vastness waited outside a small bubble, trying to ...

The image would not come; she felt vertigo. Even searching for a mental verb did not work, because each one was wrong.

She did yoga breathing, then said, "Who are the ... entities/outside/time—" Again, a flash of synesthetic experience almost disoriented her. "There is someone in this world besides the races we see, is there not?"

"Yes," Rilla said. "It requires us all to hear/taste/see/touch/ experience, it is important."

This time it was Rilla's verb that sent the wash of synesthesia through Saba.

"Why is it important?" Saba asked. "I too feel it. I need to know why this is important."

"Zhot tells us," Virigu said, "that you are the one who hear/taste/see/touch/experiences the most. All of us are a part, but you translate it for the temporal mind."

"I." Saba knew then that what she had experienced was no dream, despite fever—despite physical debilitation. It was real, and the metaphor of music was the key. For some reason, her own unique capabilities, her lifelong studies of symbol in relation to sound and sense, had made some kind of limited breakthrough. And she was not the only one who felt the sense of urgency.

"Tonight, I will listen again," she promised. "But where is Zhot?"

"There is sun," Rilla explained.

Even considering all the strange synesthetic experiences associated with terms and verbs, this was a non sequitur.

"I do not understand."

"His people, Zhot more rapidly, they become plants," Rilla explained. "It is his race's great change. Your people, they change the more rapidly, become those-who-fly-and-sing-myth." She waved to the west.

A bomb seemed to go off behind Saba's eyes. "Changes. Do all the races change?"

Virigu and Rilla both made gestures of agreement.

Rilla said, "It must be swift, so Zhot says. Until you hear, he hears best. It is because your metabolism fights the alterations, and thus you are made very ill."

Virigu again opened her long, thin fingers in a gesture of concurrence, and Saba thought immediately of her genetic makeup. Was it because of the sickle-cell gene? No way of knowing without tests. The immediate priority was to let the others know—and to get herself away, as soon as possible.

She thought again of the impending deadline. Whatever had happened to the First Team might be happening to them—and apparently it did not necessarily involve death, but mutation.

Yet the Yilayil did kill. Thinking of the Russian biologist, Saba said, "I have not dared to ask. Those who are buried in the Field-of-Vagabonds. They have been deprived-of-life. Why? For not wishing to attain ti[*trill*]kee?"

"This data can be found in the Knowledge bank," Rilla said.

"Come," Virigu spoke, rising. "We must view the records."

Rilla looked at her. Saba tasted surprise, then wondered how she had done so. Then she mentally gave herself a shake. It did not matter how, right now, or even why. She was on a data search; at last the puzzle pieces were coming together.

But the picture was not clear yet.

She followed the other two into the great computer room, and they settled around one of the terminals. None of the other beings in the room paid them any attention, as always. Though Saba had experienced great change, that apparently did not affect life in the rest of the House.

She sat, and waves of darkness washed through her consciousness, receding. She would not faint; adrenaline was serving her for now. When they finished this session, she must report to Gordon, then sleep, for she had to be physically ready for the great dance that night.

Thinking these things over, she did not watch what Virigu did to the computer, thus when she looked up at the screen and saw a close-up of one of the beings nicknamed "Baldies" by Terran Project agents, she felt shock zap through her nerves.

Virigu looked at her, her attitude one of concern, but then she turned back to the screen and her chitinous fingers blurred rapidly over the pads.

In silence the three of them looked at an ancient record—the spaceport, Saba realized. Ships of all kinds sat on the vast field, some lifting, some arriving. The reverberations of power seemed to vibrate through the screen as a great vessel lowered slowly, on a blue-white column of fierce light, to the field.

A voice spoke in a staccato language, but Virigu damped that, and brought up the Yilayil translation.

At once Saba realized she was going to have trouble with the Yilayil language. She wondered, as she grappled with meaning, if this was a very old record—if Yilayil had evolved like human languages do. Of course it would, she thought, if the culture has changed. And the Yilayil in the House would see no necessity of changing it—any more than a modern scholar of literature would change Shakespeare, or the epics of Anglo-Saxon. A scholar would have learned the early forms of the language, just as a human scholar did.

So she did not understand everything she heard, but the visual record made it clear enough: the Baldies' globe ships were among those that arrived, but suddenly they arrived in great force, and the visual record changed rapidly as it recorded a horrifically devastating war.

Great areas of the planet's islands were laid waste as the Baldies and their enemies—in this instance a race that looked like ambulatory turtles—fought viciously.

And then the Yilayil appeared, armed with some kind of energy weapons, and began killing both combatants in the war. The narrator did not give any reason for the war (as far as Saba was able to comprehend). It was enough that they were killing anyone and anything in their way.

It was not the Yilayil who ended the war; the narrator said, in flowery language, that the Yilayil were able to halt the ending of life so that the *** could alter the destroyers into harmless form.

And the rapid flow of images showed Baldies metamorphosing into sea life, and vanishing into the great waters, and the other beings altered into flying insects that settled on the mountaintops above the cloud layers.

The record ended, and Saba watched the blank screen, her mind struggling to grasp all she had heard—and consider the consequences. First, the *** term: the closest she could come in translating it was non-ambulatory-life, singular.

Something—some one thing—had caused the Baldies and the turtle-people to mutate into utterly different lifeforms. It apparently had taken many generations; Saba had not heard numbers, or had not understood them if they were mentioned.

But something, some one being, had that power. And this was the same being—or its descendant?—that was changing human beings.

"Field-of-Vagabonds," Rilla said. "Is for those who destroy life. When the Yilayil see them, they end those lives before they can recommence the destruction of before."

And suddenly Saba realized what this implied: that that poor Russian biologist, who emerged so suddenly from the jungle, probably carrying some kind of scientific tool in hand, had been mistaken for a Baldy on the attack. And since he'd not been able to explain himself, the Yilayil had taken summary action.

Now it made sense, in a weird way. To other races, the humans *would* look like Baldies. The absence or presence of hair might be too subtle a difference for other races to see; meanwhile, the similarities were strong. The Baldies stood upright, had the same number of limbs as humans, their coloring could be considered similar. They wore clothing. They carried weapons.

The Yilayil might still have assumed that the First Team—and the present team—were Baldies, and though they spoke Yilayil, lived peaceful lives, and professed to wish to attain ti[*trill*]kee, the genetic alteration was vastly speeded up—in self-protection.

But it wasn't the Yilayil who caused that, it was this mysterious ***.

They think we're Baldies, she thought as she rose slowly from her seat. A salutory realization!

What do we really know about the Baldies?

Her mind went on its relentless drive to extrapolate to the logical conclusion.

We know they flew about in these futuristic globe ships— and that they have the capability to move about in time through the gates. They are capable of extreme violence.

This, and their humanoid form, would lead anyone to conclude that the Baldies were, in fact, human beings from the future.

Her heart and spirit wished to reject that image utterly, but she forced herself to examine the evidence. What was the likelihood of humanoid races evolving on other worlds? A glance at Rilla—even Virigu—showed that similarities were certainly possible. And biologists argued for bilateral construction and other aspects of Earth life-forms being logical progressions in the chain of evolution.

But she did not want humanity to become Baldies—at least, not like the glimpse they'd had of Baldies so far. Only, was that the whole picture? The Baldies could in fact be far different than those strange beings who appeared and destroyed, as thoughtlessly as humans of the past had wiped out peoples of other races, and today wiped out various species of creatures.

She grappled for a time with vast questions of ethics and morality, and then abandoned them. There was not enough evidence. The question of the Baldies' origin was for some other team to discover—some data analysts, who had the time and resources to plumb the question with the thoroughness it demanded.

Right now she had immediate concerns—ones that must be reported to Gordon, before she prepared herself for the night's work.

She said to Rilla and Virigu, "I must rest now. I thank you for this session."

They both nodded, and moved away.

She retreated to her room, grabbed her communicator, and tapped out the code for Gordon.

He connected a moment later.

"Gordon," she said without preamble—appreciating, as she always did, that she could talk to him that way. "We are being modified at a cellular level."

"I know that," he said. "I have a report for you on the flyers, who are our First Team."

"I just found that out as well," she said, "though I haven't had a chance to think it through. But here's a poser for you: the reason all this is happening to us is because every being on this planet, including the mystery being, thinks that we are Baldies."

Silence, then laughter. It was the kind of poignantly painful laughter that Saba immediately recognized, for her own reaction had been the same.

"Well," he said. "Interesting indeed. Quite sobering."

Saba said, smiling, "I thought you'd see it that way. Now, shall I report first, or shall you?"

"Go ahead," he said, and they took turns summing up the day's findings.

CHAPTER TWENTY-SEVEN

As Eveleen made her way slowly out of her dreams the next morning, she became aware of a sense of change—of portent, almost before she opened her eyes.

It was a good feeling of portent, that much she was aware of.

When she did open her eyes, it was to see the familiar rounded, bare walls of their Nurayil dorm cell. She turned on her side, listening to the faint scrunchings the futon material made, and she sniffed the familiar dusty-laundry-room smell.

No more, she thought. Then it struck her what the portent was: they did not have to go to work. It no longer mattered. They were going to go *home*.

She laughed. Her ever-present thirst no longer mattered, nor did the weird appetite for protein. Or the headache, or the joint-ache. Home—soon, to fresh strawberries, and luxurious baths, and sanity. Home.

Ross stepped out of the fresher just then, and smiled when he saw her smiling. "Good dream?" he asked.

"No. Good wakening," she said, getting up slowly. "Shall we bother rolling this stupid mat? Oh, Ross, I am so glad we're going home. I hope Gordon got Saba already, because—"

A tapping at the door interrupted her.

"You get that, would you?" Eveleen suggested. "I'll go clean up."

She walked into the fresher, enjoying for the first time in what seemed an eternity the strange sensation of passing through the gunk that felt like plastic wrap. Never again, she thought as she stepped through, and never again, she chortled happily as she shoved her clothing through.

From the outer room she heard excited voices, but no sense of alarm accompanied them, for she recognized the high one as Vera. Vera always sounded like that.

She fingered her hair into a braid, then pinned it up off her neck; the walk through the jungle would be hot, if this day was as sunny as the one previous had been.

Stepping into the room, she saw a brief tableau: Ross standing head bowed, hands on his hips. That posture sent a pang of warning through Eveleen.

She turned to Vera, whose hands were spread wide, her round face haggard—as though she hadn't slept.

"Everywhere," Vera said, her accent very strong. "Everywhere I could think. Each Moova house. Each place we have found food. I hide from Yilayil—I do everything. No Irina."

"What?"

It sounded like someone else's voice. Eveleen grabbed her middle, which cramped suddenly. "What? Don't tell me Irina is missing."

"I won't if you don't want me to," Ross said with bleak humor, "but the fact is, she hasn't turned up—not all day yesterday, or, what is more important, last night."

"Gordon," Eveleen said, thinking rapidly. "He was talking to her when he left here yesterday morning. Does he know?"

"Yes," Vera said. "I reported to him very late last night, when I went to sleep. He was not worried—said she was probably following up on some details. So I did not worry either. But she never came back."

Eveleen nodded. "Did she show up at her job?"

"I do not know that, for we work for different Moova. She was not at our meeting place at midday, but sometimes she would not join me because she was busy. I did not really worry at that point."

"No Moova said anything to you?"

Vera shook her head. "That is not their way. We serve, they take no further interest in us."

Ross said, "I still am inclined not to be too alarmed. You said she sometimes takes off to do her data verification on her own, right?"

"It is true," Vera said, drawing in a deep breath, which she let out in a sigh. "She does not always tell me what she is working on. But this is the first time she did not return at night."

Ross glanced at Eveleen, who shook her head slightly. Eveleen realized they'd both had the same thought; Irina might have gone to see Misha—for whatever reason. But they weren't going to bring *that* one up without more evidence.

"She might even have gone out to see the Jecc place," Ross said slowly. "For the final report."

Eveleen said, trying for lightness, "Good. Then you won't have to write one!"

"Oh, won't I," Ross fired back grimly. "You watch. Milliard and Kelgarries will expect breath-to-breath detail, in triplicate."

Now Eveleen looked from Vera to Ross. "Should we contact Viktor and Misha?" She suggested with what she hoped was delicacy."

"I did," Vera said, for once not smiling. "They do not know where she is. Misha has said they will search the jungle."

Eveleen felt a spurt of worry. So Irina—wherever she was—was *not* with Misha. A romantic tryst—Irina going to spend time with Misha—would have been simple, despite the emotional fallout for poor Vera and her unrequited crush.

"Why she'd go there makes no sense," Ross said.

"To check on the positions of the First Team's camps," Eveleen said. "She always seems to need to see everything herself."

Vera looked wry. "This is true. She thinks no one observes properly." She sighed again. "Viktor is going to check the Field-of-Vagabonds in case she needed to see the biologist's grave for some reason, and Misha said that after he visits the camps, if she's still missing, he would see if he could track the movement of the ancient transport system."

"She knew about that?" Eveleen asked.

"Oh, yes, Viktor showed her when he gave her his maps. She had to see everything, she said, and so he showed her everything he could think of."

Eveleen looked up at Ross, feeling sick inside. "All I can think of is those disappearances. We're not quite to Disappearance Day—"

"But who says that it has to match up exactly with Katarina's? We already know that the others disappeared at different times than she did," Ross finished, his expression pained.

"But *after*," Vera said, her tone hopeful, as she turned from Eveleen to Ross. "All of them. After Katarina. Not before."

"We still do not know why they disappeared so abruptly, though," Ross said softly. "We know what happened to them after. But not what made them drop everything and vanish."

Eveleen asked, afraid she knew the answer. "Viktor thought also to check—"

Vera pressed her lips together. "Yes."

Eveleen finished the statement in her mind: check to see if there are any fresh graves at the Field-of-Vagabonds out loud, she asked, "So what should we do? Search as well?"

Vera said, "Gordon was very specific. He said to meet here, and no one to go anywhere, after I checked my job and hers. This I have just done. She is not there."

As an afterthought, Vera unslung her carryall and pulled out some food.

"I'm not hungry," Eveleen said, sitting down against the wall. She pressed her arms against her middle and brought her knees up.

"We have to eat," Ross said.

Vera nodded. "Must keep up our strength."

Eveleen forced herself to take a few bites, but she kept looking from one to the other, wondering if they were going to disappear next. A firestorm of emotions burned through her. Though she could not claim to have become friends with Irina—not in any sense of the word—she respected the woman as a colleague and as a very fine agent. She did not want her to have been killed, but she also did not want to find out that some—unnamed, unknown—*thing* had somehow taken over her brain and forced her to, what, run to the island of the flyers?

"The flyers," she whispered. "Then maybe that's the next place to check—and we're the ones to check it."

Vera hesitated, then said, "I promised Gordon. We must do this plan only if he concurs. Too many of us missing—" She gave a shrug. "Then the others must search for us."

Unspoken was the implication that the unnamed something would take *them* over as well.

Eveleen gritted her teeth, wondering how she could have felt so wonderful on waking.

Vera's fingers trembled as she unhooked her com from her belt. She tabbed the control, then uttered a Russian curse. "He is using his unit," she said. "We must wait."

"I'll prepare our packs," Ross murmured.

Eveleen sat where she was, hugging her arms tightly to herself as Ross moved efficiently around the little chamber, which felt more like a cell every moment. Vera sat down against the opposite wall, and did not speak as she kept tabbing her communicator every minute or so.

Finally—when it seemed to Eveleen that something must happen or she would run out screaming—Vera's face lit with relief, and she said, "Gordon! We think—what? What's that?"

Eveleen clenched her teeth.

Ross froze in the act of hooking a freshly filled canteen to Eveleen's pack.

Vera lowered her communicator and looked blankly at them. "Irina is back," she said.

"'Back'?" Ross repeated, and something in Vera's tone must have triggered an idea, because he snapped his fingers. "She went down the timeline!"

Vera nodded. "And Zina has returned with her. She has called Misha, and Viktor. They are coming, they will be here—Zina wants us to go back at once."

❧ ❧ ❧

Gordon ran up the access tunnel, puffing hard. A sharp pain in his side forced him to slow, but he would not stop, not until he reached Saba's room.

She was not in the great cavern; he would tear the place apart, he vowed, if she was not in her room.

But when he pounded on the door it opened almost immediately—and he found himself staring up into the face of a tall creature looking kind of like a sandy-skinned seal.

From beyond came Saba's voice, a little hoarse, but sane—and amused.

"Gordon, this is Zhot."

Ashe gave the being a nod, and a formal Yilayil greeting.

Zhot replied in kind, then withdrew to a corner. His movements were quick and fluid; disconcerting in so large a creature.

"Zina is here," Gordon said—in English. "We are to leave."

"I can't," Saba said.

Ashe faced Zhot, ready to demand her freedom.

"It's not anyone here," Saba said hastily, before Gordon could speak, she cleared her throat and added in Yilayil, "No one is forcing me to do anything. It is I who must do this. Zhot is here to help me to understand what it is I discovered during the Great Dance."

Gordon gritted his teeth, and when he knew his voice would come out steady, he said—in English again, "Please. Report."

Saba stayed with Yilayil. "I cannot express any of the terms in English. Some you might not comprehend, bear with me. Last night I was more ready for the experience, and I went rested. What I found out is that the other entity that I spoke to you about is in fact real, it seems to either be comprised of, or controlled by, all the plant life on this planet. Undersea, above sea, it's all connected."

"A sentient plant," Gordon repeated—in Yilayil.

"Yes. I still do not perceive how it exists outside of time. I mean, I could understand the past—but the future? Yet this is the reality," Saba said.

"Go on."

Zhot remained motionless, listening.

"It is I who was able to comprehend a portion of the entity, just enough to provide an image for the others. It—they—don't really communicate. It's too large, too vast, too *alien*. But I understood this much: what it's doing to us—to all of us on this planet, every race that has come here—is turning us into plants, or harmless animal helpers for the plants. That is perhaps what the flyers are. We've been breathing spores since we arrived, and that's making the change. Rapidly for humans, though there is great danger, but the entity was afraid that our volatility, our violence, would endanger the planet once again."

"But... Wasn't that the Baldies?" Gordon said the last word in English.

"Perhaps—or perhaps it hears our innate violence. I don't know."

"So we're being mutated—against our will."

"Yes," Saba said calmly.

Gordon struggled with the inherent moral question.

Saba went on—as though reading his mind. "It is just the same as our terraforming planets."

Gordon considered this, and though he still fought against an instinctive revulsion—as if the jungle outside the city had suddenly turned evil—he said, "No, it's more immediate than that." He thought about how he'd carelessly uprooted plants all along his rail route. "We routinely kill plants for food, for other needs, to make this city, even. Not just us, but the non-plant beings."

Zhot spoke for the first time. "The entity heals the planet."

Saba said, "It knows what I am going to do—apparently what I must do, to protect the timeline downstream. I must warn all the races on this world. Even the Yilayil do not quite know the extent of the changes, or why they are occurring. Whatever they decide to do, they have a right to know. And it must be I who tells them. I cannot leave until I do."

Gordon considered this, then nodded slowly.

"All right," he said. "Understood. Keep in, touch. I will inform Zina, and I'll get back to you on the next step. Maybe we can help you with this?"

"Some of it I can do with the Yilayil system," Saba said. "I know how it functions; what I don't know, Virigu can help me with. I will get started right away. But every race must be informed before I can leave. I see that as my own moral responsibility."

Gordon thought about the present timeline—and the flyers, weasel-creatures, and the humanoids, but before he could formulate his thoughts into a question, the com burred against his skin—in the emergency pattern.

He clicked it on. "Ashe here."

Vera's voice blared out, in Russian. "You must come! Irina is back—she went down the timeline—Misha is furious. I think he is going to strangle Irina, for she then *went up the line to the First Team!*"

CHAPTER TWENTY-EIGHT

"So Misha and Viktor are coming here?" Ross fired the question at Vera.

Eveleen felt a wash of sympathy for the tired, confused, frightened woman.

But Vera answered steadily, "Yes. Misha just said so. But they have one stop to make before they reach the transport close by."

Ross snapped his fingers. "Of course. The other spaceport station—that's not far from our terminal site. Misha will probably head right there," Ross guessed. "I would, if I was going to make trouble. The Field-of-Vagabonds is a relatively short hike from that first station." He looked at Eveleen. "Let's meet them there. We might need you to keep something stupid from happening."

Eveleen knew she could prevent Misha from strangling Irina if she had to, but she didn't look forward to trying.

But she kept that to herself. "Right," she said. "Let's."

They left, almost running down the ramp.

Outside, they were astonished and dismayed to see the streets of the Nurayil city impossibly crowded. A huge, spectacular cloud formation loomed to the northwest; the sun, unfortunately, was still in the east, and it bore down with accustomed intensity.

271

Eveleen ignored it as she, Ross, and Vera dodged around the various denizens of the city. All three avoided confrontations, by mutual and unspoken agreement. They deferred to everyone, though Eveleen could have screamed with impatience when a trio of slow-moving oboe-people maneuvered some kind of complicated machine in front of them and set it to inch forward.

They followed it only until they reached a side street that Vera knew. She pointed, and the three of them dashed into the narrow, less crowded alley. Domiciles lined both sides of the alley, Eveleen glanced through an open door to see some of the green beings just about to emerge, two of them humming a kind of dirgelike chant that set Eveleen's nerves on edge.

What was going on?

They skidded around a corner, cutting across Moova territory. Eveleen had only glimpsed this area, and had avoided it; there were many small, conical houses that all looked alike, and they were arranged in intersecting circles, not in orderly rows.

Vera led them through, threading unerringly between houses.

They emerged, panting, in an area that Eveleen recognized. Less traffic clogged the ways here; mostly the buildings were old, some abandoned, their architecture strange.

Past those, into the area that had been abandoned longest. Here, the jungle had encroached steadily. Now they dodged plants and vines and undergrowth, until they reached the ivy-choked hole that led to the ancient transport system.

Another run down the ramp. At least the air was cooler.

They reached the concourse, just as one of the flat cars arrived with a whoosh and a hiss. The foremost figure had yellow hair.

Ross stepped down directly onto the rails, raising a hand. "We'll join you," he said.

Misha waved them on, his gesture casual, but his face in the dim lighting was tight with anger.

Ross flicked a look at Eveleen, and she interpreted it to mean that she and Vera should board first.

"Come on," she murmured.

Vera followed, glancing doubtfully back at Misha, who ignored her. She settled behind Eveleen. A moment later Ross slid in behind her; he'd stayed on the rail in case Misha decided to leave before they could board.

No one spoke. The car jerked forward, moaning and vibrating, then slowed again fairly soon; the journey to the second stop was not a long one.

The car pulled up behind another one. Halfway up the ramp they saw Irina and the Colonel—the latter's square body also considerably thinner. It seemed strange to see her in this environment.

Both paused, waiting.

Misha disembarked with a vaulting leap, then turned to offer his hand to Eveleen. "Are you here as my guide or my guardian?" he asked.

"We're here," she stated, "to stop trouble before it starts."

"More fool you, then," he said, turning his back.

He was in a hot rage, obviously; his boot heels struck the old tiles as he strode up the ramp directly to Irina, who stood a little way from the Colonel, her arms at her sides.

Misha stopped before her and spoke a short sentence in Russian.

Eveleen didn't understand the language, but the meaning was clear: *Why did you do it?*

Irina answered in English, her voice, as always, clear, precise, and emotionless. "I went alone," she said, "because you would not have permitted Svetlana a choice."

Silence. Eveleen watched the impact of that realization hit Misha—that Svetlana had, for whatever reason, chosen to stay in the past.

She had chosen.

The Colonel looked from one to the other, then said, "We will discuss this. Let us go to a more convenient location."

Ross said, "The signal on the corns won't reach here."

"Then we shall go where they will," Zina said calmly.

Everyone followed, even Misha. He walked still with that tight anger, but his eyes were narrowed, their expression unseeing, almost stricken. Eveleen looked away, feeling that even a simple glance was intruding on his privacy. She slipped her hand into Ross's, and he gave her fingers a reassuring squeeze.

Out in the sunlight, Irina took over the lead. She had found a new shortcut. Eveleen recognized none of the streets, but fairly quickly they arrived back at the Nurayil dorm.

Moments later they were in her and Ross's cell—and Gordon knocked almost as soon as they shut the door.

"Saba?" Eveleen asked.

"I have lots to report," Gordon said. "But it can wait," he added, frowning as he looked round at them. A little louder he said, "Let's sit down, shall we?"

Irina remained standing. Everyone's attention shifted to her.

"As soon as I read the notebooks," she said, "I knew what had happened. I knew that it was I who effected the disappearance. It had to be so. I knew that if I told any of you, then Misha would try to stop me, or to go himself, and he would not consider the timeline, or the consequences."

Eveleen glanced at Misha, who just shrugged.

Irina went on, "I prepared my evidence, and presented it to Gordon."

At that Misha's head came up sharply. "You *knew*, then."

"Yes. We discussed this yesterday morning. I also understood her reasons for keeping her mission a secret until it was completed. Go on, Irina, give them all the details."

Irina sighed, leaning back against the wall as if her energy had abruptly drained. "What was needed were the physical tests," she said. "So I went forward and reported. We needed Valentin and Elizaveta for that; I went back to the First Team and found Katarina, and explained." Her voice suddenly went uneven. She pressed her lips together, hard, then continued, her voice harshening.

"Katarina understood. Together we went forward to the present-day timeline, and there Valentin and Elizaveta performed tests on us. The key one was bone density. The other molecular in nature. I don't understand it even now, but there is this to know: the spore interaction on the molecular level is so subtle that we do not really have instruments to measure it. But the fact is that Katarina's bone density was so dangerously altered that there was no returning. The changes had gone too far. Even removal from the spores would not restore the team to health. The changes were such that any of the First Team who returned would be forever crippled—if they survived long enough to shed the effect of the spores."

"Then we're doomed as well," Eveleen said, not even thinking. Horror seized her.

Irina glanced at her, compassion clear in her gaze. Tears gleamed along her lower lids, but she went on, "No. For they tested me as well. Our bone density is not yet at this danger point. For this we either have Vera to thank—"

Eyes turned Vera's way.

Irina said, "It is she who took responsibility for the food analysis. When we all began to sicken, the headache and joint-ache required calcium, or as near as we could find, this she decided, and she found the foods that would provide the supplement. That is in the cheese dish we all came to rely on, for it also carried a complex protein that again slowed the damage."

Zina spoke now, for the first time. "Valentin does not wish to rob Vera of credit that is due her, but there is the possibility that the spores affecting us are different than those that affected Katarina and the First Team."

Irina sighed again, a shuddering sigh that seemed completely uncharacteristic, and she said, "So when this news was complete—last night—Katarina and I went back. I knew where most were, from Viktor's findings, and Katarina knew the rest. Together we found each team member, and told them. They left their things exactly as we found them. She did not go back to her archive, but left it buried as she had when we first went forward. I showed them the transport, and they went as a group to the island to await the changes there. It was peaceful, it was not bad. They knew that they would have children. They knew that their children would fly. And they knew that someday, their descendants would see us."

Silence met this news.

Irina swiped at her eyes, then she turned to Misha. "You are not the only one to leave someone important. Katarina and I, we were in the university together. We served two missions together. We were close—we were sisters—" Her voice suspended, and she shook her head, hard.

No one spoke.

Irina then dug into her pocket. "As for Svetlana, she chose to go to the island. She did write to you: I brought it with me, so there would be no alteration in time. Here it is."

She handed Misha a paper. He took it, then thrust it into a pocket in his shirt.

Zina said, "Valentin urges us to leave now. He says daily the damage does worsen, and he does not know when the point of nonrecovery would be, but does not want to risk finding out after the fact."

Gordon stepped forward then. "It is time for my report. You probably saw the mass movements toward the House of Knowledge?"

"Is that what's going on?" Ross asked. "All we know is, everyone who could get in our way was out on the streets, just when we were trying to hurry." He cast an amused glance at Misha, who gave him a sardonic smile. Misha's eyes, though, were still somber.

"There is a mass meeting being held right now, for everyone who can cram into the Yilayil caverns. Basically the word is what we already figured out, but not the scale. Apparently the key sentience on this planet is the plant life, a vast interconnected awareness that is trying to heal itself by altering us. It's been trying for centuries to communicate; the Yilayil language and music kept evolving in the direction needed, but none of them, for whatever reason, could make the mental leap outside of time and sensory awareness that it required for even as limited a contact as Saba made last night. A being named Zhot was the closest, but he had only reached the awareness of this other entity.

A Virigu, and some of the Yilayil as well. They knew of the entity, but had never been able to communicate."

"And Saba did?" Eveleen asked.

"Yes," Gordon said. "She made the breakthrough. Her musical sense, apparently, was the last link needed, the catalyst. She feels that she is obligated to inform every being on the planet about the genetic alterations. What they do is up to them."

Irina nodded slowly. After a moment, Zina opened her hands. "It is right," she said.

No one else spoke.

"So what can we do to speed it along?" Ross asked. "About all I can contact is the Jecc."

"And I the Moova," Vera chimed in.

Gordon nodded. "Do it. The rest of us will remain here and stay in contact. Saba's colleagues in the House are telling those who came in person. Saba and one of their computer experts are busy on the communications system, letting everyone else know. They should be done about the time we finish here, for it's enough to let each enclave and race know, and spread the news in the way they think best."

Ross turned to Eveleen, who felt adrenaline—the old call for action—suffuse her body. With a clear goal, she found she could move again.

Once more they found themselves following their customary route to the transport station, but once they reached it, not surprisingly they found it completely empty. Even the Virigu was gone; the place was like a vast hangar, completely deserted.

"Jecc city," Ross said. "Up to it?"

"Of course," she replied.

They scarcely spoke as they made their way once again to the ancient transport. Eveleen realized they probably could have taken one of the rail-skimmers—but even after all this time working on them, they never had learned how to operate them. The rail-skimmers might not even reach the Jecc city.

The flat cars whooshed them speedily to the southernmost point of the island. Together she and Ross walked up to the Jecc caves, hand in hand.

They were soon sighted, and a swarm of Jecc came running out to surround them:

At first Eveleen felt a twinge of alarm; too late she realized that the Jecc might consider them interlopers or even enemies.

But the tweets and calls as the Jecc tumbled about Ross reassured her. They largely ignored her—all their attention was on Ross.

At one point one of them must have put a question, for Ross responded in Yilayil, pointing to Eveleen, "My mate."

Shrill tweets rose from all sides. The Jecc obviously found the notion of "mates" an exotic concept.

Eveleen did not try to comprehend all the various Jecc reactions, but Ross seemed to know who to listen to, for again he responded in Yilayil. "Yes, it requires one of each of us to pass on genetic material. One offspring results—rarely two or more—but we can repeat the process, just as you Jecc do..."

Eveleen felt a sense of unreality seize her; the biology lesson lasted until they reached the outer caves.

Here, abruptly, they entered civilization—but for totally different beings.

Beautiful colors were everywhere. The catwalks and pathways, the furnishings, everything was child-sized. Jecc swarmed everywhere, on all levels—for Eveleen saw, tipping her head back, that catwalks and cave tunnels were located at several levels. At the very top, she saw tiny faces peeping timidly down—Jecc children?

Then she lost sight of them as they were led beyond, into an even greater cave. Cool air swirled gently across her face as she gazed up at row on row of great murals painted in realistic, glowing colors all round the stone walls. This was what she had glimpsed from the upper vent—but it was far vaster, and more beautiful, than she had conceived.

Sudden silence brought her attention downward.

The Jecc had settled into rings, with old wrinkly Jecc closer at hand, and others outward in widening circles.

One of the Jecc greeted Ross formally, using all the Yilayil deferences.

Ross said back, "I have come to make certain you were aware of the new people recently discovered."

The old Jecc trilled, "We know of the world-being. We know now why we have changed."

A weird, sighing whistle went through the ranks of Jecc; Eveleen felt hairs prickling on the back of her neck. The emotions caused by the sound were intense—loss, isolation.

"Then you can decide what you want to do," Ross said. "This is why I came."

"What do you do, Ross of Fire Mountain?"

"We have a ship, we will go back to our world," Ross said.

Again a sound swept through the Jecc, this time a susurras of high-voiced whispers.

"We have a ship," the old Jecc said at last. "At Harbeast Teeth Island. It is secret all these generations."

"One ship?" Ross repeated.

Rapidly the Jecc explained—and Eveleen began to understand. That sense of unreality still pervaded her mind.

She seemed to be watching from somewhere else, observing this exchange between two utterly different races, using the language of a third race, to talk about spaceships from the past—a technology not yet attained by Earth civilizations.

Comprehension worked its way slowly into her head. The ship the Jecc had was a kind of shuttle, hoarded against the day when they would return to normal. Apparently they had a great ship up in space, circling around. Eveleen nodded to herself; of course it would be unmolested. The mysterious plant entity only controlled what was on the surface.

How many other races might have motherships circling around in orbit?

No way of knowing.

Suddenly the conversation ceased. Ross turned to Eveleen. "Come on, we're done," he said.

In silence they walked past the ranks, and out of the caves.

Neither spoke until they reached the transport.

"So are they going back home?" Eveleen asked. "I confess I didn't follow it all."

"They don't know," Ross said. "Some want to, some don't. Others want to stay—and a fourth group wants to find another world."

"That same debate must be going on all over the world," Eveleen commented.

Ross sat back. "I don't know why, but the whole damn mess makes me sad."

He activated the control, and the flat car zoomed forward, relieving Eveleen of having to think of anything to say.

"Let's get out of here," Ross said when they reached the Nurayil dorm for the last time, and found everyone gathered—Misha having also just returned from an unnamed errand.

"I am going to need help transporting Saba," Gordon replied, looking relieved that they were safely back. "She's by far the weakest of us all. Her body has—we believe— been resisting the changes, and her immune system is at a dangerously low ebb."

Eveleen watched Ross's face brighten. Now he had orders, impending action—a clear need, one that he could meet, even if it was just to carry a sick woman on a stretcher.

"There's a transport near the House of Knowledge," Misha began.

"Found it," Gordon said. "Everyone needs to get their gear, and meet at the transport near this dorm. Come on, let's move."

Under cover of the sudden springs of conversation, Eveleen heard Misha address Gordon. "So it was a false trail you sent us on—the island, the Field-of-Vagabonds."

"I needed to keep you busy," Gordon said. He hesitated, then added, "You'll have to admit even a needless trip is better than sitting with nothing one can do, counting off the seconds."

"Ah." Misha shrugged. "So you claim empathy as your reason?"

Gordon only laughed. "Go. Get your gear."

Eveleen watched Misha vanish through the open door.

She knew that whatever Svetlana had said in her letter was not going to be shared with anyone; nor would Misha permit anyone to see him reading it. She thought about being separated forever from Ross, and even though the Russians' relationship might not have even remotely been like what she and Ross shared, for the first time, she felt pity for the blond agent.

She kept her thoughts to herself as she packed her few belongings. To her surprise her emotions were mixed at the thought of abandoning forever the little cell.

Ross and she were alone. She was not aware she'd sighed until he said, "You can't be wanting to stay."

"No," she said. "But I hate feeling that I could have done better. That this mission was so strange, so..."

"Nightmarish? Long? Boring?" Ross prompted, looking amused.

"Oh, I don't know," Eveleen said. "Confusing, I guess is the best term. Is it only going to get harder, Ross? Suddenly I feel, well, *old*."

"You're sick. I'm sick. We're going home," he reminded her. "C'mon, help me get our sticker off the door. I hope the next inmate has a better time—"

"If there is one," Eveleen said. "How weird. It could be that we are the ones who caused the evacuation."

"Except we still have three races down the timeline, two of them nothing anyone would want to be," Ross reminded her.

They laid their palms op the screen, then pressed the control that they had learned meant *vacate*.

"Uh oh, we forgot to check our credit rating," Ross joked.

"Oh, I'm sure we had enough for half a ride," Eveleen joked back, trying for lightness.

They kept up the banter as they threaded their way through the crowded street.

This time there was a difference. Unasked, various beings offered them deference. Again and again the other races withdrew, permitting them to go first. No one spoke to them, and expressions were as impossible to read as ever, but somehow their status had changed.

Eveleen was still pondering this when they descended the ramp to find everyone waiting.

Everyone—even Saba, who looked so frail Eveleen felt her heart start pounding. But Saba's dark eyes were clear and smiling, and she held her head at a proud angle as she leaned on Viktor's and Gordon's shoulders.

Together they all rode the last car to the station near the parkland.

Half an hour's hike, through misting rain, and they reached the time apparatus.

Zina stepped forward and worked the controls.

Eveleen watched, waiting impatiently for the doors to open.

Lights flickered on the little console. Zina frowned, and punched the code more carefully.

Impatience turned to alarm.

"What now?" Ross asked, then he cursed under his breath.

For answer, the doors slid open.

And framed there were two Baldies, blasters in hand.

CHAPTER TWENTY-NINE

Quicker than an eye blink, Zina slammed her hand on the door controls and they shut on the Baldies.

She poked at the manual lock, saying over her shoulder, "Fast. Out of here."

Misha led the way.

Gordon picked Saba up; Ross fell in step right behind them, in case Gordon, who was breathing heavily, should falter. Ross glanced down, saw Eveleen at his side.

"They must get that same vertigo right after the transfer," she panted.

Up ahead, Zina turned. "I counted on that." She gave them a faint smile.

Under his breath, Ross said to Eveleen, "She's fast. Give her that."

Eveleen chuckled somewhat breathlessly. "You mean the rest of us were going to stand around like zombies."

From behind came the keening noise of blaster fire.

"They're out," Misha said with mordant humor. "And hunting us."

"Quiet." Zina's word was not loud, but her voice carried command.

No one spoke. Ross's mind roiled with questions—guesses—plans as he plunged along the pathway behind Eveleen.

Viktor took over the lead, and in silence they wound along trails and under hanging ferns, coming to a stop in a deep little grotto.

Gordon bent, and Saba slid to the ground, where she sat with her eyes closed. It was hard to see her expression; the light seemed muted.

Ross blinked, surprised to discover that night was falling.

The rain had ceased, but the sky was covered by a heavy bank of clouds.

Everyone was breathing hard.

Ross said, "If they've got the machine, that means they've got the camp upstream."

Zina gave a tired nod. "It means they might have the ships as well." She turned to Gordon. "Your surmise was my own, that our tampering with the navigational wire must have sent out some kind of signal we were never aware of."

"Where do we go now?" Vera asked. "Back to the city?"

"Then we lead them right to the others, and they'll start shooting everyone," Eveleen protested.

"They will find their way to the city anyway," Zina said. "And they will shoot until they find us. I think we must go ahead, and warn the Yilayil. Now, so they have time to prepare."

Viktor gave a single nod, and plunged into the undergrowth.

A short time later they came to the transport, and both Viktor and Misha checked the area carefully before they emerged from the protective screen of shrubbery and dodged down into the partially overgrown entrance.

"This ought to buy us a few hours," Ross commented as they half skipped, half ran down the steep rampway.

"The lights will draw them," Misha responded.

"Whom do we tell to get the fastest action?" Zina asked.

Saba said, "We must return to the House."

The car was still there from earlier; they all dropped into it, Gordon hovering protectively near Saba. The two of them conferred in quiet voices as everyone else found a seat and leaned back.

Misha worked the controls. The car lurched, then began to pick up speed, pressing Ross back into his seat. He rather enjoyed these things, but he'd always liked roller coasters— the more dangerous the better.

They passed their old station and continued to the House of Knowledge station.

This one, Ross noted with grim surprise, did not seem as dusty and neglected as all the others. Who in that place used it—and why?

Useless to ask now.

When the car had come to a stop, Gordon helped Saba out, and in a group they proceeded up the ramp.

There they found a clean, dry tunnel. At the exit doors, Saba turned. "You'll have to wait," she said. "No one's been permitted inside. Even with all the changes, I don't know what it might mean to break that rule."

Zina said, "We will be much better here. Gordon, go with her. The rest of us will remain here until you return."

Ross promptly dropped his pack to the tiled flooring and sank down with his back to the wall. He pulled out his canteen, took a deep drink, then offered it to Eveleen, who also drank.

Vera sat down on Eveleen's other side, and Viktor beside her. They began to converse in quiet Russian. Zina and Irina had embarked on another conversation, also in Russian. Ross, lifting his head slightly, saw Misha standing at the other end of the tunnel, his back to the group, his body tense. Reading his letter, of course. Ross shook his head, and returned his attention to his immediate surroundings; from time to time, he saw his wife sending covert and compassionate glances Misha's way.

It was not long before Gordon and Saba abruptly returned.

"They know," Gordon said. "And if I understand right, they are prepared."

"Then here our responsibilities end," Zina said. "Let us return to the time-shift apparatus. We have to see if they still hold it."

"We have to take it back," Ross said grimly.

Misha turned around. "You don't," he said with all his old sardonic humor, "want to see what happens?"

"And how can we do that?" Eveleen asked, hands on hips. "I'd as soon not have a ringside seat, especially with blasters providing the special effects."

"No," Ross cut in. "Let me guess: another of these transport stations will give us a perfect view?"

Misha smiled, and Viktor laughed.

"The other tower. The spaceport tower," Misha said. "It was probably a military outpost of some sort. You can see over the entire city from it."

Zina hesitated, then gave a nod. "If it's quick. We'll have a better report, maybe a better understanding of what happened."

Again to the cars, and this time they proceeded farther up the line. Ross realized he was getting a feel for the geography of the transport system; if he was right, the Yilayil city had been much, much bigger in the past.

They disembarked and walked out into an empty street, partially overgrown. All of them used their flashlights, making their way after Misha.

The tower turned out to be one of the ones Ross and Gordon had found in the far future—the tall red one wherein the savage weasel-creatures had built their lair. They had not been able to explore farther.

This time there was an elevator to take them up, silent and slow but still working. Bluish lights flickered in it, faint but still working from some long-term power source.

At the top, there were a number of devices that turned out to be zoom lenses. A central control area with a huge screen above must have been a video linkup of some sort—but age had destroyed that system.

The lenses were manually operated. The one Ross chose had dust and some tiny fungi growing tenaciously in it, but it worked well enough. He could see more clearly down into the dark street than he could with his naked eye. The principle was not infrared—he couldn't figure it out. Everything looked shadowless and curiously flat, but discernible.

"Hey!" Eveleen's voice was sharp. "They're right below us!"

"The spaceport," Zina said. "Of course. They would check there first—"

"What do we do? We haven't any weapons," Vera asked, looking from one to another.

Ross saw his wife in her fighting stance, her face tense but calm. Misha had not moved.

He suddenly looked up. "Watch now." He pointed downward.

Ross pressed his eye to his viewer, in time to see not two Baldies, but a team of ten of them, walking in single file up the empty street, firing at anything that moved. They also shot away any plants in their way, blazing a trail that anyone could follow.

And had.

As Ross watched, the lead Baldy tipped his head back and stared right up at the tower—seemingly at him.

"You think this was *their* tower, long ago?" Eveleen murmured.

No one answered—everyone was watching.

From behind came a group of six tall, four-armed figures, all of them in flaxen robes.

"Yilayil," Saba murmured, easily heard in the silent room.

The lead Baldy swung about, lifting his weapon, but before he could fire, the Yilayil all raised long tubes to their mouths. Ross could see their furred cheeks puff as a cloud of particles that glowed with odd colors streamed out of the tubes; he didn't know if the colors were real, or some effect of the lenses.

The Baldies got off two shots, and two Yilayil collapsed to the street. Then the Baldies stopped firing. Looking around wildly, they slapped at their faces and bodies, tried to run, but moved as though wading through glue. The ground seemed to be sticking to their feet. Involuntary wormlike motions lifted their arms into the air, splayed their fingers, and tipped their heads back. Within a minute, they stood frozen, and horror suffused Ross as he saw thin green tendrils curl out of their ears, mouths, and noses.

He hastily looked away, swallowing rapidly. Whatever had happened, it was no more pleasant a death than the blasters had been.

Zina's voice was flat. "That's enough. Let us retreat."

"Just as well," Ross said tightly, "we don't have to go out there."

Eveleen gave a quick, wincing nod.

They withdrew in ordered haste, glad of the tight air system—for whatever that spore had been that the Yilayil had used might still be permeating the air.

No one spoke on the return—either on the transport ride or during the night hike to the time-transportation apparatus.

Misha and Viktor checked ahead—but they found the transport hut deserted. The rest of the group emerged from the jungle, Gordon still helping Saba, and Zina once again pressed the controls.

And again nothing happened.

Ross felt Eveleen's hand slide into his. It was obvious what had occurred. The Baldies had either changed the codes or else had jammed the apparatus. Either way, unless the team up the timeline figured out what was going on, they were stuck here forever.

"We assume that a signal brought them," Saba said at last. "Why do you think they came?

"To rescue that scoutcraft," Gordon said in a tired voice. "Remember, the globe ship belonged to the Baldies originally."

"Then..." Eveleen said slowly. "Then we are the bad guys here, not the Baldies?"

Silence met this, but Ross sensed everyone's attention turning her way.

They all sat in the dark, forming a semicircle around the transport doors. No one lit a flash—too dangerous a lure.

"Think about it," Eveleen said. "I mean, I'm scared of them, and I know the horrible things they did. But we came here on their ship, and we know that the crews on these globe ships all died. How would we feel to get a signal from one of our craft, and follow it up to find a lot of aliens on it—and our crew gone, presumed dead?"

"They brought the war to us," Ross said.

"We don't know if it was a war. Oh, they seem to be shoot-happy, but then so have we been in the past, and we've always seen ourselves as the good guys."

"So we're the Villains?" Misha's voice came out of the darkness, cool and amused.

"To them we are," Eveleen said, her voice steady. "We don't know anything about the Baldies' motivations. Boris—everyone—thought that the globe was a scoutcraft. That argues that at least some of their missions were not war-related. Their encounters with us have involved their deaths as well as our own."

"So their action on Dominium—the old timeline—was self-defense?" Ross asked.

"No," Gordon said. "That was warfare, all right. But we don't know when those Baldies appeared from. Their cultures might vary as much as ours have. All we really know about these people is that they are hairless humanoids, that they have interstellar travel, that some of their foods can be ingested by us, and that they have time-travel capabilities. We don't know what their grand strategy is, we don't know their motivations, emotions, loyalties, or what they consider threats. Nothing."

Just then a hum filled the air, lights flickered on the transport—and the doors slid open.

In the dim light, Valentin stepped out. "Ah! Did we manage well?" he asked.

Voices talked, laughed, whooped, a spontaneous expression of relief—and release. Neither Gordon nor Zina said anything about maintaining silence as they helped Saba in first.

Ross squashed his primitive but urgent instinct to shove his way forward and make sure he was next. Instead, he waited, and Irina and Vera were sent next; after that he and Eveleen stepped inside.

As soon as the doors closed, Eveleen sighed and leaned against Ross. "I just want to go home," she said.

He tightened his arm around her.

The vertigo seized him then, and a moment later the doors opened. He stumbled out, Eveleen with him, and there, in a lit clearing, were other members of the team. The acrid scent of burned vegetation singed his nose; he sneezed as the doors closed behind him.

"What happened?" he asked, finding Case Renfry standing nearby. "Baldies hit you guys first?"

"Wait," Renfry said, sounding as tired as any of the agents. "We'll brief everyone at once—and we'd better hurry, because more of them might show up at any time."

"I take you to ship." That was Gregori.

Ross and. Eveleen fell in step behind him, letting him lead—and make all the decisions. Suddenly Ross felt exhaustion grip his head, and he forced himself to walk at a smart pace.

Still, it seemed forever until they reached a clearing, and there was the ship. The Baldy ship. With a weird mixture of emotions skittering through him, Ross walked up the ramp and straight to the galley.

The weird mysteries of the universe could wait—first order of business was some hot coffee.

The welcome aroma of fresh brew made him realize someone had been ahead of him here, too; he looked up to see Gordon pointing silently to a row of mugs, just set out, judging from the steam curling up lazily.

Grateful beyond words, Ross grabbed the nearest and slurped, not caring that his tongue scalded. Tears sprang to his eyes, but the coffee made its warm way down inside him, imparting a sense of well-being that he hadn't felt for an eternity.

He was partially aware of the others crowding in behind, and the row of mugs diminished to just one left over.

"Are we all here?" Gordon leaned in the doorway, trying to count heads. The galley was crowded with bodies, but no one seemed to want to move. "Case, why don't you fill us in on what happened?"

"They landed at the space station, luckily," Renfry said. "Elizaveta was over that way doing a last check to make certain we'd collected all our analyzing gear, and saw them come down. She hightailed back here and we shut the ship down so they couldn't get whatever homing device had brought them. Unfortunately, they must have some kind of signal on the time devices, because they found ours, and of course we had the time set to your year. There was no way to warn you."

"Well, they won't be following us back," Irina said, her eyes wide and dark with strain.

Ross frowned. Eveleen was not looking at him. She stared down at that one last mug of coffee, her lips parted.

Ross realized then that someone was missing.

Quick glance—Misha was missing.

Irina said in her precise voice, "Mikhail Petrovich reset the time to the First Team. He said he was going to destroy it when he got there. The Baldies—those the Yilayil don't get—will be trapped back where we were."

Ross whistled. "He went back? To the First Team?"

Irina's nod was short, her face now blank. "With Colonel's permission."

Zina turned to Boris. "We are here, and since the transport is ruined, there is no need for a last equipment run. Let us take off."

Gordon looked at Zina, his face strained. Then he turned to the crew. "You heard. Coffee break is over—strap down in your bunks."

Ross retreated, taking his coffee with him.

Gordon was apparently going to stay in the control cabin, as Ross found himself alone. He climbed into his bunk and gulped the rest of his coffee before strapping in.

A short time later came the unpleasant sensations associated with takeoff, but this time he thoroughly welcomed them. His mood was so good it must have made him get over the effects faster, because as soon as they had reached nullgrav, he unstrapped and launched himself out of the cabin.

He was not the first, though.

He found Irina at the screen, her face turned away, her shoulders hunched, and her hands gripping her arms as she hung in the air, watching the planet dwindle into a tiny point of light.

Finally she said something in Russian, her voice broken, and Ross hastily pushed himself back, glad he had not made any noise.

He found Eveleen at his shoulder—and Gordon.

"What did she say?" Eveleen asked when they reached the rec room.

Gordon winced. "I have lost them," he said slowly. "I have lost them both."

CHAPTER THIRTY

Ross was surprised when Gordon offered to room with Viktor—and Viktor accepted. This left Ross alone, but only for a short time. Eveleen appeared, duffel floating beside her, half an hour later.

She grinned as she tossed her bag in the direction of the bunk. Ross watched it gyrate in midair, then bump gently against the cabin wall as he said, "Not that I'm not glad to see you, but what about Saba?"

"She's the one who needs the most sleep. We just talked, and although she's so invincibly polite I thought we were going to go around and around forever with the 'Whatever you prefer,' no, 'Whatever *you* prefer' routine, I finally got the impression she'd just love to have the cabin to herself so she can sleep, sleep, and then sleep some more." Eveleen wrinkled her nose, and sniffed. "Your sinuses clear? Mine almost are. When I think of those spores…" She mimed a shudder—and since she wasn't holding on, she accidently began spinning gently in the air.

Ross laughed, and grabbed her in a hug.

A little later, he went out in search of food. He was ravenous almost all the time—and he wasn't the only one, he noted.

After he got his meal (and he was determined to eat as wide a variety as possible, if for nothing else but to get rid of the taste of that one food they'd eaten for weeks), he cruised directionlessly.

Hearing voices from the direction of the old study cabin, he paused. There he heard Gordon—and Viktor.

The conversation was a mixture of Russian and English, with an emphasis on the former, but in it Ross heard Misha's name several times—and once the name *Travis Fox*.

It was Gordon talking. Has he finally made his peace with Travis's disappearance? Ross thought. Because one of the scenarios the big brains back at HQ had come up with was that Travis had not suffered any kind of traumatic death, but had chosen deliberately not to return. Gordon had seemed to take this personally—as if he were responsible, as if he had failed the Apache agent.

Now another agent—a part of Gordon's team—had deliberately made the same choice. His motivations were different, but the effect was the same.

Misha had chosen never to return home again.

Misha's choice kept coming back to bother Ross from time to time as the ship days slid measurelessly into one another.

He slept, ate, played games and watched videos. The entertainment stuff brought along had been used minimally on the way out, but on the way back, they all seemed to have the same idea. It wasn't just the lack of a mission to focus on; they were all soul-hungry for scraps of home, even stupid movies. Ross found himself watching action flicks over and over, just to listen to English.

The return trip passed without incident.

They landed, refueled, and no one was waiting to attack them. The globe ship lifted again, obedient to the mysterious tape that unknown minds had designed and programmed, and arrowed them unerringly straight for Earth.

When they landed, it was still winter in Russia—deep winter. The journey back was the same, only in reverse: a truck to the cargo plane, a cargo plane (this time it was heated) back to the landing strip, then a train to St. Petersburg, where they were quarantined until Russian and American scientists had determined that the spores were gone from their bodies. During their time in quarantine they continued to eat voraciously, and their recovery progressed fast. And it was true that Saba had suffered the least alterations; her damage had been to her immune system. About the time that Ross began to feel desperately restless they were released from quarantine.

And Zina came through on her promise of a celebratory tour. They spent a couple of days visiting historic Russian sights. Ross looked at some of those ancient Byzantine mosaics and wall paintings. The strange eyes that gazed down at him from those old paintings somehow reminded him of the Jecc.

What had happened to them? Weird to think that whatever it was had already happened by the time these paintings had been made.

Ross wanted to go home.

He kept his mouth shut. Eveleen clearly appeared delighted with everything; Gordon was interested, and Saba, who still tired quickly, insisted on not missing a single tour. She gazed about her, those intelligent, far-seeing eyes sometimes going diffuse. But she never stopped smiling.

Ross found the baroque palaces and fabulous art collections interesting, but what he really enjoyed was seeing human beings all around him—hearing a human language, even if he couldn't understand it. Normally impatient of crowds, he now welcomed humans all about him.

He did get unexpected reminders, though; seeing children darting about in a snowy park, his thoughts were drawn yet again to the Jecc.

And to the present timeline, which Ross, Gordon, and Renfry had first discovered.

In the present timeline, there were those three races: the flyers, who knew they had to stay. The humanoids, who were probably the Baldies caught back in time. And those Yilayil who—for whatever reason—refused to leave the planet. Or had been forced to stay?

So many unanswered questions! At least for now, he thought one night, after they returned from a ballet. He sat down and opened his laptop, resolving—now that their return to the States was mere hours away—he'd better get started on his report.

The first note that popped up was his surmise about the feathered cats.

Feathered cats.

Who brought the cats? he thought. We never saw any, and we know the two teams never brought any. It argued yet another expedition, for whatever reasons. And the planet's great entity would start altering these little predators into, what, the birds that they hunted?

He closed the laptop, grimacing. No, he'd deal with reports—and memories—when he had to. For now, he was on vacation.

Two days later, they stepped off the plane in Washington, D.C. All around them were people speaking English!

Ross's euphoria lasted well into the expected battery of debriefings, medical and psych tests.

During the interview portion of his reports, he startled himself by frequently resorting to Yilayil to express certain ideas. He realized that one cannot completely shed one's experiences; good and bad, they shape one permanently. In conversations he—and Eveleen, Saba, and Gordon—frequently resorted to whistle/drones for certain words and verbs that really were better expressed in Yilayil.

"It's a habit we're going to have to drop," Ross said to Eveleen as they prepared for bed that night. "Unless we want to be talking a secret code."

"Not in front of other adults," Eveleen said, smiling. "But in case we have kids—so much better than spelling the crucial words out, don't you think?" She grinned in fun.

"Kids," he repeated. "Is that what you want to do?"

"Don't you?" She still smiled, but her brown eyes were serious.

He shrugged, a little helplessly. "I don't know—I hadn't thought. Is this something you want right away?"

Eveleen shook her head. "No. We've invested too much time in our training, and the Project needs us. And the work we do, even when we fail, is good work, I believe. I've been thinking about this a lot, ever since we lifted ship. I think we need to stay with the Project, at least until they don't need us."

Ross considered. "I had such a bad childhood," he said slowly. "I just never considered kids...But I do know how I'd raise them, which would be the opposite of how I was raised. Or not raised," he finished, laughing ruefully.

Eveleen grinned. "Well, we have plenty of time to consider our options." Then she narrowed her eyes in that familiar assessing look, and added, "There *is* something. Did I upset you with the idea of kids?"

"No," he said. "Surprised, yes. I was so used to thinking about us being stuck on Yilayil—and if we were stuck there, would we eventually have mutated offspring..."

"Yes, me too," she murmured.

"It's Misha," Ross said. "And his staying behind—"

Eveleen waited as Ross struggled to articulate.

"I—am I warped somehow? Has my background done something to me—" He shrugged. "This is stupid. I don't know if I can express it, or even if I should."

"Talking things out is good, we agreed on that," Eveleen said. "You can't shock me—I've seen too much in my own single years."

"It's Misha," Ross started again.

"Misha? Go on."

"Not him, but what he did."

"Ah!" Sudden enlightenment widened her eyes. "Is it that you don't think you could have made the same decision, given the same circumstances, only if I were on the First Team instead of Svetlana?"

Ross grimaced. "If I found out you were prisoned there for the rest of your life I don't know if I could willingly join you, knowing there were no options. Does this make me—"

"It doesn't make you anything," she said fiercely. "Stop it. Stop. You can't torture yourself with 'what if questions because the circumstances are not the same. For one thing, both Saba and Gordon are convinced he meant to go back and stay, if he found Svetlana, and further that choice was made from the git-go. I guess they talked a lot about it. Not surprising, considering they both lost agents to past timelines."

"How do they see that?" Ross asked. "Because Misha wangled his way onto the mission?"

"That could have just been his sense of adventure." Eveleen laughed. "I don't know all their reasons. One thing Gordon brought up was Misha's own psychological state. He was so much like a man suffering from combat fatigue. Too much violence, too many dead companions, after all those Baldy attacks on the Russian stations. It makes people see life differently."

Ross nodded. That he could understand.

"There were other things, though I didn't ask for them. Here's what convinced *me*. All that flirting before we left, and on the ship. It was so...so empty. I really think it was his way of blinding us all to what he meant to do if he could. After all, once we got to the planet, he could have carried on with both Vera and Irina. Each of those women would have welcomed him. But he didn't. He'd closed everyone off by then, and he was angriest when he thought that Irina had closed off his access to Svetlana. But at the end—" Eveleen shrugged. "He finally saw the way he'd looked for, and the fact that Zina let him do it meant not only that she'd seen how the destroyed machine would keep us safe, but that he'd refuse to come back. He'd thought it all out ahead. It was not a moment's decision, made in anguish."

Ross sighed, and cut right to the real issue. "Would you go back?" he asked.

She turned her head away, her brow furrowing slightly. "I don't know," she said finally. Then she smiled at Ross. "It works the same for me as it does for you. Unless I knew all the circumstances—unless they were *real*—I have no idea what I'd do."

He kissed her. "Then let's drop it, and move on," he said.

She grinned, and they finished getting ready for sleep.

Later on, when he thought over the conversation, he suspected that she did indeed know what she would have done, but she was wise enough, and generous enough in spirit, to at least pretend to match his ambivalence.

That's real love, he thought sleepily. She's a couple steps ahead of me—but I can learn. And it will grow, and change, and make new people of us both.

All we need is time.

ABOUT THE AUTHORS

Andre Norton was one of the best-loved and most famous science fiction and fantasy authors of all time. She was named Grand Master by the Science Fiction Writers of America and was awarded a Life Achievement Award by the World Fantasy Convention. She wrote over a hundred novels which have sold millions of copies worldwide, including her Witch World, Beast Master, Solar Queen, and Time Traders series, among others. She passed away in 2005.

http://www.andre-norton-books.com/

Sherwood Smith was a teacher for twenty years, teaching history, literature, drama, and dance. Before that she worked in the film industry for several years. She writes science fiction and fantasy for adults and young readers; she has been working on the Sartorias-deles fantasy series all her life, beginning with the CJ Notebooks, then continuing on as her main protagonists began to grow up and become active in the world.

Though known primarily as a fantasy writer, Sherwood along with author Dave Trowbridge collaborated on Exordium, a five-volume space opera, with Rachel Manija Brown on the young adult "hopeful dystopia" series called The Change, and with Andre Norton on four books listed elsewhere.

https://www.sherwoodsmith.net/

About the Publisher

This book is published on behalf of the author by the Ethan Ellenberg Literary Agency.
https://ethanellenberg.com
Email: agent@ethanellenberg.com

Made in the USA
Coppell, TX
21 October 2022

85088903R00179